Falling Sky: Book One

THE DEADLY CROCUS

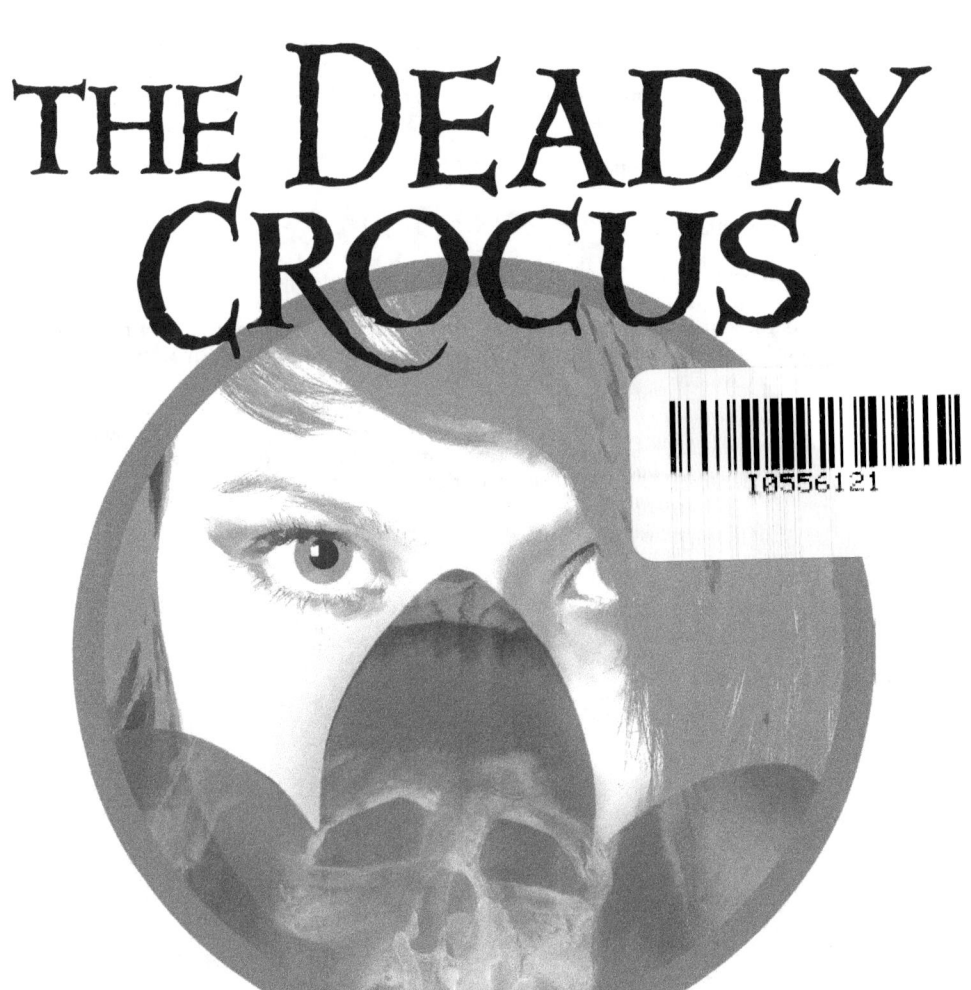

E.T. Ellison

© Copyright 2019 by E. T. Ellison

ISBN: 978-1-7348036-1-7

www.etellison.com

A more modest and substantially different version of this story appeared as a novelette called *Night Funnels* in the science fiction/fantasy webzine, *Singularity*, in 2002.

Book, cover, title page and map designs by E. T. Ellison.

Published by Clownbox Press
216 Mt Hermon Road, Suite E-233
Scotts Valley, CA 95066

025180

cLoWNβoX
P ʀ ɛ s s

A Wyn of Wonder

BESIDES SODBUNNIES
and humans, the Island of Wyn in the
planetoid called Hallah is home to a
number of extraordinary creatures:
pranksies, windsharks, butterwings,
perfins and squarms, just for starters.
And not to forget the oh-so-helpful
help-fairies who are still mostly
human.

UNTIL THE FIRST
skyfall blasted a huge hole in it,
Hallah was the sort of planet just about
anybody in their right mind would
like to live in. Now something – or
someone — who's a huge fan of crocus
flowers is killing Hallah. On purpose.
Now Hallah urgently needs a hero, and
who could be a less likely planet-saver
than a naïve young Quincian Queen of
Niceness named Glix Larue? But there
are some odd things about Glix ....

FALLING SKY
is award-winning author
E. T. Ellison's outlandishly
imaginative, action-packed new series
for readers youngish and older.

Dedication

To the young — and younger — women of the planet Earth who must battle demons of all shapes, sizes and genders to become all that they can be. I hope things will be better someday. One of these young women — my youngest daughter — inspired the idea of night funnels all those years ago. Thanks, Corwyn: this tale could not have existed without you.

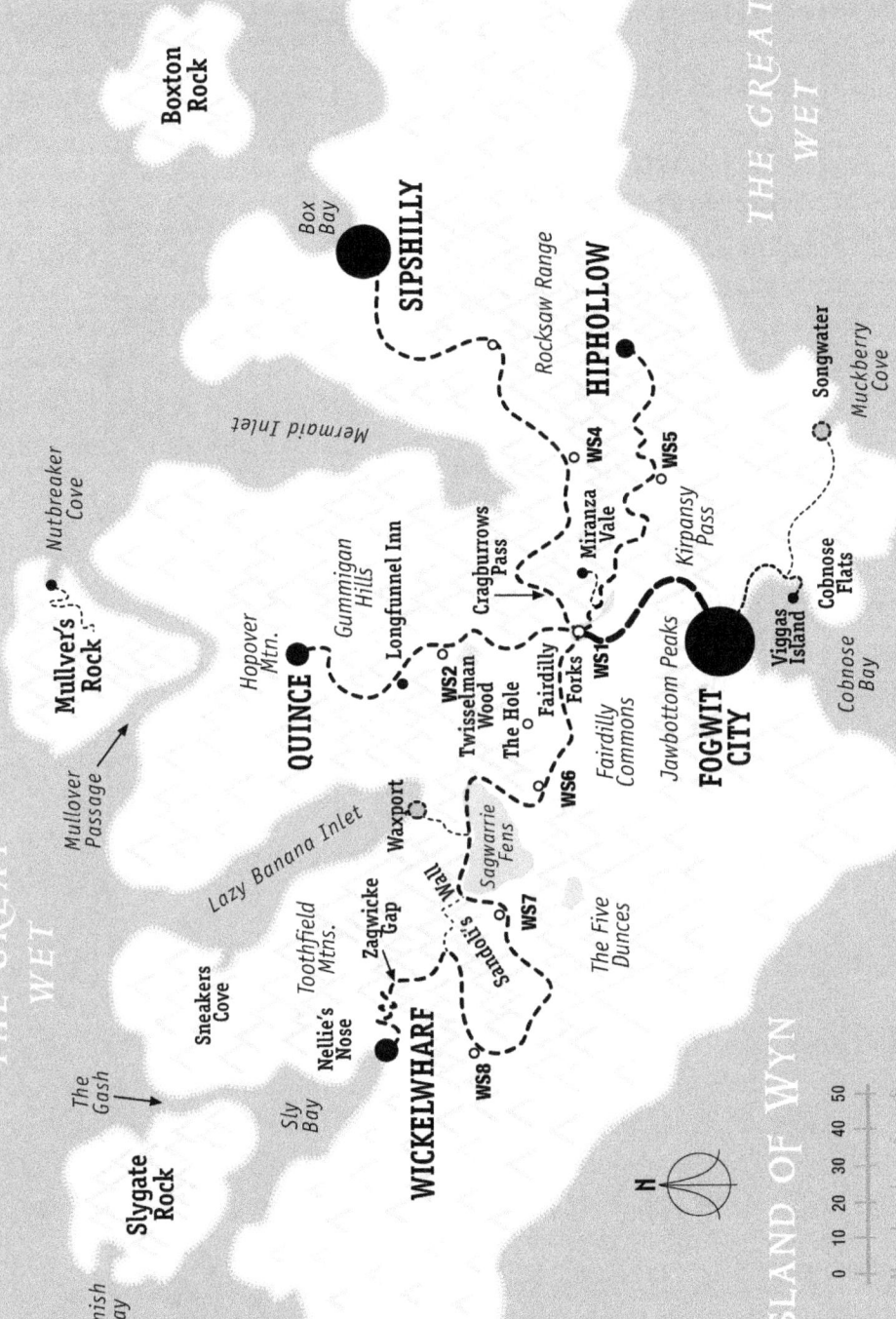

THE GREAT WET

THE GREAT WET

Boxton Rock

Box Bay

SIPSHILLY

Rocksaw Range

HIPHOLLOW

Songwater

Muckberry Cove

Mermaid Inlet

Nutbreaker Cove

Mullver's Rock

WS4

WS5

Miranza Vale

Kirpansy Pass

Cobnose Flats

Gummigan Hills

Longfunnel Inn

Cragburrows Pass

Hopover Mtn.

QUINCE

WS2

Twisselman Wood

The Hole

Fairdilly Forks

WS1

Jawbottom Peaks

FOGWIT CITY

Viggas Island

Cobnose Bay

Mullover Passage

Lazy Banana Inlet

Waxport

Sagwarrie Fens

Fairdilly Commons

WS6

Sneakers Cove

Toothfield Mtns.

Zaqwicke Gap

Sandoul's Wall

WS7

The Five Dunces

Famish Bay

The Gash

Slygate Rock

Sly Bay

Nellie's Nose

WICKELWHARF

WS8

N

ISLAND OF WYN

0 10 20 30 40 50
M I L E S

Nevergate Cycle Books
by E.T. Ellison

The Last Nevergate Chronicles:

The Luck of Madonna 13

The Mask of Madonna 13

The Ghost of Madonna 13

The Ashes of Madonna 13

The Axe of Madonna 13

The Cult of Madonna 13

Genesis ... and Then Some

    (The essential companion to the Last Nevergate Chronicles)

The Falling Sky series:

The Deadly Crocus

The Well of Life

The Black Door

Travis One-Shoe thrillers:

Treasure of the Holy Quincunx

Contents

Prologue

THE MORNING WAS WARM and calm to a fault: only the impatient movements of the coronation watchers stirred the air. Far to the west, the sun just had crested the Five Dunces and now grazed a lazy arc across a crisp blue hemisphere. The gleaming snowcaps of the five tallest mountains on Wyn really did look like five, bright dunces, or so thought the next queen, just a bit nervously.

A burnished humming tickled the air; a pair of frisky juvenile butterwings flew up out of yet another large box, their long gauzy gowns trailing like golden mist-ghosts. Only their colorfully-patterned crests set them apart from each other. The butterwings hovered over the next queen's head for several moments, then, in a most stately fashion, slowly settled the copper funnel-crown on her head without mussing her bristle of orange hair even a little. This orange-haired queen was known by the name Glix.

A quick nervous smile zipped across Glix's cream-colored face. She made the proper shallow curtsey, waved a nice little wave to the crowd, then stepped back into the line.

At the final fanfare, the portly Grand Funnelmaster waddled to the cusp of the stage and inspected the crowd. Under a gaze as heavy as his drooping belly, the Quincians stilled their gossips, whispers and mumbles. In due time the Grand Funnelmaster nodded, raised his arms and bellowed the traditional benediction: "Let the Queens go forth and carry the niceness and honor of Quince out among the fairgoers."

As if following a cue card, a cannon blast punctuated his remarks with an earsplitting exclamation point. The rolling grassland that was Fairdilly Commons lurched violently and the air vibrated like a church bell hammered by Goliath himself. Far above the fairgoers' heads, the distant sun flickered, sputtered and went dark.

The cannon blast was surely not a cannon blast. No cannons are known to exist on the island of Wyn. Maybe the sound was more like the great grandfather of all sonic booms. But there was also the odd sproing that could be heard through the echoes of the Boom of the Century, as it was labeled the next day by the headline writers of the *Fogwit Morning Lobster*.

Almost everyone present at the Fairdilly Fair clapped hands over their ears and looked up at the abruptly darkened sky, as if they might actually see where the light had gone. Of the ten freshly-crowned Queens of Quince, only Glix did not look up. A nice little mindvoice said to her: "Looking up is not only graceless and uncool, it is possibly the very essence of un-niceness. Besides, it might be some kind of test. Or it might make your crown fall off."

The clunking of copper crowns to the wooden platform was just a teeny bit satisfying to Glix, who, despite being wrapped in blackness had maintained both her innocent, straight-ahead smile and her crown. If it hadn't been utterly dark, some people might have seen a hint of a self-satisfied smirk flicker across Glix's face.

Tangled up with lingering echoes of the boom and the sproing, Glix heard such diverse comments as "whoa, where'd the sun go?" and "that's not a very nice trick" and "where did I put my flashlight?" and a lot of other things you might imagine that people would say when the sun abruptly blinked off on an otherwise perfect morning.

Then two things happened: the sun blinked back into existence and a shriek like a thousand banshees burst out of the sky and into the ears of the fairgoers. It was so loud that it drowned out all the expressions of relief at the prompt return of the sun. The torpid air came to life in restless gusts from every direction. A shrieking gusher of sonic agony kept it company. Hats spun away, hairdos were mussed, skirts defied gravity. In the screams, bellows and urgent whispers that sizzled through the crowd like static electricity, the word "cyclone" was heard more than twice.

A tiny speck of bright light fell from the sun, trailing a fuzzy dark line. The speck blossomed into something you would probably think was a good-sized meteor, but wasn't. Nor was it a cyclone. But whatever bright, burning thing it was, it was heading on a zig-zaggy line right for Fairdilly Commons, where the annual Fairdilly Fair was just getting underway. The bright thing was now a lurching fireball with a curly pigtail of black smoke.

3

In mere moments, the fireball came to dominate the sky, so bright that all the lush green of Fairdilly Commons seemed to fade to the color of old hay. As if by mental telepathy, thousands of fairgoers shook off their shock and all decided at once to sprint for the only possible protection: the Bones.

Proctors did their best to avert a full stampede and for the most part succeeded; many were muddied, but none were trampled. The folk from Quince, of course, did the nice thing: they allowed all the other fairgoers to precede them down steep trails that lined Fairlaken Trough and into the caves that wormed their way through the Bones.

Sometimes it is dangerous to be nice. By the time the too-nice-for-their-own-good Quincians reached the edge of the trough the fireball seemed ready to plunge into the fairgrounds. The wild gusts of wind that accompanied the fireball filled the air with decorative hairpieces, hats, helmets, spectacles, corsages, green-glazed popcorn and cones of sticky green cotton candy torn from the fingers of young fairgoers. The very frightened clump of young ladies that was Glix and her fellow queens had to hang on to each other just to keep their feet while they searched for a trail down into the Bones.

Before they even located a way into the depths, the Fireball of the Century slammed into Fairdilly Commons. Anyone silly enough to be standing was blown off their feet by the blast. All of the queens and most other nice Quincians were in this group.

A thick gray snake with a billowing hat rose into the sky and a rain of hot mud and chunks of fiery detritus peppered the fair-grounds. This hellish rain made holes in tents, dents in carriage roofs, scorch marks and splotchy brown messes wherever it landed. Animals bleated, whinneyed or snarfled with fear and outrage at being battered and stung. Otherwise, the brief rain of hot mud caused surprisingly little damage.

No one noticed the small, burning black orb that splashed into Longbottom Well.

By sheer good luck, the fireball had hit a dozen or so miles to the west. Naturally, this spot came to be known as the Hole of the Century, a magnificent three hundred foot deep crater. Fairdilly Fair and the fairgoers were spared.

The upshot was this: the fair went on, only a smidgen of time behind schedule. And, all of that year's fairgoers had much more to talk about than usual. Even better, they all had a once-in-a-lifetime experience to exaggerate a few days later in their reports to the stay-at-homes back in their various home towns.

• • • •

Some months later in the home of Glix Larue, the middle queen, a ceramic bottle was sitting in its usual place on the nightstand next to the hand-mirror with the twisty copper frame. "Evernice," said the nice-colored lettering on the bottle's otherwise plain white label. The bottle, the mirror and the nightstand sat quietly in a sparsely decorated bedroom next to a bed topped with the usual sorts of bed-clothes. An odd polished copper crown hung at just the proper angle from a padded copper hook.

The crown was fashioned from an inverted copper funnel embellished with elaborate copper swirligons, fleurets and cabochons of blue azurite. The effect was impressively royal, and even more so when the funnel-crown sat comfortably on the head of its orange-haired queen.

On this particular sulu evening, the queen was downstairs and the bedroom was empty of living things. Well, except for a green sod-bunny napping in a padded wicker basket in a corner by the open window. Then a vague, shadowy thing appeared next to the bed. Where did it appear from, exactly? A mystery.

The shadowy thing wasn't really what most people think about when the subject of shadows comes up. This one was more like a formation of rippling air that was ever so slightly darker than the air in the queenly bedroom lit only by a single glowpot. If you looked sideways just right you might conclude that the ripple in the air had a shape that was vaguely human, with a head topped by a broad-brimmed, hat-like shimmer.

Footfalls fell on the stairs outside the door. The vague shadow made a flurry of quick motions, replacing the bottle of Evernice with another bottle of Evernice that was identical to the first except for what was inside it. What was inside it was not only not Evernice; it was not nice at all.

The not-quite-shadow melted away just as the bedroom door opened. In the corner by the window, the sodbunny still napped, oblivious to the switcheroo of a moment ago. As a watch-sodbunny, it was useless.

Not so long after that, a tiny copper night funnel with a soft rubber tip was gently inserted into the queen's left ear by a kindly woman. The queen was careful not to move as two drops of candle-warmed, not-at-all Evernice entered her ear through the night funnel.

The very next morning the queen's almost perfectly nice queenly life started coming apart at the seams.

6

1

Distant Scream

THE MIDDLE QUEEN'S BREATH came in choppy, impatient spurts, so loud that she feared to rouse the sleepers in the house up ahead, the last house before freedom. She leaned forward and rested her hands on her knees.

"Well, Cinder," she whispered, "I don't see the thing that's been following us and we're almost out of Quince. Are you excited?"

Hearing his name, Cinder wiggled in the cozy confinement of a pocket in her cloak. Queen Glix took the movement as a "yes."

Panting in the protective shadows of a clump of ironpalms, she spotted something that could be a big boost to her escape.

Un-nice thoughts nibbled at the corners of her mind like hungry mice. Was she willing to steal to improve her chances of escape? She said things to herself like "it would be handy, but …" or "I really shouldn't, but …" or "he really owes me, but …." Nonsense like that.

But it was the perfect place for a theft, said her practical self. Only this single run-down dwelling stood near the gate at the very edge of Quince; she could be away in seconds. The first moon, Lumo, was still low over the western hills and the starless sky overhead was a deep indigo. The queen could barely see, much less be seen. Still, she was nervous.

Had she been really followed?

Silly idea, but ….

The queen sucked in a stealthy breath through clenched teeth.

From the deep pool of darker dark under the ironpalms she squinted her eyes and peered back along the meandering, little-used trail she had taken to get here. Nothing seemed to be moving, but a gnawing feeling said something was watching her from the shadows.

It wasn't the first time she'd had that feeling in recent weeks. Or the second, or the tenth. But since nothing ever seemed to happen, she made an effort to just stop thinking about it and worry about other things.

She pulled back the hood of her cloak and cupped an ear with her copper-gloved hand. Was there an out-of-place sound? A faint crunch of gravel, a twig snapping underfoot, the abrasive swish of fabric or leather brushing against shadowy leaves? Not now. Only crickets sawing at their legs and the neah-neah of a goat in the paddock on the other side of the hedge.

She stared at the shrubbery across the road. Despite the need to be on the move again, her courage seemed very slow to heat up. One more time she wondered if she dared to add "theft" to her growing list of crimes. This sort of theft would qualify as a "Felonious Challenge to Total Niceness" in Quincian terminology.

A feeling of unease started to grow in her and it had nothing to do with becoming a thief; the hideous black mark on her left palm had begun to tingle. The sensation was not exactly painful, but it instantly got her full attention. A vague premonition told her to look up.

Shielding her eyes from the white disk of Lumo, she stared straight overhead.

About midway up the northern sky, almost directly above Hopover Mountain, the middle queen spotted something that didn't belong there. A tiny dot of light where no light should be. And it was growing. Another skyfall? What else, she answered herself as a sick feeling bloomed in her stomach.

She tracked the tiny point of light as it moved down the black hemisphere. It grew fast, but it didn't seem to be headed in the direction of Wyn, the largest and most populous of the islands. So far, only the first skyfall had crashed into land. The hideous sight and sound of that one was burned deep into Queen Glix's memories. Worse, a tiny fragment of the shell — what they called a cinder-egg — had changed her nice life forever, a thought that rekindled her anger at the sheer unfairness of it all.

Bad idea, the anger. Just thinking those angry thoughts now caused the sinister black mark to sizzle with a ferocity she hadn't felt since that fateful day at the Fairdilly Fair. A yelp of pain sprang up from her throat and escaped her lips.

9

Silently cursing herself for letting that happen, she looked again at the last house. No lights came on, but nearby she heard rustlings in the paddock ... but no hoof sounds. She forced her attention back to the sky. The speck was now a blob of yellow light and it now had a glowing tail. Glix watched until it disappeared behind the jagged range of lower mountains just west of Hopover. The earth beneath her feet shook for a few seconds and a stiff gust of wind sprang up, rustling leaves and stilling the crickets. Queen Glix listened for a boomy sound, but if there was one, it was too far away to hear.

This piece of sky must have landed somewhere out in the Great Wet. At this realization, the pain under her glove dwindled to a dull ache and she became aware that she was getting cramps in her legs from crouching. Slowly, carefully, quietly she rose to a standing position. Only then did she look again at the lonely, forlorn object half-hidden behind the featherbush across the road.

Glix waited and listened some more, but heard only crickets, goats and a distant scream of a hunting nighthawk.

10

2
....

That Was the Plan

THE RUSTY THING had a long forgotten look in the moonlight. Still, it had a perfectly good seat that supported only moss at the moment. Of course, she knew it would be decidedly un-nice to just take it. Well, not so much un-nice as just wrong. On the other hand, the forlorn object's owner had committed many offenses against her person over their years of school together: drooling in her hair a hundred times, for example. Wasn't a proper balancing long overdue? In that case, stealing an abandoned bicycle wouldn't really be stealing, would it?

The queen smiled a tiny smile at her mental gymnastics. Was that what they had called an Insidious Rationalization in her "Impediments to Total Niceness" class at the academy? The queen thought it probably was, but she was too desperate now to care about such niceties. Just not quite desperate enough to actually commit the theft. So she waited. For what, exactly? She didn't know.

Cinder had tired of waiting. Possibly he was anxious to return to Hiphollow, the place of his birth. Or possibly he just needed to make a nugget deposit. No matter. He crawled out of her pocket, caught hold of his mistress's belt with monkey-like paws and crawled around to her back.

Ka-ching! The mechanical coin dispenser at the queen's back spat out a disc of starglass. The coin slid down the back of her many-pocketed tan traveling skirt, breaking the protective silence with a musical clink as it hit the gravel. Several seconds later, a familiar thwap-thwap of wings and strange, squeaky jibber-jabber also broke the silence.

Through a surge of un-nice thoughts at her bad luck, Queen Glix looked up to see the dark undersides of a pair of butterwings no more than a dozen feet directly overhead. Their wings were a moonlit golden blur and she thought she could see the outlines of a glidesack full of scroll-letters slung between the pair.

Had they seen her? They were no doubt gossiping in their weird language, but butterwings — even airpost butterwings — had a reputation for being incredibly nosy busybodies. Would word of a sinister figure lurking near the town gates reach the wrong ears? Wrong ears in this case would mean just about any ears in the town of Quince.

"Cinder, what are you *doing* back there?" chided the queen in an urgent whisper. "You don't want butterwings to notice us, do you? We're right under their mail route and a pair just flew past us. They might tell somebody, and then ...."

Her "and then" was interrupted by another almost electric sizzle under her glove. She shook her hand again in pain and agitation. Even a glancing thought about the inquisition that her traitor of a doctor was planning for tomorrow morning now made the black mark on her palm go crazy. Or was it something else that caused the sizzle? She was starting to realize that quite a few things would make her palm go crazy these days.

Then an idea belatedly triggered by the clink of starglass redirected her mind and prompted the queen to finally take action. In seconds the rusty, moss-covered bicycle was back in use. In the pair of depressions its tires had left in the soft earth there now sat a pair of small starglass coins. Balance achieved.

She pedaled through the ancient gates that flanked the only road in and out of Quince, taking special notice of the way the white light of Lumo glowed a golden orange when it shone on the curly "Q" of polished copper cradled by the black ironpalm uprights. It was beautiful in a stern but magical way that kindled a surge of pride in the three qualities for which Quince had earned great renown through-out the island of Wyn: copper craft, chocolate making and niceness. Glix had never seen the gate by moonlight and would probably never see it again. Her moment of community pride morphed into some-thing else and a small trickle of tears seasoned the bittersweet savor of the moment.

The copper funnel-crown in her backpouch suddenly seemed heavy and she felt stupid for packing it. Other sour feelings piled on and threatened to make her turn around. Maybe she had overreact-ed. Maybe things wouldn't be so bad after all. But then maybe they would be worse. So instead of turning around, she pedaled hard-er and hoped the squeaks and clunks of the old bicycle couldn't be heard by any ears but her own.

A mile down the road, the realization began to sink in that she had actually left Quince behind and was completely and totally on her own, all because of things that weren't her fault. She thought of her little sister Wixit and the tears began to flow again. But she crammed that thought into a tiny corner of her mind and thought about her destination instead. People in Hiphollow wouldn't insist that she remove her glove and expose her shameful brand. She was very sure of *that*.

The insubstantial, mostly invisible shadow-thing that followed her might have chuckled at this thought ... if shadow-things of this nature would actually trouble themselves to chuckle.

A vague tingle arose from the mark under her glove, but Glix ignored it and pedaled harder along Fairdilly-Quince Road toward what she hoped was the safety of the Gummigan Hills in the distance. Later she would shinny up the slender trunk of a waxbark and spend the night hidden in the shelter of its high branches. At least that was the plan.

13

14

3

Lost in the Night

LUMO'S COOL radiance transformed the countless potholes on Fairdilly-Quince Road into ghostly windows to who-knows-where; with diligence and luck, Queen Glix was able to avoid most of them.

She also avoided every other night-traveler for the simple reason that there were none. There was absolutely no good reason for anyone to travel this road by night. This was fortunate because she'd much rather ride on the potholed old road than on the swampy trail that followed Laundry Creek off to the left.

With no warning, two things happened at the same time. A distant buzzing sound interrupted her thoughts and her palm developed a sudden itchy-tingly sensation that wasn't pain. A warning, she decided. But what was it warning her about?

The buzz was getting louder and seemed to be coming from up ahead where the road made a bend and disappeared into the pass through the Gummigan Hills. There was an odd quality to the buzz that reminded her most of help-fairy wings. Why would lots of help-fairies be flying at night?

The last thing she needed right now was a bunch of black-cloaked women trying to be helpful to a runaway queen of niceness. Not the kind of helpful picture she wanted to imagine. In a moment of panic that might actually have been wisdom, she dragged the bicycle off the road, bumped her way down a rocky incline and into the tall swamp-grass that bracketed both sides of Laundry Creek.

As a child, Glix had been allergic to swampgrass. A fit of sneezes confirmed that she still was. Dragging the bike across the shallow creek, she sneezed her way through the swampgrass on the other side, crossed the old trail and thrust herself into the woods to a place she could see the road but not be seen. At least that was her hope.

She waited, panting and doing her best to stifle her wayward sneezes. Presently a mass of long, black torpedo-like shapes came into view. They were flying perhaps a dozen yards above the road, accompanied by a raucous chorus of raspy buzzing. Windsharks. At least a dozen.

Riding them in a tight formation were black-cloaked help-fairies, their own wings tucked back and unmoving. Glix had never heard of help-fairies that rode windsharks. It just didn't seem very, what ... helpish? She couldn't say exactly why, but these also looked somehow different from the help-fairies she had met during the annual family outings to the Fairdilly Fair. And it wasn't just the blue sashes around their waists.

Then they were beyond her view, taking their noisy buzzing with them. Struck by a sudden fit of curiosity, Glix lurched out of her hiding place, crossed the creek and scrambled up the slope to the road. She hid in a thicket of roseberries and watched the strange group recede into the night, veering away from the road to skirt the town of Quince well to the west. Then even the sounds were gone.

Riding along the trail was much slower going than the road had been, but felt safer. There had been no more windsharks yet, but she wasn't about to risk the road again. She stopped and checked her polished copper pocket watch: three minutes past midnight. She gulped a deep breath; the very nice village of Quince was now far behind, but not yet far enough behind. Mr Hipskander and the welcoming folk of Hiphollow were still more than a hundred miles away. So she chewed a yumstick for energy, remounted and pedaled south into the night, still wondering about the strange group of black fliers.

Many yawns later, the trail ended at a mountain of broken bricks, tangled metal and dirt. No more trail tonight. She got off the bike and

walked it past the huge piles of debris that were all that remained
of the Longfunnel Inn. Then she came upon a small clearing not far
from the road. Poking up from its well-tended grass was a gleaming
forest of copper baskets set on top of short ironpalm poles with copper bands just below the baskets. Grave markers ... and new enough
that they still had an orange shine. Here she paused for a moment.

The Longfunnel Inn had been a place of many fond memories.
The rambling, quaint brick structure sported many gables and tur-
rets clad in polished copper. A maze of weathervanes, dream-traps,
gremlin-sticks and lightning rods had sprouted from its ancient roof-
lines. In the past, luminous smoke had risen in lazy curls from its
funnel-capped chimneys. In the nose of her memory, that smoke had
always been alive with the aromas of baking bread, roasting roasts
and crackling hearth-blazes.

Then a wayward shard of sky blew it all to smithereens. And
not even a *big* piece of sky ... nothing like the one that had blasted
the Hole of the Century in the grassy downs of Fairdilly Commons
during the opening ceremonies of this year's fair.

According to the eyewitness account of a funnel buyer from
Fogwit City, the fragment sliced into the north wing like a monstrous flaming pie pan. After blasting ancient bricks into clouds of
russet-colored dust, it burrowed a fifty-foot deep hole in what had
been the back gardens. Then the rest of the structure had collapsed
in upon itself, burying several dozen unfortunate guests under tons
of brick, wood, metal and glass. In almost no time the clouds of pul-
verized and baked material had settled over the wreckage, depositing
the look of ancient ruins that it had now.

Seeing this ghostly shambles in Lumo-light sent a small flood of
tears running down the runaway queen's cheeks and sniffles to her
nose. And she couldn't help comparing it to the wreckage of her own
nice life. She brushed away the tears while her mind tried to hold back
a different flood, a flood of recent memories that were better left un-
remembered. If she could pluck them out of her brain, leave them by
the road and ride away from them, she would do exactly that. But she

settled for pushing the bicycle back to the road and just riding away. Presently the sad ruins of the Longfunnel Inn were lost in the night.

4

The Safest Place

QUEEN GLIX was now at Waystation 2, three miles south of the wreckage of the Longfunnel Inn. Bright Lumo had left the sky and the dimmer red-orange glow of Rhomo was only a rising haze on the other side of Hallah's starless sky. Glix decided she could travel no longer. She just couldn't. Unaccustomed to bicycle riding, her legs felt like wobbly soup-straws and her bottom felt, well, uncomfortably over-used. That was until it went completely numb. The urge to sleep grew stronger with every second as she stood in the shadows on the far side of the road, watching and listening.

A sinuous ground-mist wrapped the scene in undulating shapes that sent an electric chill up her spine and then back down again. All the windows were dark and the Waystation appeared empty but for one cottage, which had a decrepit freight buggy parked next to it. On the porch of that cottage a trio of shadowy figures hunched over a glowing brazier. Aromas of cooking meat wafted past her nose and made her stomach growl. Glass instruments shimmered with orange reflections from the coals and sent slow, wavering harmonies into the mist.

Hollow and eerie, the music made Glix shudder. These must be glassblowers, most likely from Sipshilly. Odd folk according to her father, who nevertheless admired the marvels they created with furnace, sand and air. A thin sigh escaped her lips to be whisked away by the strange music. She shuddered again: time to leave.

A few miles down the road, Glix wished she had been brave enough to spend some coins on one of the empty cottages, glassblowers or no glassblowers. She could barely pedal hard enough now to keep the bike from falling over. After one near spill, she dismounted.

Spotting a small grove of towering waxbark trees perhaps a hundred yards to her right, she made a decision. She would shinny up the smooth bark and spend the night in one of those giants. It wouldn't be the first time, after all. In nicer times, she and her friends had dared each other to sleep in a tree, and Glix had actually done it. But those nicer times were gone: here she was, alone in the forest of night, wondering how and why her nice, smooth life had turned lumpy and rancid.

Finally, she tore herself away from such sorry thoughts. Finding a safe place to sleep was all that mattered now.

Picking the least wild of several faint wildlife trails that seemed to lead toward the grove, Glix started pushing the bicycle into the woods, then stopped. Obvious tire tracks might ruin her escape, a notion that the mark under her glove immediately found objectionable.

Shaking her hand and hissing an unqueenly comment in the general direction of Quince and another in the direction of Fairdilly Forks, she hefted the bicycle onto a shoulder and soon had it hidden in a thicket of flockleaf bushes. Then she got down on her hands and knees and tried to shmoosh away any evidence of tire tracks.

The queen stood, wobbling on her soup-straw legs and waving her flashlight here and there. It was hardly a perfect shmooshing job, but it was the best she was going to manage tonight. What mattered most to her at the moment was sleep.

Only a few more minutes along the trail, then some climbing, then sleep. Finding a tiny reserve of unused energy, she trudged toward the trees. Thirty-four minutes later the trees seemed as far away as ever. Had she been walking in circles?

Glix stopped, her vision now feeling as wobbly as her legs. Closing her leaden, gritty eyes for a few moments, she let her other senses wander in this place. Wherever she was, her senses reported that this place felt different in some hard-to-describe way from where she had hidden the bicycle. Too quiet, for one thing. No owls hooted, no crickets chirped, no small creatures rustled in the underbrush. And the air felt, what, thicker?

Something wasn't quite right, but she was just too tired to try very hard to figure out what it was. But she was also too tired to panic, so she opened her eyes again and gave the area another once-over with the flashlight. The beam grazed something square-ish then moved on. Square-ish?

She found it again, not far off the trail near a clump of shadows tinted a pale orange by Rhomo. It was a sign ... and not an old one. The wooden rectangle smelled freshly painted, a dull pink background and squiggly, deep orange lettering that spelled out these words: "Lost Wayfarers Cottage — One Minute Ahead." A squiggly orange arrow pointed along a not-at-all-overgrown path that she had somehow missed before.

Forcing her legs back into action, she presently discovered that the sign had not been joking. She now stood before a tiny, apparently windowless cottage that was almost completely encircled by misty forest. Where the trail ended, two stone steps led up to a wooden door with a pink sign over it. "Night Door," it said in the same almost persimmon colored characters as the sign by the trail. Too exhausted to be suspicious, the runaway queen grasped the handle and twisted. The door opened without even a creak.

Her hand fumbled automatically for a light switch where it thought one ought to be. Click ... a pleasing yellow glow now suffused the one-room cottage. Somehow, the inside seemed bigger than the outside. It also seemed very familiar. And why not? The room was an exact replica of her very own bedroom in her family's very own house in Quince, the very capitol of niceness on the island of Wyn.

In her strange state of mind, this familiarity did not trouble queen Glix one smidgen. In fact, it made perfect sense to her to remove her copper funnel-crown from her backpouch and hang it on the special padded copper hook her father had made for it in the funnelshops.

And it made perfect sense to say "good-night Dear Self" to the haggard reflection in her hand-mirror with the twisty copper frame that sat where it always sat on her nightstand, and to fiddle a bit with the tiny night funnel on its post. Most of all, it made perfect sense to pull back the bedcovers, crawl into the soft bed and fall instantly asleep, not giving even a single thought to the white bottle of Evernice that was missing from this room's nightstand.

She slept a sleep of innocent bliss, completely undisturbed by the scraping and shuffling sounds that might have caused a lighter sleeper to lurch awake in alarm.

Cinder heard everything Glix didn't, so he curled up next to safest place he could imagine: his mistress's cozy neck.

22

5

Wherever

THE SCENE IS picturesque and familiar. A ring of age-polished gray stone surrounds a bottomless pool filled with water the color of forest shadows. The pool is a gemstone set in a dell of emerald grass, but the dreamer sees it differently. Because of what she knows already, the dreamer sees a sinister black blot polluting the center of a friendly grassy commons. As dusk settles impatiently over the scene, the dreamer notices that a solitary youth now occupies the stone wall that earlier in the day had supported dozens of excited participants in the annual Bottlefishing Derby.

A copper funnel-crown partly covers a mass of orange hair that the pert youth with the button nose has fashioned into a fishtail braid that hides the faint swirl of pink behind her right ear. Her hands hold a fishing pole, its line dangling limp in the water, her listless feet dangling over the edge, almost touching the black blot. She is waiting for something, but not sure exactly what or why, and not so happy about it.

The dreamer knows the youth as her un-dreaming self of several months ago, knows that the place is called Longbottom Well, knows that she is waiting for five bells, knows that the flittering Picters Guild butterwings currently pointing their eyebuttons at this and that are about to feel the crackle of blue magic from the brown-sashed help-fairy who shoos them away as a favor to the smelly proctor from Wickelwharf. It's coming, dreams the dreamer, her dream-heart pounding, her dream-stomach churning.

The dreaming queen has replayed this scene from the Faird-illy Fair a hundred times in her waking mind, but she has never dreamed it until now. Actually, she has never dreamed anything until now because nobody dreams in her hometown of Quince, the place she has just escaped. Not ever. Period. That's because of the Hacklebee dream-traps that protect every man, woman and child of Quince from the unpredictable un-niceness of dreams. But the Lost Wayfarers Cottage has no dream trap, and Glix is having the very first dream of her life. Thus, we can forgive her dreamself for expecting the dream to play fair, to be a precise playback of the events that afternoon on the Fair's last day.

That's when the dream goes haywire, leaving the reality script in the dream-dust and playing the next sequence inside out and backward. Well, not exactly, but something like that.

There is an unfamiliar steel gray face twisted in agony, there are gray spider legs writhing in a mad dance; there is a rain of spinning sky-shards and another rain of blue flowers. There is also a familiar body that lurches backwards off the wall, a bouncing ball that shoots up from the water, a face that splats in a puddle of cool mud, a tall man with an Adam's apple like a goose egg in a rubber hose who juggles sodbunnies.

Then there are the five stern-faced men who question the dream-er about a missing cinder-egg, a copper glove fad at the Academy of Niceness that comes and goes, a hand that shoots up to catch the bounding black ball that is not really a ball, a copper crown that goes wobbling, the evil demons that stage a takeover of the middle queen's speaking apparatus and cause her nice world to fall apart....

The dreamer and her real self agree on at least one point; the horrid bit of sky-junk that everybody wants to calls a cinder-egg is causing all this strangeness, the same impossibly living thing that burned and permanently scarred her left palm during the few sec-onds she held it. It's the thing that filled her mind to overflowing with scenes she can't possibly understand and finally signaled two mysterious numerals — two and seven — over and over and over again.

But there's more to it, realizes the dreamer for the first time. In the dream the cinder-egg knows her and she knows it: and it isn't just an "it." It's not "knowing" in the sense of "understanding," but there is an attunement, a bond between the undreaming Glix and that living node of her living planet. And with that attunement comes a power ....

Zap! Every nerve ending in her body seems to have gotten plugged into a separate electric outlet ...and the sizzling pain makes her eyes want to escape their sockets. But then her dream sky explodes into clouds of pink and orange stars that almost instantly smother the pain in colorful aromas: oranges, rose blossoms, cinnamon, guava, cantaloupe and bubblegum ... just for starters. The dreamer snaps her eyes open and the clouds of pink and orange aroma fade, replaced by a gigantic green face with huge green eyes and long whiskers.

• • • • •

If this place was still the Lost Wayfarers Cottage, it had gotten a major make-over overnight. Or maybe a make-under. Glix's memory from last night was of a place that was a dead ringer for her own bedroom, but this was not it. It had shrunk, for one thing. And a musty chill now seeped up from cracks in the wood floorboards while vagrant slivers of sunlight painted sharp yellow-green shapes on it from gaps in the roofing.

She crawled out of bed and stood up, a little shaky and not yet realizing that she had just woken from her very first dream. Her feet crunched on grains of black rice scattered on the floor, but she barely noticed. She *did* notice that her joints felt creaky and ancient, that every muscle in the lower half of her body was registering an achy complaint. Better to sit down for a while, she decided, except that there was no furniture in the Lost Wayfarers Cottage this morning and the "bed" she just crawled out of had lost all appeal.

What last night had seemed to be her very own soft and cozy bed was not a bed at all. It was just a rectangle of mouldering, dirt-crusted burlap sacks loosely stuffed with straw. It reeked of mold, mildew and something else. What the something else was finally registered.

The little black rice grains were not rice grains after all, realized the small part of her brain in charge of realizing such things. Gaack! The floor must have recently hosted a convention attended by every mouse within a hundred miles. The only place not dotted with droppings was directly in front of the cottage's door.

Glix scrunched her face into an imitation of a pale prune. The door was in the opposite wall from where she thought it should be. Where the Night Door had been was now just a blank wall of rough planks separated by lumpy horizontal streaks of decaying gray plaster. No door, no light switch, no soft glow from wall sconces. Other things she remembered from last night were also not there: no bedclothes, no nightstand, no hand-mirror, no night funnel, no post, no padded hook holding up a copper funnel-crown. And no chair, no table and no shelves covered with carefully arranged this and that.

Her crown now hung from the wooden handle in the door with the pink sign over its lintel that said "Morning Door." That was exactly all the invitation she needed to scoop up her sodbunny and make a hasty exit from the Lost Wayfarers Cottage into, well, wherever.

6

No Such Luck

WHEREVER turned out to be a small clearing in an otherwise dense and unfamiliar forest. Not a single giant waxbark tree was in sight. Basically circular, the clearing was no more than fifty feet in diameter and carpeted in low-growing clover dotted with poppies and clumps of flowering silvergrass. In the very center stood a circular stone well with a quaint conical roof and a copper-handled crank to draw up a copper bucket on a rope.

A vast tidal wave of thirst surged up from Glix's toes and without a moment's forethought, she ran to the well and began cranking. Somewhat alarmed by this sudden action, Cinder leaped from Glix's arms and scampered toward a lush patch of tall clover.

Glix barely noticed his departure. In almost no time she was slurping down water from the copper ladle attached to the bucket by a copper chain. The facts of the water's slight effervescence and faint aromas that hinted at such things as watermelon, peaches, cinnamon and strawberries did not even register until her thirst was slaked. Then her brain started up again.

The oddness of the situation now began to register, as did the shadowy portal in the tangled vegetation at the far edge of the clearing. There was also the sign.

A few strides later the hungry but no longer thirsty Glix stood frowning at a low sign marking the beginning of the only trail into the wood. Or anywhere, actually. Today, the quaint lettering said, "Enter All Runaway Queens Who Love a Good Prank." In smaller letters were the words, "Secret Entrance to Twisselman Wood." Glix looked around for another exit, but tanglethorn was everywhere.

Pranksies! That realization was enough to send shivers up and down the middle queen's spine. According to local history, little good came to humans who tangled with the hyper-mysterious pranksies, a nasty breed of not-so-human creatures that was legendary for unpleasant pranks and secret knowledge. Twisselman Wood was where they lived. A recent conspiracy theory involving pranksies bubbled up from Glix's memory.

She had been confined to the headmaster's Quiet Room for the trouble with Miss Smittsgood during her Nice Moments in History class earlier that afternoon. Of course it wasn't nice to say, but what she blurted out was exactly true; when Miss Smittsgood talked, her chins really did look as though they belonged on the underside of an ancient nanny goat strutting along on her hind legs. Just why she had felt the need to blurt this out completely baffled her now. Even six months ago she would never have blurted anything un-nice to anybody for any reason at all.

So Glix had been sitting in the Quiet Room mostly being quiet when a highly unlikely theory popped into her head; perhaps pranksies were the cause of her recent troubles. In this theory Twinker Gidlet had hired the colony of pranksies that lived in Twisselman Wood to ruin Queen Glix's mostly perfect life. Silly theory, really, but that didn't stop Glix from taking it seriously. Lots of otherwise intelligent people take silly things seriously.

Glix had been so certain of this conspiracy that she had been ready to borrow a bicycle that very day and ride all the way to Twisselman Wood to set things right, once and for all. Then she recalled the Purple Noodle Incident and settled for grumbling to herself a lot and continuing to make un-queenly insults in the direction of just about everyone who crossed her path. Except Twinker: she steered quite clear of Twinker.

Well, here she was at Twisselman Wood and as her sore bottom would unhappily testify, she had gotten here on a more-or-less borrowed bicycle. Strange? Very! But now she didn't feel at all like going in and confronting pranksies.

Twisselman Wood was not at all like the cheery little clearing behind the Lost Wayfarers Cottage. Glix stood under the sign and contemplated a dense, swampy jungle dominated by knobby carbuncle trees. Webs of slimy moss sagged from the tree branches. To her nose, the stench emanating from the murky place smelled like ancient furry leftovers two days after you take them out of the fridge on the way to the compost bucket.

She wrinkled her nose, backed away from the entrance and circled the clearing again hoping some other way out would magically open up. No such luck.

30

7

Only Sputters

GLIX HAD NEVER known of anybody from Quince who had actually ventured into this place ... at least not since a group of older boys returned from an expedition into Twisselman Wood with foul-smelling purple noodles dangling from their heads instead of hair. Fortunately, a few days later the purple noodles fell out. Unfortunately, the hair that repopulated their naked scalps was the color of neon blueberries. For a person like Glix who had lived her entire life with carrot colored hair, going through life with purple hair didn't seem all that bad. Most people, however, thought otherwise.

That had all happened several years back and now Glix was about to repeat their error. Not smart. On the other hand, it didn't seem that she had many choices. Once she was outside, the Morning Door had swung shut and refused to open and let her back in ... even when she'd kicked it. And the tanglethorn-infested forest that hemmed in the cottage on both sides had proved painfully impenetrable. As a last resort, she scrunched up her face in her customary caricature of deep thought, hoping that something wise would come of it, but nothing did. So in she went.

If she ignored the stench, the air in Twisselman Wood seemed stiff and tired, as though it had been painted into the spaces between the trees by a very old painter with a very old brush using very old air. Glix took a deep breath and walked as many steps as she could before exhaling and having to take another. Slow work. But at least the focus on breathing helped her ignore the unsettling sounds.

Twisselman Wood was alive with eerie creaks, chitterings, rustles, hoots, slithers, smackles, plops, grunts and other noises that might well have given Glix a fright. For good or ill, she was too busy managing her breathing to give them much notice.

The unsettling sights were harder to ignore. The place was alive — if "alive" was the right word — with vague, shadowy shapes that seemed to flit in and out of existence. They felt both familiar and totally alien at the same time, so she kept her eyes focused on the trail and worked even harder on managing her breathing.

Her mind found itself retracing recent troubles, beginning with that fateful morning at breakfast with her mother, father and little sister, Wixit.

Her favorite breakfast was in front of her, as usual: a bowl of steaming niceberry porridge and a glass of fresh-squeezed yum-yum juice. For absolutely no good reason she could think of afterward, she had scowled and blurted out these exact words: "I totally *hate* niceberry porridge. It's totally barfish and makes me want to spew! I want a sleazeburger, and with green sleaze, not yellow! And I want toadwater instead of yum-yum juice!" She stated all this ever so emphatically and without even a droplet of good humor.

Her father had dropped his spoon into his porridge, which splashed and made a small mess. "Beg pardon, Glixxie? What did you say?" Wixit giggled and their mother frowned a puzzled frown and stuck a finger in her ear.

Glix had been instantly struck by a gut-lurching embarrassment that is so many times worse than standard embarrassment that the emotion probably needs its own word. She knew exactly what she had said but she couldn't believe she had even thought it, much less spoken it. And toadwater — whatever that was — sounded far too yucky to flush one's toilet with, much less to drink. So she looked down at her bowl and forced her mouth to mumble something like, "the porridge is very good this morning."

32

Then later that day at the Quincian Academy of Niceness, there was a lunchtime discussion around the absurd idea that there can possibly be too much niceness. To the jaw-dropping astonishment of all present, the normally sweet, placid and exceptionally-nice-to-everybody middle queen rubbed her dessert — a big piece of fresh, gooey, greensugar pie — in Twinker Gidlet's yellow hair. "Possibly your nice yellow hair is too nice and too yellow," shouted Glix. "Garfish gooey green is really *your* color!"

When shocked tears welled up in Twinker's eyes, Glix stormed away, snit-like, waving her arms in silly, shaggy circles and having second thoughts about the sense of wasting a perfectly good piece of greensugar pie in that way.

Her oh-so-nice life had been in a downward spiral since that day, when what she now thought of as her "speech problem" first surfaced for no good reason at all. Of course there actually *was* a good reason, but it was so impossibly weird that Glix wouldn't have believed it anyway.

It is the fashion in Quince (as in many other places) to believe that every nasty, awful, unlucky thing that happens to someone happens for a reason. And the reason that oh-so-nice Quincians most like to believe is that the victim must have deserved whatever happened. And that was how it was with Queen Glix and her new speech problem. It was ug-ly!

The here-and-now Glix slogging through Twisselman Wood would have rehashed her sequence of unhappy events yet again if it weren't for the fact that the trail came to an abrupt end. She was almost disappointed, actually. She hadn't even gotten to the part in her rehashing where the blubberiest bozo in the academy "accidentally" sat on her lunch-sack and loosed a noisy and vile-smelling flatulence to many enthusiastic compliments from his comrades. But the sloggy trail had ended and the rehashing would just have to take a vacation for a while.

Raised above the swampy forest floor by three tiers of river rock chinked with moss was a circular platform paved with mossy

33

brownish-green flagstones. It was empty of trees or any other sort of vegetation except moss. A sign at the entrance to this clearing said, "You're Here. Now What?"

Festooned in slime from the top of her hood to the tips of her boots, Glix must have looked like a monster from a cheap scare-show. Certainly she didn't look like a Quincian and even more certainly not like a Queen of Niceness...or even a tarnished, runaway Queen of Niceness. Still, she was here and that was that.

The air at the edge of this clearing had lost its dreary staleness; in fact, Glix's nose now found it to be unusually sweet and laced with a tang of ripe vitality. Very strange.

Shafts of watery greenish light washed the center of the platform. In the center of this natural spotlight was a watery, shadowy shape she hadn't noticed before. It had a vaguely human form and was hunched over a round, flat stone that looked like a huge flat toad-stool with a polished cap. The shape was indistinct enough that Glix couldn't tell for sure if it was facing her or had its back to her. Either way, it seemed to be using the stone as a table for some sort of game involving the stacking of small, carved bones into elaborate, fanciful structures.

Whatever or whomever it was that was moving the bones around, was also completely ignoring its moss-slimed visitor. Glix felt an irrational anger boiling up inside her but before it reached her tongue, the figure stood up, stretched and placed what might be watery translucent hands on the top of its watery translucent head. There was a sound like pulling two strips of Velcro apart as the thing tore its watery, translucent shadowy form into two pieces, like some sort of weird semi-visible husk. The thing inside bent forward, stepped away from the pieces, sat back down and resumed its stacking game without ever looking up.

Glix's mouth gaped. Finally her lips moved but no words came out. Only sputters.

8

....

Coy Dimples

WAS THE THING that emerged from the husk a pranksy? Its face was hidden in the shadow of a broad-brimmed snakeskin hat worn at a rakish angle and sporting a dozen feathers that were so brightly colored that they almost glowed in the gloom. Most of creature's body was hidden by a cloak made from polished snakeskins that reflected back the murky greens of the forest with a sort of metallic shimmer that Glix found most remarkable. Sleek snakeskin gloves hid both hands.

All in all, the effect was quite dashing. And surprising. Glix had expected pranksies to be stumpy, fat, gnome-sized creatures with mottled, warty skin, leathery bat-style wings and really bad teeth. That was how the purple noodle boys had described them. This pranksy sported wings that looked more like the wings of giant butterflies painted in a contorted design featuring overlarge cat eyes against a swirly background design that, if you looked closely enough, was comprised entirely of ears. As the pranksy worked at its collection of bones, the wings moved in a sluggish, hypnotic flutter.

"Well, then. Who have we lurking at the edge of my office?" inquired the pranksy without looking up from its game. Its voice was rounded and refined, but frosted with a layer of sardonic amusement. "No, let me guess. It is Lord Bush, the splay-toed fritterwit from the slime-caves of the third moon of the fourth planet residing in the spleen of the Frump-God. Am I right?"

Tinkling laughter erupted from the dark edges of the clearing.

Glix was speechless for perhaps five seconds. Then the anger she'd been suppressing boiled over and her speech problem reared its ugly tongue. "Stop sucking your wallow-bones and look at me, Puppy Boy! You grow up in a stink-farm or something? If you're going to act like a third-rate slug-charmer I will just take my feather and go back home." Almost as an afterthought her tongue added: "And may a putrid perfin piss on your pantaloons."

A low chorus of "ooooh" and "oh-my" rippled around the clearing.

Glix gulped. Yes, she was angry at being ignored and then ridiculed, but maybe the peeing perfin curse was a little over the top. And feather? She didn't even have a feather. Rivulets of nervous perspiration trickled down her neck as she tried to construct a proper apology.

"Well said, well said!" exclaimed the pranksy, who had still not looked up from his precarious construction.

"Clearly you are no fritterwit." Then he twisted his head to the right and whispered an exaggerated stage whisper off into the shadows. "Look close, my fellows! Here before us is the legendary Queen Glix, the current middle queen of nice-as-greensugar pie Quince. Evidently she has run away from her unappreciative fellow Quincians and come to pay us a visit. Dare we brave her chainsaw massacre of a tongue and ask 'why?'"

Murmurs of "imagine that" and "la-di-dah" and "whooo-pee" and "uh-uh" came to Glix's charbroiling ears and she thought one of the cat eyes in the pranksy's wings winked at her.

She made a lame shrug, shuffled her feet and bit her tongue. How had the pranksy known her name and that running away was exactly what she was doing?

"Ordinarily, Queen Glix from Quince, we humble folk of Twisselman Wood prefer that guests arriving by the secret entrance knock three times before entering, then state their names and their business, then bow twice and last but certainly not least, present lavish and clever gifts that will amuse us endlessly."

A rumble of whispers that might have included "first-I-ever-heard-of-that" punctuated the pranksy's declaration.

"Read the rules, people. Read the rules," exclaimed the pranksy using his stage whisper again. Then to Glix: "Rules, schools, fools! Who needs any of them?"

The cat eyes on his wings winked again.

"Still, lavish gifts are always welcome. What do I mean by lavish? One of those remarkable three-headed meadowlarks would do just fine. Too bad your father didn't buy one when he was loitering around the Fangler Pavilion at the Fairdilly Fair. You wouldn't have liked it, of course — any more than you liked the clever little Invisible Spy Ring he gave you. I see you're wearing it on the wrong finger. Always wear an Invisible Spy Ring on your right ring finger. The left ring finger being the right one in this case. Where else?"

Glix had completely forgotten that she had put on her Invisible Spy Ring before making her hasty getaway from Quince. And for a fact, those rings are quite invisible indeed, which makes them difficult to keep track of and is no doubt good for Invisible Spy Ring sales. As she frowned at her left hand, she saw nothing but the copper glove. She was about to ask the rude pranksy how he knew about the Invisible Spy Ring when he held up a hand in a stop gesture.

"The other left, Queen Glix. It looks exactly like a huge invisible wart on your right index finger. Check it out." The pranksy still hadn't looked up from his bones. "One good thing about a three-headed meadowlark is that you would never get confused about which finger you should wear it on," he mumbled.

"Another good thing is that you could have brought it here to your new friends, the estimable pranksies of Twisselman Wood. And because we are ever so fond of three-part harmony, we would have been so cooperative and helpful. Possibly even useful.

"Of course, that well-behaved sodbunny in your cloak would also be a fine present. They are brighter than they look and not nearly as useless as they seem ...."

Glix was about to say something much stronger than "no way, Puppy Boy," but before the words came out, the Viceroy held up his hands and mumbled in his stage whisper, "No sense of humor, this one."

To Glix, he said, "Now please, please, *please* stop gawking at me from the doorway, Queen Glix. Come on in, pull back your hood, sit by the fire and warm your slime-buttered soul."

The pranksy punctuated his speech with a yawn, then tumbled his construction and swept the carved bones into a pocket. Unfolding himself to full height, he flicked an invisible fleck of dust off his cloak and exclaimed, "Come, come. Pranksies don't bite ... except when provoked, of course."

Glix blinked. Where the toadstool table had been were now two comfortable looking padded chairs on opposite sides of a round fire pit. Orange flames cast sinuous, dancing flickers on the pranksy's hat and cloak. A cautious Glix mounted the tiers to stand before the pranksy. To her surprise, he was her own height, not gnome-sized. In other words, the pranksy was exactly as tall as a girl her age whose height was categorized as "medium plus" by her traitorous family doctor.

The pranksy plucked a bright pink feather from his hat, bowed and presented it to Glix. "The Viceroy of Twisselman Wood, at your service. Or am I supposed to be Emperor today? I forget."

For the first time, the pranksy's face was no longer hidden by the shadows of its hat. If Glix's jaw could have dropped to her belly button, it would have. Except for the fact that the skin on this version of her father's face was the exact color of the moss that hung everywhere along the path through Twisselman Wood, the face of the Viceroy — or Emperor — of Twisselman Wood was exactly her father's face. Right down to the mole on his chin and the coy dimples in his cheeks.

9

An Unwanted Habit

"GOTCHA!" exclaimed the Viceroy through a grin that stretched her father's mouth from ear to ear in a most unnatural way. As the area erupted in raucous laughter, the dapper pranksy jumped up and down and capered a sly little fist-pumping victory dance. Glix's face turned the color of a pickled strawberry.

"Enough!" boomed the Viceroy in a voice that might better have belonged to someone the size of the portly Grand Funnelmaster of Quince. On the instant, the clearing became as silent as tundra.

"Since you brought no lavish gift, didn't knock three times, et cetera, we had to enjoy a little prank at your expense. Surely you expected some such thing from pranksies? And I'm quite certain that your father won't mind wearing my own handsome face for the duration of our interview. I stretched it for him so it would fit properly. Most likely his funnelmaking fellows will remark about his improved appearance.

"Of course right now his face is doubtless sporting a vapid expression of worry — not easy to do with a Viceroy's face. I just hate it when they do that." One of the eyes on his wings winked again. "And he's naturally joining up with the posse that's about to start searching for you. Tsk, tsk, tsk. Total waste of time, that. But we won't tell them you're amusing your fine new friends in Twisselman Wood and refuse to be found." The pranksy cocked his head in that irritating way that parents have when they're about to pose a fake question that kids have no choice about. "Will we?"

More raucous chortles from the invisible gallery.

"Did I hear the word 'refreshment'? Yes, I believe I did. Suitable refreshment always mutes the sometimes over-serious tang of wise counsel. Wouldn't you agree, Queen Glix of Quince?"

At the word "refreshment" Glix's empty stomach woke up and cast its vote for refreshments of the food variety. "Groy-yoy-yoy," it rumbled.

Before Glix's face could work up another blush, the Viceroy's hands opened to reveal a pair of thick dark brown squares with a funnel molded into the top of each. "Take two of these and call me in the morning. Quick, now, before they melt in my hand and not in your mouth."

It was as though her ungloved hand had grown a mind of its own; in slightly less than an instant the wonderful Quincian chocolates had been stuffed into her mouth. Her eyes closed and a blissful expression adopted her face until the melting was complete.

While Glix floated in her chocolate haze, the Viceroy reached both hands into the fire pit and pulled out two glowing goblets containing a pink-orange liquid that swirled and twisted like liquid flames. He held the goblets up to the wan light dusting the clearing and gave the contents a careful inspection.

Sensing something, Glix opened her eyes again. With a sober expression, the Viceroy held a goblet out to Glix. "You may find that goblets are a more civilized way to imbibe this essence than slurping it from a copper ladle," remarked the pranksy.

A flicker of a frown crossed the Viceroy's face before he continued. "I believe you will find this most stimulating, possibly even more stimulating than the best Quincian chocolate. We pranksies — and certain lesser creatures — sometimes call this remarkable essence 'Blood of Hallah.' I'm sure you'll agree that Blood of Hallah has an infinitely more dramatic ring to it than, say, 'quess.'"

40

Except for knowing that Hallah was the name of the planet she lived in, Glix had no idea what the Viceroy was talking about. Still, she suddenly realized she was hugely thirsty and took the offered goblet of liquid flames with her copper-gloved hand. To her surprise, the goblet was cool, not hot. A complex fragrance that hinted of peaches, sassafras, tangerines, rumwood flowers and other scents of a generally pink or orange nature tickled her nostrils. Her mind was so engulfed by the odd mixture of scents and the fringes of memories that were just out of reach that she completely missed the pranksy's toast: "To interesting times."

When she saw the pranksy raise the goblet to his lips and down the contents, Glix hastened to do the same. For all its delicious aromas, the draught tasted more like a slightly sweet-tart version of the bubbly mineral water from Seltzer Springs than anything else. And equally much like some other slightly fizzy water she had tasted recently, but that currently had a "Don't Remember Me" tag on it.

The pranksy tossed his goblet into the fire pit and Glix followed suit.

"Nothing like a little Blood of Hallah to quench a chocolate thirst and enliven the senses, eh Queen Glix of Quince? Now let us be serious. Item one: you are running away and got lost on the way to wherever you thought you were going. If it will make you feel any better, your arrival here was more about being found than getting lost. Against our better judgment, we wanted to meet the human who spoofed the simpletons of Quince with that copper glove fad. Brilliant, actually. Who but the one and only Glix Larue could have invented such a clever stratagem for hiding that beautiful blotch on your palm?"

The Viceroy tipped the brim of his hat, bowed slightly and said, "For that amusement, we tip our collective pranksy hat to you.

"Moving right along to item two, you have suspected us of complicity in a conspiracy to ruin your nice Quincian life, a moronic conspiracy not worthy of a hack novelist with his literary shoelaces tied together." It was a statement, not a question. The Viceroy continued before Glix could find the wit — or bad judgment — to respond.

"Forget that idea. It's got 'stupid idea' written all over it. It's a haircut-for-a-bald-person kind of idea, if you know what I mean."

Glix thought she had a vague idea of what the Viceroy meant by that.

"You see, Glix of Quince — note that I'm dropping the silly Queen business, by the way. Dear, innocent, misguided, hopelessly bamboozled Glix, if you think you've got troubles now, just wait a little while. Things are going to get really interesting, if you get my meaning. The business with what those yo-yo Notables called a cinder-egg and the stigmata on your palm? Zero, zip, nada! Your entertaining new speech affliction that has made you the Quincian Pariah of Niceness? You ain't seen nothin' yet, to borrow vernacular from another time and place.

"If you had a dozen lifetimes and lived each one differently from this point onward and were blessed with not too much help from the helpful help-fairy crowd, you might get out of your life alive. But — and this is a very important but — now that you have taken our feather, you are entitled to a choice of answers. You may not think you've asked your question yet, but just humor us, it's how we do things around here ...."

The Viceroy paused long enough for Glix to notice that the pink feather was now clamped between her own clenched teeth. She wanted to spit it out but her jaws refused to open. All she could do was wrinkle her nose and pucker her lips. It tasted relentless and sour, exactly like an unwanted habit must taste.

10

We'll Call You

"BUT FIRST," said the Viceroy, "don't you think you should tell us all how it felt to have your hand sizzled by that quantode? The one and only one of its kind that escaped being smashed to muckle-dust when that sky fragment landed in Fairdilly Commons, leaving that fried dirt stench hanging in the air for days? The very same item that you first thought was a lucky perfin egg and even more laughably still call a cinder-egg? We also want to know what the significance of the digits two and seven could possibly be?"

The stage whisper again: "That would be ever so entertaining, eh my fellows?"

This time, the Viceroy's invisible fellows were more muted in their response. Glix thought she heard "she's in for it now," and "that'll teach her to be born human," among the murmurs, but she decided they were just trying to scare her and tried to ignore them.

Glix recognized the look now on the Viceroy's face — her father's, actually. It was the one that showed up just before her father delivered a factoid he thought was particularly important. Her father loved delivering factoids.

"By the way, those big spidery things are called Keepers by folks in the know," explained the Viceroy before pausing again to inspect the girl's face.

"Smart of you to have kept the quantode's blast of information to yourself. The five yokels on the Council of Notables are self-important buffoons to a one...and at least one can be a very dangerous buffoon when the mood is on him. Lucky that the mark hadn't revealed itself yet or you wouldn't have been able to get away with that copper glove ruse of yours."

Glix found herself unable to come up with a worthy denial to these statements, which were all true anyway and shouldn't have needed denying. But with so much effort having gone into one particular deception, some part of her wasn't about to publicly admit that there was an ugly black scar-tattoo on her palm. So lacking anything creative — or at least inspired — she settled for a really lame denial instead, which she delivered with the most innocent expression she could muster under the circumstances. "Mark? What mark?"

"Silly girl! The human hasn't been hatched that can fool a pranksy for even a nanosecond. The mark that was hiding under the copper glove, of course." The Viceroy of Twisselman Wood fished around in a pocket of his cloak, then pulled out a copper glove and waved it in front of Glix's eyes. "This copper glove."

Glix swung her eyes toward her naked left palm: absolutely gloveless. Pulses of anger and shame rippled across her face: the ugly, swirly black whatever-it-was that she had worked so hard to hide from everybody was right there in full view. Except that now it didn't look quite as ugly as she had previously thought. If she had known anything about fractals, she might have recognized the pattern as one of those. Very orderly and beautiful in a paisley sort of way.

"Quite handsome, isn't it?" murmured the Viceroy, half to himself.

Glix opened her mouth, expecting something masterfully nasty to roll off her tongue, but the Viceroy held up his hand again.

"If I didn't know better, I'd say you were extremely, once-in-a-millennium lucky to come away from an encounter with a living quantode having only a pictoid of a certain Mandelbrot set burned into your palm and a few quazillion mysterious scenes burned into your graymatter. But then that lucky orange hair of yours and the cute little pink swirl behind your ear probably saved your life. Most likely the quantode thought you were one of the Specials from way back when. Or at least a genetic hiccup of one. Or maybe just a freak of nature with the raw material to maybe do something worthwhile someday. And soon. Maybe. But since I know better than to call you lucky to your pert little face, let's just drop it and get back to why you came here — and the whole choice business.

"Your choice is this: A, we will answer whatever silly, stupid, possibly even moronic question you think you want to ask, or, B, we will tell you where all your good answers are going to be hiding. How's that for a deal?"

Glix blinked and wished that scratching her head in public wasn't such a violation of niceness. She suddenly felt hugely stupid and clueless. Still, it seemed that a question was required and had decided to just go with ....

"But wait!" interrupted the Viceroy. "Are you aware that, despite what most clueless humans like to believe, there are almost never only two choices? What if, in your particular case, there was a third choice? This would be a very dangerous, risky choice that would involve doing battle with ELVIS."

A chorus of "you-just-made-that-up," "the-king-is-dead-long-live-the-king," and "you-ain't-nothin'-but-a ..." and such filtered down from the invisible hooting gallery.

"Quiet down, you hapless hound dogs. Not *that* Elvis. The *other* ELVIS, of course: Egregious Lazy Vain Ignorant Silliness. The knuckleheaded ELVIS unconspiracy that's just standing around twiddling its fingers while this once important planetoid destroys itself. If this really was a third choice, it would involve a bit more involvement with quessedness and ...."

The already dank air in Twisselman Wood dankened further and the already murky light tilted several more degrees in the direction of dark. All in the wink of a cat eye on the Viceroy's left wing. At the very same moment, every sound — even the unheard sounds of earthworms tunneling in the soil under the Viceroy's office — seemed to have been squeezed out of both the air and the area. You could have eaten that dank and murky silence with a spoon ... but you would probably have spit it out on account of the taste.

The silence went on and on and Glix found herself holding her breath while trying to remember something. Then there was a faint floral aroma; a gentle rain of blue petals fluttered down out of nowhere. Crocuses, thought the part of Glix's brain that knew her flowers.

The Viceroy held out a hand and a large blue crocus flower settled onto it. For a time he seemed to be studying it. Then his hands became a blur of motion; in a matter of seconds he had woven a wreath of crocus blossoms and placed it on Glix's head.

Glix blinked at this odd behavior, but said nothing as the pranksy cocked his head and studied her. "Our employer thinks a crocus crown would look good on you. Me, I'm not so sure about the blue and orange: a little too garish. But no matter. Our employer also thinks quess is a no-no: violation of the First Protocol. So let's just forget about a third choice, shall we?"

As he spoke, the pranksy looked up into the morass of vines and branches far overhead and seemed to be talking silently to no one in particular, but a particular no one in particular ... if that makes any sense. But the whole time he was looking up, all the eyes in his wings were winking at Glix.

When his gaze returned to Glix, he held out two closed fists. "Whatever your question might end up being, it's time to make your choice of answers. In this fist, Answer A. In this fist, Answer B."

Glix was about to make her choice when something burbled up to the top of her mind. It had been tugging away at the back of her mind in the same irritating way that small children do when they're trying to get a parent's attention. She just blurted it out. "You're the shadow that's been following me. You are, aren't you!" It wasn't a question.

The Viceroy with her father's face gave her a proud fatherly look. "Well guessed indeed!" He turned his head away and said in his annoying stage whisper, "For all the good it will do her, eh my fellows?"

Glix rolled her eyes, suddenly very tired of whatever silly game was being played here.

The Viceroy nodded, as if reading her thoughts. "Time to choose," he murmured.

Her next-to-the-last recollection of Twisselman Wood was of the Viceroy whispering a single word in her right ear after she had changed her mind and pointed at the fist containing Answer B. That single word was "dreams."

Her final recollection was the Viceroy's image wavering as he smirked out the words, "Don't call us; we'll call you."

48

11

Out of Sight

GLIX DREAMS about a white door in a wall made entirely of blue crocus flowers. The doorhandle is shaped like an uncoiling snake and endless streams of cockroaches scurry back and forth under it. Because there are no cockroaches at all in Quince, a little bubble in the dream shows a picture and some text describing the history and characteristics of the species Blatta orientalis. *Now cockroach-aware, Dream-Glix's sharp eyes notice that each cockroach has the letter "A" on its back in blocky white type.*

Hmmm, mutters Dream-Glix to her dream-self. She reaches out to twist the handle and sneak a peek inside, but is whiskered awake by sodbunny whiskers before her dream-fingers can even touch the writhing handle.

• • • • •

She blinked a groggy blink, sniffed the spicy aroma of waxbark leaves and felt a jab of panic. Where was she? Certainly not in a bed or a bedroom. A waxbark tree?

Light filtered through velvety deep green foliage that she now recognized as belonging to a flockleaf bush. Next to her was a certain rusty bicycle. Memories of her night ride flooded back from wherever memories do their napping. Alas, they did not include any recollections of crawling into a bush and going to sleep. In fact, they ....

Cinder's nimble fingers distracted her and Glix couldn't help a small smile. Her sodbunny held out a wad of breakfast: half-chewed

windwillow leaves from a cheek pocket. Evidently he'd been out forag-
ing already. Glix shook her head ruefully, reminded of her own empty
stomach, but grateful to have such a generous traveling companion.

Thoughts of hunger were swept aside as her ears belatedly woke
up and noticed a familiar sound filtering in through the dense shrubbery: the whoosh-whoosh-clack-clack sound that could only be a
General Steam steam-buggy.

Her heart skidded to a stop for an instant. Had they come looking
for her here already?

An important memory seemed to be on the verge of asserting
itself when some little door slammed shut in her mind. All memories
since hiding the stolen bicycle — including her night in the Lost Wayfarers Cottage and yesterday's events in Twisselman Wood — tucked
themselves away in some hidden brain-closet. And a smattering of
other important memories as well. She knew something was, well,
amiss, but not exactly what it was. Exasperating.

Glix frowned, absently brushed twigs and dried leaves from her
hair, and tried harder to dredge up whatever memorable memories
might be missing — if any were, in fact, missing. Some minutes later
she realized that the characteristic steam-buggy sound was gone, but
now there were other non-forest sounds. Switching mental gears, she
began to imagine being caught and hauled back to Quince and the
horrid Dr Runcipool's planned medical inquisition. The mark under
her glove sizzled a reminder to avoid this topic, making Glix somehow feel like a trapped animal.

Suppressing a sudden insane urge to lurch to her feet and flee to
nowhere in particular, she instead made a stealthy crawl to a nearby
sheltered spot where she could see the road.

Parked by the roadside was a standard cream and copper colored Transport Guild wagon, occasional puffs of egg-shaped steam
still popping from its stack. A hose snaked away from its water tank
and disappeared toward the Little Twisselman River. A groink-scup-
wheeze-groink-scup-wheeze sound came from that direction. Definitely not a search party; more likely a load of copper things bound

for somewhere or other. But what was that noise?

Creeping through the underbrush toward the source of the odd sounds, Glix spotted the driver; it was Jobie Arkaway, the uncle of the fat boy who, at the urging of Twinker's nasty older sister Jaynin, had squashed Glix's lunch-sack under his massive buttocks as payback for the pie-in-the-hair episode.

A squat, burly fellow, Jobie was working a seesaw pump that refilled the steam-buggy's water tank from the river. Why would he need to stop for water so soon? Scuttling back toward the steam-buggy, she spotted a growing puddle she had missed before.

Her current hiding place was about thirty feet away from the buggy. Quiet as a snail, Glix worked her way in slow, hunched-over steps toward a blackberry thicket at the edge of the road, then slid under the buggy for a quick inspection. A steady dribble was leaking from a dent in the belly of the tank, but the storage rack for extra wheels only had one wheel in it instead of the usual two. It was ahead of the spot with the leak and it looked like there might be space behind it for a person her size. Looking once in Jobie's direction she crawled underneath and pulled her body into the cozy little space. If a sore bottom could smile, it would have smiled at that moment; there would be no bicycling today.

Questions about the wisdom of this possibly rash act were quick in coming. Where was Jobie's load going? Had her absence been discovered yet? Were people looking for her already? Was Wixit putting too many greensugar lumps in her porridge again? Did the masses of sharply carved clouds mean it was going to rain hard today?

Dull scraping sounds interrupted the assault of miscellany and second thoughts. Glix guessed that Jobie was now winding the buggy's water hose back on its stow-hooks. Then she heard a wheezing grunt, a metallic clatter and something that might be a latch being latched.

Overcome by a moment of panic, she was starting to wiggle out of her perch when a door closed, springs creaked, levers scraped and pistons whump-whumped back to life. Before she could move any further, the steam-buggy whistled, lurched and made its way back onto Fairdilly-Quince Road.

Glix gulped and hauled herself back into her hiding place. Maybe it would work out after all. Her escape from Quince may not be going as she originally planned, but at least she hadn't been caught ... and she was neither walking nor bicycling.

It wasn't long before she began to think seriously un-nice thoughts about stowing away in this place. Every puddle splattered her hiding place with brown goo that smelled of fresh horse droppings. If Glix's sense of humor had been intact, she might have thought the layer of fresh, horsey mud made a good disguise. But she was too chilled, wet and battered by the bumpy ride to find humor in her predicament.

And her stomach was making empty noises that she feared could be heard even over the chuff-chuff-rumble-rumble. The thought of a chewy yumstick remained only a thought; she couldn't wiggle around enough in her cramped quarters to dig one out of her backpouch.

Although she was not good with distances and times, she convinced herself that Fairdilly Forks could not be far away: two hours further at the very most. The crossroads at Fairdilly Forks, with its copper dome and tall, fluted columns, was where she planned to drop to the ground, avoid being squashed by the big wheels, scurry out of sight and resume walking toward Hiphollow as soon as the coast was clear. No problem.

In fact, Glix was quite looking forward to walking again; much better than becoming a black-and-blue human sculpture dipped in smelly mud. To distract herself, she attempted to identify familiar landmarks along the road from the odd perspective of the buggy's undercarriage. It was neither easy nor fun.

Spatters of rain began and soon became an army of enemy raindrops marching to wha-whomps of thunder. With each bellow of thunder, Cinder made a pitiful whimpering sound and tried to burrow even deeper into her left armpit. His whiskers tickled.

By dint of much twisting and squirming Glix managed to pull the hood of her cloak over her head, which seemed like an excellent and cozy idea for a very uncozy spot. The hood kept most of the water and mud away from her face. It also kept the light away. After a time, the darkness, the warmth, the rocking motion, and the rhythmic creaks of the buggy combined to make Glix drowsy.

For a while she thought fondly of Mr Hipskander, the juggler at the Fairdilly Fair who had juggled Cinder to her as a present. She smiled to herself as she next thought of Mr Hipskander's shy son, who had stared at her hair nonstop while his father was juggling. She couldn't recall his name, but remembering his eyes and his smile kept her awake a little longer.

Then she slipped into slumberland, dreaming of the mysterious cinder-egg that had shot up from Longbottom Well and ended up in her hand.

• • • • •

The shriveled black thing is no longer shriveled or black. It is plumped up fat and smooth. Pulsating with a vibrant reddish-gold hue, the cinder-egg is floating down a thick river of golden sweet-runket pudding. As she watches it float away, tiny streams of sparkling crystal motes spew from its surface in a hundred directions. Somehow she knows the motes are tiny bits of information about something important. Oddly, she doesn't find this at all odd.

Realizing that chasing down the golden orb has become extremely important, Dream-Glix suddenly finds herself in an orange kayak. She paddles very hard to catch the cinder-egg, but it always stays just out of reach. From time to time, she stops paddling to scoop up a handful of pudding, which tastes precisely and perfectly wonderful. Twinkly motes settle like tiny loving caresses on her arms and cheeks, each imparting a tiny spark of information to be absorbed into her hungry brain.

The rowing, pudding-scooping and knowledge bursts continue for a long, long time, but Dream-Glix never seems to tire of the experience. After another eon of dreamtime, she realizes that the tiny sparks of information are starting to tell her something.

Shudder-clunk-hiss-clatter-whoosh. As these new sounds penetrate her awareness, the river stops flowing and the cinder-egg sinks out of sight.

12

Into a Steamy Night

MAJOR WRONGNESS! Glix shook her head awake to a gnawing feeling in the pit of her belly. There was no steam-buggy noise and no motion. Her ears detected only a steady drip-drip-splash-splash. And it was dark, a thick close darkness heavy with the smells of hot metal and lubricants.

Silly me, thought the enshrouded Glix as she twisted around in her cramped hideout and finally peeled the hood back from her head, exposing her eyes to light again. That made exactly no difference: darkness remained.

Then a distant thunk that might be a closing door made her heart thump like a drum in her chest and the hair on the back of her neck bristle.

Stifling a dozen groans, Glix extracted herself from the steam-buggy's undercarriage. For a time she lay on the cold smooth surface beneath it, just staring into the dark and listening. She must be in a building, one that creaked and groaned as if it were very old and cranky. Faint scurrying sounds came from her right, but didn't seem close enough to worry about.

Finally she slithered out from under and began to unwind kinked muscles and a spine that seemed to have forgotten how to straighten out. Her head ached, too. The whole running away caper had gone horribly askew and she couldn't imagine how it was going to get any better. In this mood, she sat back down against the steam-buggy, cradled her throbbing head in her hands, closed her eyes and tried not to think. About anything.

Instead, she thought about everything, all at once. Her throbbing skull seemed to be a writhing nest of hammer-headed snakes and there was nothing she could do about it. Then something changed. An odd remnant of her latest dream resurfaced; with it came the magical aroma of sweetrunket pudding. Then her mouth was filled with the taste of it, smooth and creamy and laced with just enough sweetness. Essence of sweetrunket pudding swirled through every corner of her mind, swabbing all the dark corners with golden light.

When the golden light faded, it left behind a vague sense of general well-being laced with the lingering aromas of her favorite dessert. It occurred to her that the head-snakes were gone and the headache, too. Weird, but a nice weird for a change.

Glix had no clue at all where that nice weirdness came from; nothing like that had ever happened before. Even the nasty blotch on her palm had taken a break. In fact, she had the strange sense that it was purring like a cat. Double weird!

Glix inhaled a deep breath, smiled, hauled herself upright again and opened her eyes. From far overhead, shafts of blue-white light cast awkward renditions of skylights on the concrete floor. She saw that the steam-buggy was parked inside a large storehouse of some sort. Strange smells prickled her nose and her empty stomach responded with a loud gurgle that left a dwindling trail of eerie echoes.

She pressed herself against the vehicle and waited for an outcry, but after a minute that seemed more like an hour, there was only the scurrying of tiny feet. Apparently safe for the moment, Glix cast around for an exit. The shadowy outline of a garage door was not far away, with a smaller, people-sized door beside it. She tiptoed away in that direction.

Through a crack in the doorframe, Glix peered into a misty gloom that must be early evening. Somewhere. But whatever somewhere this was, it was definitely not Fairdilly Forks, which contained only a crossroads, a colonnade and a Waystation, after all. No buildings like this. And this place hardly meshed with the mental pictures she had painted of Hiphollow.

She wasn't really surprised by these realizations, but she was certainly very angry. At herself. Idiot! Idiot! Idiot! railed her mindvoice. How could she be so stupid as to let herself fall asleep while being endlessly jounced around and splattered with stinky mud?

Her escape plan — if something that hasty and vague could be called a plan — had only involved getting to Hiphollow, where she knew at least two nice people. Certainly this place was anywhere *but* Hiphollow. Maybe Sipshilly, maybe Wickelwharf, maybe even …. Here Glix's mental self-trashing paused, hesitating to even mentally say the words Fogwit City. If half the stories were true, Fogwit City was by far the most disreputable and abhorrent place on the island of Wyn. Surely she wouldn't be so unlucky as to end up in Fogwit City. She pushed that horrid thought completely out of her mind.

Sipshilly, probably. Or maybe Wickelwharf. She knew absolutely nobody in either of those places, but at least nice Quincians didn't think poorly of those two towns. Still, she shuddered at the thought of so many strangers, none of whom, being non-Quincians, would have any reason at all to be nice to her, much less help her out of this stupid situation her long nap had gotten her into. She screamed an untranslatable mental scream and then started to wind down.

She recalled the therapeutic effect of her sweetrunket pudding dream and after a time she was calm enough to do something more constructive than berate herself. What was done was, unfortunately, done. Now something else needed to be done. Getting out of this place would be a beginning.

Inch by inch, Glix pushed open the smaller door and crept out onto a paved sidewalk next to a paved street. The moonlight revealed that it was lined on both sides with hulking brick buildings standing shoulder to shoulder. A warm and humid night pressed in on her and swirls of steamy mist gave the air a thickness she had never experienced in Quince. She didn't much like it.

Her heavy cloak was now out of the question. Brushing off as much of the remaining mud as possible, she rolled it up as tightly as she could and stuffed it into her backpouch. Then she squared her shoulders, mustered what courage she could muster and walked into a steamy night.

13

Or Would They?

LUMO WAS a lazy orb just cresting the tops of the structures and fa-
voring the mist with a silvery sheen. While she was nervous about being in a strange town all by herself, it hadn't yet occurred to her that
she might actually be in danger. She would be just fine in Quince,
after all.

The narrow street twisted away in two directions: up and down.
Down seeming an easier walk than up, she set off to her right. Clever-
ly painted garage doors seemed to be the fashion on this street. Some
were geometric patterns, some were complex swirly designs, some
depicted scenes with unfamiliar places, people and objects. Even in
the moonlight, all were colorful enough to skirt the very edge of garish. And entirely foreign to her bland Quincian sensibilities.

While her eyes were occupied with painted doors, her mind tried
to puzzle out where she was. She was pretty sure by now that it had
to be either Sipshilly or Wickelwharf. Both were harbor towns on the
Great Wet, which might help explain the muggy air with the odd tang.

The Hiphollow that Mr Hipskander had described was situated
in a mountain valley high in the Rocksaws. The town itself was located on an island in the middle of a place where five fast-flowing creeks
merged to become a river. Hiphollow folks mostly lived in home-
grown ildrits tucked among the hills and spent little time in town. At
least that was how she remembered the gangly juggler's words; now
it sounded far too far-fetched to be true. She pinched herself hard as

punishment for falling asleep and missing Fairdilly Forks, where she should have slipped away from the steam-buggy.

She was passing a dark, narrow gap between two buildings when a knee-high yellow-brown dog stepped out and stopped. Glix stopped, too. "Well hello there. I hope you are having a nice evening, wherever we are." It was the kind of thing you could say to a nice Quincian canine and get a nice waggly tail in response.

This dog growled, sniffed the air and growled again. Perhaps detecting the scent of Cinder wrapped around her neck like a green muff, it growled again. Cinder squirmed and the dog growled again, this time showing slavering jaws and rows of sharp teeth.

Glix took a quick step back and looked around for something like a stick. Nothing. The colorful street seemed as clean as new toothbrush. Falling back on niceness, she was about to say, "go home, nice doggie" in her very nicest voice when the dog upped the ante with a surly snarl and a small lunge in Glix's direction.

"YARRGH! Get back into your slimy dung-wallow, you scruffy pusswad, you mouse-brained eater of purple underpants! You-hear-me? I said GET!"

Those very words snarled forth in a meaner, nastier, downer-and-dirtier voice than you could ever imagine being uttered by a runaway Queen of Niceness. A twisted, squint-eyed expression and a threatening, I'll-whomp-your-pointy-nose-into-a-pancake gesture of her copper-gloved fist rounded out the package. And to emphasize her intentions, Glix snapped her fingers, hissed between her teeth and pointed. The dog whimpered, slunk down and ran up the street with its tail tucked so tightly between its hind legs that it might well have been stapled there.

Glix shook her head in disbelief. Had she really said that? She didn't even know what a dung-wallow was. Where did that come from? And purple underpants? The runaway queen grinned in spite of herself: wherever they came from, those un-nice words had worked ever so nicely on the dog. But it probably wouldn't be a great idea to say things like that to the *people* of this place. Or the people of any place, actually.

Presently she rounded a bend and came to an intersection illuminated by a streetlamp. To her right the streetscape became more varied. Nearby were closed shops, but further down a haze of lights and vague sounds suggested human activity...and possibly food. Her nose confirmed this and her stomach did a happy somersault of anticipation. And, yes, her treasured coin dispenser was still strapped to her waist.

In the other direction, the street was lined with dark buildings much like those she had just passed, but without the painted doors. Straight ahead, the steep street got even steeper before it bottomed out at a broad plaza. And beyond that was a waterfront lit with a thousand lights. Piers lined with sea-vessels stretched far out into a moonlit harbor where countless other sea-vessels rested at anchor. Here must be the Great Wet, the sea that covered most of her world. Twinkling lights on the sea-vessels gave the scene a picture-book appearance that Glix found most charming indeed.

Her eyes were now attracted to a distant mass of lights on an island in the eastern curve of the bay. It looked fuzzy in the mist, but seemed to be a solid mass of tall buildings all crusted with blinking lights: red, green, blue and yellow, mostly. And some of the lights formed shapes. Was that a golden butterwing with...a crown? And there; could that be a mythical horned misthawk? Some of the lights near the tops of the structures seemed to form words, but they were too distant to be readable through the hazy murk.

A memory from her class in Not-So-Nice Geography surfaced and a sick feeling blossomed in the pit of her stomach: Viggas. Was this spectacle of lights the legendary Viggas Island? An involuntary shudder shook her slender frame; Viggas Island held the very throne of infamy in the minds of most Quincians. Even worse than Fogwit City itself!

Why couldn't she at least have stowed away on a steam-buggy headed for Sipshilly, she grumbled to herself? She tried to look away, but Viggas Island was a truly magnetic sight. Only the urgings of her stomach eventually pulled her eyes back toward lights closer at hand.

Now Glix noticed the signs mounted below the streetlamp. "Street of Painted Doors," said one sign in plain letters. That explained the painted doors. "Cobnose Bay Drive" said the cross-street sign.

Of course.

Cobnose Bay was what Fogwit City was built around. The bay got its odd name from a famous operetta about a bloody pirate of Old Earth named Captain Cobnose the Red, who lost his nose in a sword fight and had it replaced with a nose carved from a corn cob.

If hearts could really sink, hers would have sunk at least to her knees. Now she would have to somehow backtrack many miles to get to Hiphollow. Probably hundreds of miles. And without the aid of a bicycle it could take days or weeks. To her surprise, this realization wasn't all that horrible. At least she was far away from Quince; Dr Runcipool would just have to perform his stupid inquisition without her. And nobody from Quince would ever think to search for a runaway Queen of Niceness in a place like Fogwit City. Or would they?

14

Under a Rock

BOISTEROUS LAUGHTER and conversation thickened the air like flour in gravy. Glix had rounded a bend in Cobnose Bay Drive and everything came alive. People were everywhere. Hundreds of them, maybe more. Glix felt a gentle wash of relief — and also a not-so-gentle pang of fear. How would a runaway Quincian girl fare in Fogwit City? No way to know, but the prospect of finding out was hardly inviting.

Rimming the edge of the street was a dense mass of colorful shops of all sorts, all crammed together shoulder-to-shoulder with no space between them. Many were closed and dark, but a brightly lit sweetshop, an assortment of pubs and eateries and several small inns were all still open for business. Certainly she would be able to find a meal and a bed tonight in Fogwit City.

A few minutes of wandering told her that the real action was in the large park lassoed by Cobnose Bay Drive. Trees on the periphery were lit by clusters of tiny lights, giving the area a lively, almost magical illumination. Must be glowinkles, concluded Glix — or whatever they called them here. Even stodgy, traditional Quincians hung up special bait in their trees to attract glowinkles during evening festivities in their backyards on pleasant sulu evenings.

The park was clotted with humanity. Some people just seemed to be wandering aimlessly while others clustered around men or women standing on stools. The stool-standers spoke in bellowy voices and made energetic motions with their hands. Still others stood in lines at kiosks that sold refreshments: ales, sweet-drinks, fried sea-snails, roasted nuts, gummy fruit-sticks, takeetoes and other stuff she had never even heard of in Quince.

Her stomach rumbled and her hand went to the coin dispenser on her belt. She fumbled around for a moment before she found it under her backpouch. The practical side of her decided it would be easier to use if it were in front. So she slid it around and in no time had exchanged several small discs of starglass for something familiar from her family's annual visits to the Fairdilly Fair: honey-roasted almonds, sweet-onion crispies and a dark, sweet, bubbly beverage called kola that had been outlawed in Quince when it was discovered that it caused the teeth of goats to dissolve.

Glix stood by herself at the edge of the park, munching, gulping and watching folk walking by or chatting in small clumps. Most ignored the girl with the bright orange tangle on her head and the bright green sodbunny around her neck, although odd looks or frowns were occasionally aimed in her direction.

The busiest frowners were a trio of girls a little older than Glix. They pointed at the shiny coin dispenser at her waist, giggled, tittered and made snide what-haywagon-did-you-ride-in-on looks. Overhearing bits of their conversation, Glix reddened; perhaps she should have left the coin dispenser where it was. She focused her attention on getting the last tiny bits of crispies out of the bottom of the bag and tried not to look in their direction. But she couldn't help looking. No one in Quince was that rude — well, not usually, at least — and no one in Quince dressed like that. Not even close.

For one thing, these girls all wore nearly identical outfits. Their legs were wrapped in glossy black leggings, topped by short skirts that seemed to be made entirely of shaggy strands of multicolored glass beads that tinkled when they moved. Higher up were tight sleeveless black tops made of a stretchy ribbed material that accentuated curvies and left midsections bare. Each girl sported glossy black lips and all were bejeweled with necklaces, bracelets and anklets made of the same beady stuff as their skirts.

At this distance, the only way Glix could tell them apart — besides their heights — was by the color of their braided hairpieces, which were evidently dyed to match the color of gum-bubbles their mouths were blowing.

Confronted with this bombardment of sneering Fogwit girl-fashion, Glix squeezed her lips together and made a hasty getaway into the nearest mass of older Fogwits.

The girls followed, continuing to point, snicker and giggle. Except for the tallest, haughtiest and shapeliest of the three, the one Glix had heard being called Zellah by the others. Zellah was having an intense whispered conversation with a trio of strangely-dressed boys, a conversation spiced with sly glances in the direction of her coin dispenser. Under her copper-gloved palm, the blotch began to tingle, a sensation Glix was able to ignore thanks to her fascination with the three boys.

Like the trio of girls, this trio wore nearly identical outfits. There were blousy-sleeved black shirts of a coarse fabric, wide leather belts studded with this and that, and tight black trousers tucked into shiny black longboots that looked quite expensive to Glix. For dramatic effect, all wore curvy black boat-brimmed hats decorated with all manner of shiny oddments. Topping the costumes were long black capes covered with patches that looked more decorative than functional. Apparently the capes were purely a fashion statement, since the weather was entirely too hot and muggy for cloaks and capes. Their right ears sported large gold rings and their faces bore the sneery expressions favored by bullies everywhere. Well, two of them did.

One stood out in some way that the others didn't. Partly it was his height: he was the tallest by several inches at least. But he also maintained a subtle distance from the others, almost as though he would rather be somewhere else. And he didn't sport the sneer. Then she noticed that he had a long wooden flute slung over his shoulder on a leather strap. Hmmm. Maybe he would prefer to be sitting under a tree amusing a runaway Middle Queen from Quince with a sad, haunting melody. And he was kind of good looking, actually.

Despite her fascination with the flute-boy, Glix decided it was time to be elsewhere. Even if she was in this strange city, she was still a Quincian, not a Fogwit, and she suddenly felt foolish for being here at all. Particularly when she would probably be in Hiphollow by now if she hadn't fallen asleep. "Sorry, Cinder. I bollixed this escape, didn't I? But we'll get to Hiphollow someday, somehow." Cinder only shifted his position around her neck.

66

Dodging all manner of people she soon found herself at the opposite side of the plaza, where a group was marching in a circle around a smoking brazier while chanting something about the sky. All wore heavy-looking sky-blue helmets painted with stylized clouds. Inside the circle a tall, dour man with a long blue-dyed beard, long blue-dyed hair and blue-dyed skin performed an odd ritual. Draped in a sky-blue robe and several necklaces of blue crocus flowers, he alternately threw sharp-smelling incense into the fire and made swooping motions with his hands, as though to hasten the acrid smoke into the sky. Nobody in Quince would do things like this in public and Glix found herself entranced and unnerved at the same time. Only half against her will, she drifted closer to the circle. For no apparent reason, the man abruptly stopped his swooping and began to peer intently at the various people in the crowd. His gaze stopped at Glix.

In Quince, people didn't just all of a sudden start staring at you for no reason. It just wasn't nice. But there was something about this strange man's gaze that made her stare back despite the un-niceness of it. For just an instant it was as if those four eyes were connected by an electric current. Then a tiny smile curled up the corners of the blue man's dour face. He winked at Glix and abruptly returned to his swooping. The spell was broken, but a link had been forged ... a link that would matter someday. She just didn't know it yet.

Glix blinked and shook her head in the same way a doused dog shakes off water. Then she shrugged: no wonder Quincians think Fogwit City is such an un-nice place.

Several other helmeted and be-flowered members of the group walked around distributing leaflets and speaking earnestly to anyone who would listen. One short young man with a bulbous nose offered one to Glix. "Thank you, kind sir" she said in her best queen of niceness tones. "Could you tell me who the blue man is? The one doing all the swooping?"

"He is Midas Blue himself, of course ... the emissary of Lady Crocus, the sky goddess. He came here from Songwater to bring her message to the people of Hallah."

"Oh," said Glix. Although she was not particularly interested in messages from sky goddesses at the moment, she was afraid she was going to hear it anyway.

"What the sky giveth, the sky can taketh away," said the young man with the bulbous nose. "Or something like that. 'Pay heed, the Time of the Crocus is upon us'. That's another thing Midas Blue says a lot."

"Oh," said Glix, smiling sweetly and slipping away into the crowd.

When she felt she was safe from Bulbous Nose, she stopped and noticed the leaflet in her hands. Her attention was immediately captured by the title: "Recent Sky-Fallings." According to this list, eight other bits of Hallah's sky had fallen since the Boom of the Century. The leaflet listed the date, time, location and classification of each one. None had evidently been as large and dramatic as the event at Fairdilly Commons, but then none had landed on land near populated areas, either, which possibly explained why people in Quince hadn't heard about them. Only two hadn't landed in the Great Wet.

The most recent had struck a tiny, unoccupied island to the north, about halfway between Wyn and the Loopskelter Archipelago. It had come down three nights ago. This fact got her attention: had this been what she had seen while she was contemplating the theft of Mookie's old bike? And how could that have happened three nights ago? Had she left an entire day under a rock during her escape from Quince?

68

15

Embarrassed Again

THE MARK on Glix's palm throbbed as if it had been whacked with a hammer. The pain knocked the matter of the missing day completely out of her mind. Before she realized what was happening, her eyes snapped shut and a waking dream took over her.

• • • • •

The scene is a dusty, arched tunnel that stretches away to a pin-point of nothingness. High overhead a pulsing, glowing tube basks the tunnel in a mottled pinkish-orange light. She now realizes that the image is moving, and fast. Imagined wind rustles through her hair, a feeling that is more exhilarating than frightening. Under-neath these physical sensations is a strong feeling that some great mystery is about to be revealed.

Just then something shakes her shoulder and wrenches her back to normal reality.

• • • • •

The captivating scene in her mind dissolved into the face with the bulbous nose. "Are you all right?" asked the blue-helmeted young man, his voice quaking with concern.

Glix blinked, frowned and felt as if she had been dragged kicking and screaming from a magical moment by the sting of a wasp. Her tongue responded with a sting of its own. "The real question, booger boy," she hissed, "should be 'Exactly what possessed you to touch me with that blob of slob-jelly you call a hand. And then stick your boogery red onion of nose in my face?' What made you think I need a boogery onion massage? Why don't you and your stupid flowers and your blue chamber pot go pester somebody else!"

The rant was hardly what one might expect from a sweet-faced, orange-haired innocent. The short young man with the bulbous nose blushed and stammered, "I...I...guess that m-m-means you d-d-don't want to make a donation to the C-C-Cerulean Society." He gave her a wide-eyed look that could have meant a dozen things, then slunk away to pester someone else.

Glix looked around and saw that her tongue-lashing of the hapless Cerulean had not aroused the ire of nearby folk. Quite the opposite. Three people winked and nodded, two grinned and winked, and four gave her thumbs-up signs. Still, now would probably be a good time to move on. Once again, she sought safety and anonymity in the jostle and bustle of the crowd.

She pushed herself past several dozen locals before she got to the inner fringe of a circle around two boys engaged in a pushing and shoving contest. They were two of the three boys she had found so fascinating earlier. She didn't see the tall one with the flute because he was standing right behind her.

Glix was stunned by both the public display of rude behavior and the fact that the crowd was cheering and jeering for their favorite ... or maybe just out of sheer nastiness. Ugh. What a horrid place was Fogwit City. Nothing like this would ever happen in Quince.

As if to underline this point, the three nasty Fogwit girls were directly across the circle from her. The same three that had been making fun of her were the loudest and most emphatic of the rabble-rousers. Glix was working on a dark scowl when the taller of the two boys suddenly grabbed his opponent's boat-brimmed hat and threw it directly at Glix.

Even as she lurched back into the crowd to avoid it, the hat smacked into her face. In the chaos that followed she was tackled, tussled and nearly trampled. Several loud whistles caused the chaos to dissolve almost instantly, thanks to two large, gruff-looking men in green uniforms and copper whistles. For those who might be un-deterred by their bulk and their whistles, the men waved short clubs in an authoritative fashion.

Glix pulled herself to her feet, dusted herself off and pretended that nothing had happened. The last remnants of the crowd trickled away, as did the men in green uniforms. Glix trickled away, too, but in the opposite direction of the bulk of the crowd; Cinder clung to her neck as tightly as if he had been stitched there.

A tall, airy framework at the very center of the park caught her eye. It was made from polished ironpalm poles, beams, struts and gussets, all bolted tightly together. On top was a platform supporting a large, flattened rectangle of glass filled with something like mud dotted with aimless flickers of colored light. Feeding unknown sub-stances into the top of the tank was a row of complicated looking copper hopper-funnels. Glix recognized the work of master Quincian funnelmakers. Latest models. The fact that her father had worked on them made her just a little proud.

This must be some kind of special toob, Glix surmised. Quincians have a sort of love-hate relationship with toobs. On the positive side, all toobs needed intricate, precisely made copper hopper-funnels. This keeps the funnelmakers of Quince quite busy and reasonably prosperous. The flip side was that Quincians generally do not ap-prove of the idea of people sitting gape-jawed and goggle-eyed, suck-ing in the colorful nonsense that was rumored to be displayed on toobs. Other rumors suggested that very un-nice things could also be seen on toobs. That explains why the only toobs allowed in Quince are the test-toobs in the Funnelmakers Guild laboratory.

Glix wasn't thinking about any of this at the moment. Since no-body seemed to be noticing her, she decided to explore the structure as a possible place to store her backpouch. Not only was it heavy, it branded her as a traveler; no one else in the park sported a backpouch. Finding no better hiding place, she tucked it under some shrubbery at the foot of one of the heavy poles supporting the toob-platform. Were this Quince, her backpouch would be perfectly safe.

Somewhere in the distance, a bell sounded three loud peals. This was evidently some sort of signal, as the scattered park-goers became a crowd again and converged upon her very location. Evidently something was about to happen here.

A clue might be the large banner hung between two nearby trees. "Sillydilly Follies: Special Show Tonight," said the whimsically ornate lettering. Glix craned her neck to look up at the toob. The flickers of color were now forming shapes. She backed up to get a better perspective, stumbled on a tree root in the turf and fell flat on her back. Her breath blew out with a whoof!

The turf was cushiony and except for having some difficulty breathing, she didn't seem to be hurt. Well, if you don't count the moon-sized bruise on her self-esteem; finding oneself on the grass for the second time in less than an hour can do that.

Cinder sprang from his mistress' shoulder before her landfall and made a zig-zaggy run through a dangerous moving forest of feet, legs and shadows. But before Glix even noticed he'd been gone, he was back, wiggling his way under her shirt.

Glix was just getting her breath back when a sizzle from under her glove prompted her to look up. Cowled figures in black robes and brown sashes now completely encircled her, their faces hidden in shadows. The cowled heads bent forward in unison. She felt cowl-hidden eyes focus on her as if she were some kind of large insect in need of their helpful scrutiny. Glix pressed back against the turf in an irrational hope that it might protect her from so much concentrated helpfulness. For a fact, the looming figures seemed far more menacing than helpful. And why were they all pointing at her glove?

Hands emerged from the folds of black robes and began to reach for her. She screamed for about half a second before one helpful hand clamped itself over her mouth. She tried to bite it but her teeth couldn't find a grip; worse, the soft, clammy hand was shutting off her air supply.

From under Glix's frilly orange shirt, Cinder heard his mistress' brief scream and panicked. He began to dart back and forth across her chest trying to find a way out.

Startled exclamations hissed from behind the cowls; there was something wild and possibly dangerous here ... something unexpected. At some secret signal, the black-robed ones all lurched back and melted into the crowd.

The scream Glix had started was now morphing into semi-hysterical giggles. Had there been a contest in Quince for Queen of Ticklishness, Glix would have been a front-runner for that crown, too.

"Stop it right now, you little green shirt-weasel!" whispered Glix between giggles, still lying flat on her back. Did that help? Not even a squidget. Cinder was too busy darting and squirming to be stopped by mere words. She had to clasp both hands to her chest before the sodbunny finally stopped his frantic movements. She lurched to her feet, still giggling and not yet realizing she had become part of the evening's entertainment.

Scattered titters, chuckles and chortles trickled out of the crowd and Glix's face flushed in response. At least the help-fairies were gone and her palm was no longer on fire.

A brassy fanfare put her embarrassment on hold and distracted the onlookers. The pompous music blared from an array of large horns attached high on the framework. Overhead, the random patterns of color in the giant toob resolved to an aerial view of the wind-shark races at recent Fairdilly Fair and a title: "Sillydilly Follies." The toob-show had begun and Glix was about to be embarrassed again.

74

16

Carried Off

SLIPS, FLOPS, FLUBS, mess-ups, pratfalls and such drew hoots, jeers and catcalls from the crowd. Glix was totally absorbed by the toob-show, feeling equal parts annoyed and fascinated. At the end of each incident, a subtitle displayed a snide synopsis. Not fair, thought Glix. And pointlessly un-nice, too. This toob-show gave the impression that everyone and everything at the annual Fairdilly Fair was nothing but clumsy nonsense.

The crowd's next whoops and hollers came at the expense of none other than the kindly Mr Hipskander of Hiphollow, the juggler who had gifted her with Cinder. His gangly physique, animated larynx and green hat with a brim like a giant pancake were clownish enough to evoke plenty of rude comments. But then he accidentally dropped a sodbunny. It was during one very difficult over-the-shoulder-and-behind-the-back juggling routine, but the toob-watchers applauded his mistake as though he had done it just for their amusement. Glix's irritation became a simmering anger.

But the sequence wasn't finished. As Mr Hipskander made a jerky, awkward movement to avoid squishing the creature, the sodbunny scampered at just the wrong moment and got stomped under a quaint black shoe. The Fogwit crowd burst into frantic belly laughs as the sad-eyed man stopped juggling and bent down to pick up the twitching green form.

The living sodbunny wrapped around Glix's neck made a pitiful, strangled sound. The subtitle appeared: "Hiphollow Stick-Man Discovers New Formula for Green Goop." Glix's simmering anger came to a rolling boil.

Very, very, very un-nice thoughts were straining like sprinters in their starting blocks at the tip of Glix's tongue. It took icy buckets of willpower to keep from screaming at these Fogtwit jerks. Then the view shifted to the Bottlefishing Derby at Longbottom Well.

The day was waning and only a single youth still fished for a fortune-worm in a bottle. This youth wore a frilly orange shirt decorated with blue funnels, had a mass of wavy orange hair and wore a copper funnel-crown on her head.

The horns up on the framework belched out a silly, blurpy sound just as the youth made an abrupt backward lurch. The scene went into slow motion and the backward lurch became a lazy, syrupy back somersault. The scene slowed even more and zoomed in on the face of the somersaulter just as it went splat into the puddle.

The Fogwit crowd erupted, and then hushed itself just as quickly. The image split into two parts, one frozen on a goofy-mouthed mud-faced girl with a huge brown droplet suspended from her button nose. The second followed the wobbly progress of the crown. It slowed, slowed some more, and then teetered on the edge of a mud puddle.

Ratchety music wound up to a dizzy crescendo then stopped short. Dead silence. The crown made one last wobble, then flopped upside down into the puddle. A sound-effect from the horns made a single, loud "plooop." The subtitle appeared: "Queen of Quince Shows Niceness to Puddles."

The crowd roared. And roared and roared. Glix was speechless. The image gradually dissolved and was replaced with lettering that said simply, "The End." After presenting a list of credits that meant zilch to Glix, the toob went back to random spatters of dull color against a field of muddy gray. Evidently the show was over. Glix turned her back on the horrid toob and stood, arms akimbo, staring at the crowd that was now applauding with great gusto.

Gradually the applause trailed off and the crowd began to break up. The toob-show and the crowd's response were so utterly un-Quince-like, that Glix just stood in shock. She wasn't even embarrassed at the image of her own muddy face on the huge toob. Actually, she had to admit she would probably have laughed at that, too. But not at a poor sodbunny being scrunched by a foot that was desperately trying to avoid it. Never that!

While she was occupied with these thoughts, she didn't notice the small clusters of the remaining Fogwits pointing fingers in her direction and whispering things among themselves, like:

"... really from Quince?

... what they do with funnels, don't you?

... the one on the toob?

... no piddledripping funnelhead gidget would dare come here ..."

Glix gradually became aware that comments were being aimed at her and looked up to see that some were coming from the trio of rude girls and their bravos. The tall girl called Zellah wore a sneering smile and held one arm in the air. Something familiar dangled from it: her very own belt with her very own coin dispenser.

Almost as an afterthought she put her hands to her waist: no belt, no coin dispenser. And no starglass, either.

The final thread of Glix's fraying tolerance for Fogwit City and its horrible people snapped. Her arms made wild, closed-fisted gestures that might have been threatening had they been made by someone much older and much bigger and much less innocent looking. Then out of her mouth spewed a sizzling blast of slurs, insults and invective, leavened with occasional bits of scatological slang. Such magnificent vehemence had never, ever been heard in Quince and was rarely heard even in Fogwit City. At least in public. Impossible to believe that this all erupted from the mouth of a Queen of Niceness.

Glix wound down. Now she just glowered at the shocked faces in the crowd. Some were slack-jawed with surprise. Others frowned in puzzlement. Several had eyes that squinted with evil intent. The six culprits had disappeared, but as if by some silent command, even nastier elements in the crowd began to come forward and press around her. She could feel the heat of angry eyes; hear the threats and rumbles of malice. And was that metallic glint really the tip of a dagger?

For the first time, her uncontrollable tongue had gotten her into truly dangerous territory. Where were those help-fairies when she really needed them? Worse, a sudden prickling of her left palm seemed to be telling her something. She had an ugly sensation that some dark force was looming up behind her. Trapped and helpless to do anything about it, her anger surged back and she spun around to face whatever was behind her.

The dark force she had sensed was a tall man dressed in an elegant formal black suit. He had a powerful, square-jawed face with an aquiline nose and glittering black eyes that seemed to be boring holes into her forehead and calculating the number of brain cells in the crowd at the same time. On top of his head sat a sleek black tophat. Glix could not repress a shudder at the sheer power the man exuded. There was nobody even remotely like that in Quince.

A restless hush fell over the crowd. The silence stretched on and on until the tension approached the inevitable breaking point. Then into that ominous silence there came a sound, a sound so sudden and so unlikely that Glix almost fell over backwards again. The man in black brought his huge hands together and began to clap with great enthusiasm.

Five burly men in black turtlenecks accompanied the man in black. These men began to clap with equal enthusiasm. The remaining Fogwits in the park got the message and began to outdo each other with the fervor of their handclapping ... even those with malice in their eyes and evil in their hearts.

After a time, the man in black held up his hands for silence. The man's five burly assistants also held up their hands. The crowd instantly settled into an uncertain silence.

"Good citizens of Fogwit City, the Fates are indeed smiling upon us tonight. As your Mayor, I wish to express my appreciation to each and every one of you for supporting your city's first Toob-in-the-Park program. And what a program, eh? Not only has Berlyn Twick shown us her most masterful reality cutting to date, she has also gifted us with a splendid moment of live theater to round out the program. Let's hear it for Berlyn Twick!"

The crowd roared, just as requested. At just the right moment, the Mayor once again held up his hands for silence.

"We have also witnessed a sneak preview of Berlyn Twick's latest discovery, a new Rising Star. A young Rising Star, the likes of which Fogwit City has not seen since young Merrigold Wynter sailed away with a prince of the faraway Loopskelter Archipelago. Has any among you seen a more splendid anti-parody of Quinceness? I think not." The Mayor frowned and slowly, gravely shook his head.

The Mayor's five burly assistants all frowned in caricatures of deep thought and moved their heads from side to side.

Fervent head-shaking rippled through the crowd, even though few, if any, had ever heard of an anti-parody before.

"Now, let's have a great big Fogwit City hand for Berlyn Twick's latest Rising Star ... Miss ...." The Mayor looked down at Glix and paused — possibly for dramatic effect, possibly to buy time to think — then bellowed, "Miss Tangerine Cream!"

At a signal from the Mayor, two of the five burly assistants hefted Glix high into the air and then settled her onto their shoulders. One pinched her leg and hissed between his teeth, "Wave to those morons if you know what's good for you. And make it look sincere."

Glix waved. And made it look sincere.

As the mystified runaway queen from Quince was carried to the Mayor of Fogwit City's long black steam-carriage amid deafening cheers, a new Fogwit Rising Star was born.

The backpouch with its funnel-crown and the belt with the coin dispenser were each carried off in other directions altogether.

80

17

Around Her Neck

THE MAYOR of Fogwit City popped another large roasted blicker-nut into his mouth, crunched it once and swallowed. By Glix's count, that made ten since they had steamed away from the toob-crowd. Glix had never seen anybody in Quince eat more than two in one sitting for fear of becoming over-energized, a condition Quincians called "blickered." In most Quincian families, children weren't even allowed to eat them at all. And on the odd occasion that they *were* allowed, it would never, ever be at night.

The Mayor sat between two of his assistants in a padded black leather seat. Glix sat across from him between two more assistants. A fifth sat in the forward compartment with the driver. For a man of such awesome personal power, Glix thought the Mayor seemed restless and unsettled. How could that be?

He had stared at her once or twice, then frowned and looked at the night sky through a window in the roof. He had not yet said a word. Nor had his assistants. Glix felt confused and more than a little frightened, but she was determined to never open her mouth again except to eat. She sat with her lips pressed tightly together, focusing on the carpeted floor as if it were a map to a fabulous treasure horde. Cinder clung to her neck and shuddered occasionally for no apparent reason.

From time to time Glix looked up from the floor and out the window. The powerful headlight beams slashed away the night like glowing broadswords, leaving spooky afterimages in Glix's brain. Was she was being taken back to nice old Quince? To a Fogwit place for stupid girls who talk too much? To a ....

With no warning whatever, Glix's stomach interrupted her thoughts with a groy-yoy-yoy-yoing noise. Glix's brain might have forgotten all about being really hungry, but her stomach had not.

The Mayor cocked his head and looked at Glix. "Hungry, eh? Well, if you can hold out a few minutes longer, you and I are going to have a nice grilled redfish dinner. Just in from Sipshilly, the redfish. You like redfish, of course." It wasn't a question.

"Meanwhile, have one of these." The big open hand held five or six hard-glazed blickernuts. In Quince, blickernuts like that were only bought for fancy dinners with somebody like the Grand Funnelmaster.

Glix knew she should say something like, "No thank you, Mr Mayor. I'm not allowed to eat hard-glazed blickernuts after dark... or ever, actually." But she kept her lips squeezed shut. Her stomach, however, repeated its plaintive groy-yoy-yoy-yoy-yoing.

"Come now, pretty Queen of Niceness. You're not in Quince and you don't have to follow silly Quincian rules. Listen to your stomach if you don't want to listen to me. Now have one. Or have two. Actually, have as many as you want. There's more than you could ever eat in that bag over there. Got a special supply in from my own plantation up on Mullver's Rock. Now hold out your hand."

Glix shrugged and held out a hand while the Mayor dropped three blickernuts into it, each with a different colored glaze. They sat there for only two seconds before all three were stuffed into her mouth at the same time. Anyone who has tried to chew three golf balls at once already knows what it's like to chew three hard-glazed blickernuts at once. Glix mumbled something that would have been a courteous thank-you if the blickernuts hadn't gotten in the way. The Mayor nodded, winked and went back to staring out the roof window.

Glix's mouth was still suffering from blickernut overload when the carriage shuddered to a stop in front of a pair of tall, heavy-looking gates. Outside, one of the Mayor's burly assistants was conversing with an equally burly uniformed guard. The gates slid aside and the steam carriage moved forward only to stop again a minute later. When the carriage doors swung open a servant in sleek black livery escorted Glix up a long, heavily landscaped walkway to a majestic structure on a hill overlooking Fogwit City and Cobnose Bay. To the bulging-cheeked Glix, the Mayor's mansion looked every bit as large as the Longfunnel Inn had been. Actually, it was much larger.

By the time dinner was served, the blickernuts had taken effect. Glix was now wearing an elegant-but-itchy black velvet dress supplied by the Mayor's staff, but pumped up by the blickernuts she felt anything but elegant. More like jump dancing or windmilling her arms or turning a dozen front flips. Instead she bit her lip, sat politely, controlled her wide-eyed energy as best she could ... and ate.

The broiled redfish was seasoned with sweet herbs and minced redroot, a popular Fogwit City spice that made her lips pucker and the top of her head tingle. Very un-Quince-like, but the effect was not unpleasant. An assortment of glazed fingerbreads and hickwort pickles also found their way into her mouth. It was just possibly the best meal she had ever eaten.

Cinder ate a salad of fresh windwillow leaves, lulubean pods and sliced sod-tubers, with a garnish of wiggly glowinkle grubs. Evidently the Mayor's kitchen knew exactly what sodbunnies like best.

In addition to stuffing her mouth, Glix talked. The Mayor asked just enough questions to keep the conversation in the vicinity of the recent Fairdilly Fair, which seemed to interest him.

Somehow the conversation always came back around to the cinder-egg. Glix's responses to the Mayor were no more detailed than her responses had been to the Council of Notables right after the incident at Longbottom Well. And anyway, Glix would much rather talk about Mr Hipskander and sodbunnies and watching windshark pod-races and cheering for her favorite hoop-jumping bluefish. And she did.

She also talked about being Queen of Niceness and how nice that had been until the troubles her sudden speech affliction had caused.

There were some tears when she talked about pedaling away from Quince, sleeping under a flockleaf bush and sneaking a ride in the steam-buggy's undercarriage. The Mayor offered his pocket kerchief to blot her tears and made properly sympathetic noises. She went on at some length about the general rudeness of Fogwit folk and about the particular rudeness of the Fogwit teens that had stolen her coin dispenser and all her starglass coins, upon which the Mayor frowned, nodded and made a significant gesture to one of his assistants.

Glix was so wired and chatty that she might have even mentioned her visit to Twisselman Wood and her disturbing experiences with the pranksy Viceroy, but that chunk of time was still tucked away in a locked closet somewhere in her memory. So she didn't.

Dessert was being served when the Mayor scratched a thick eyebrow, furrowed his forehead, pointed at her left hand and said, "A most exquisite glove, Miss Larue. Is it really copper?"

"Yes, it's copper thread mixed with glassworm silk. And thank you for inquiring, Mr Mayor," replied Glix sweetly. "Fashion statement. Mrs. Gidlet made it." Glix hoped that information would satisfy the Mayor, and apparently it did, for he just nodded and said no more about it.

When she could stuff not one additional morsel of sea-lime pie into her mouth, she looked the Mayor in the eye and spoke in a kind of whiny-surly tone that most people would be wise enough to avoid using with the esteemed and powerful Mayor of Fogwit City. But Glix, being more than a little blickered, couldn't think very wisely.

"What is it about that stupid shriveled cinder-egg thing, anyway? Nobody in Quince would say one stupid word about it except my father that one night when I overheard him say that somebody stole it and something about rug-splattered fairies. Who would care enough about that stupid piece of junk to steal it?" Except for Glix's overuse of the word "stupid" it was possibly the right thing to say at the time.

The Mayor ignored her tone and smiled a big, I'm-your-best-friend type of smile that showed a mouthful of large, white teeth. "Well you're a clever girl, Glix: you tell me. All I know is that they're very rare. Anything that's very rare is very interesting to me; I'm a collector, you see. Let me show you my Museum of Rare Things — when you've quite finished eating, of course. No need to rush."

The energizing effect of the blickernuts was wearing off and Glix was suddenly very tired and also a bit wobbly, possibly from the several petite glasses of sweet wine that had been served with dessert. As the brain-twisting events of her last twenty-four hours collapsed in on her mind, she teetered forward.

The Mayor held out a hand to steady her. "Tell you what, Miss Larue; let's tour the Museum some other time. You've had a very long and very eventful day, and I'm sure a good night's sleep will do you a world of good. Tomorrow, I'll have Professor Nardowil deal with your 'speech problem'. He's from the Collegium and is the best physiomage in all Hallah. Fortunately for you, he happens to be in Fogwit City for an emergency conference on the matter of Hallah's falling sky. He and I go way back and I am certain he will have your Quincian niceness restored very soon, possibly, um, quicker than you might wish."

Glix blinked half-lidded eyes at the Mayor. "I don't understand …"

"Nothing to trouble yourself about. It's just that as of this evening you've become a celebrity. So far as anybody in Fogwit City knows, you're Tangerine Cream, a Rising Star with a remarkably, uh, shall we say 'colorful vocabulary'. Here in Fogwit City, most celebrities like their bit of limelight. But if you want your drab old Quincian niceness back, I'm sure Professor Nardowil can do the job. So rest easy tonight, Glix from Quince. All will be well."

Glix wasn't at all sure all would be well and she didn't quite trust the Mayor. But she soon found herself lying in a huge, soft bed in a huge room with walls of scrolled plaster the color of butter and carved furniture made from honey-colored wood with a swirly grain. It also had its very own huge bubble-tub in its very own private alcove. Wide windows and a spacious balcony overlooked the city and the harbor, and the lights of Viggas Island twinkled reddishly in the glow of Rhomo. She barely noticed. As she snuggled the soft comforter around her, echoes of "all will be well" danced through her head, bringing a rainbow of relief to her battered brain; the moment Cinder curled himself around her neck she was asleep.

18

Iced on the Instant

BERLYN TWICK sat in the sumptuous breakfast room of the Mayor's mansion and fumed. It was absolutely *not* where she needed to be at the moment. What annoyed her the most was the bin of valuable unpeeled eyebuttons at risk of getting stale back in her toob-lab. The Mayor had promised that a butterwing would be here any minute to take instructions back to her lab-boy. Any moment, my butt, thought Berlyn Twick. If they spoiled, somebody would pay. Big time.

Next down on her annoyance list was the fact that she had been roused out of a sound sleep late last night by two of the Mayor's burly assistants and then driven to the Mayor's manse where she spent the night in the fabulous Cobnose Suite. The only explanation given was this: "The Mayor would like to personally congratulate you on your masterful work with the Sillydilly Follies. Now."

If those irritations weren't bad enough, her creative integrity was being compromised by this absolutely outrageous Mayoral whim. And by the dull-as-a-pigeon, carrot-topped, barely pubescent twit of a Quincian nicebody sitting across from her. Flix or Schmix or Brix or something. What was it with Quincians and the letter "x," anyway? Some kind of mindless "nice" thing? Fogwits never used "x" in their names. Berlyn Twick had previously had dealings with two funnel salesmen from Quince and each had an "x" in his name. She glared across the table at Glix with unrelenting hostility, as if names with "x's" were the runaway queen's fault.

Actually, there was one tiny spark of potential amusement to leaven Berlyn Twick's hostility: the upcoming "therapeutic exercise" with Professor Nardowil. The much-celebrated Fogwit City auteur now gave Glix a small, just-wait-until-you-see-what's-in-store-for-you smile.

Glix's response to the strange purple-skinned woman's hostility was to scrunch her lips tightly together, shrink a little deeper into her red velvet seat cushion and focus her attention on getting a glazed slickberry onto her two-tined dessert fork. Not easy, that. And no easier to keep her lips zipped. A thousand insults, curses and un-nicenesses from every category were impatiently awaiting release. Really, only the echoes of the Mayor's "all will be well" and the fact that Professor What's-His-Name would be here soon kept her mouth sealed.

The electric silence was broken by a bland comment from the Mayor. "I wish you could have seen that crowd, dear Berlyn. They were most fascinated by your new Rising Star. In fact, I would go so far as to say ...."

"No no no no no no NO! Is that quite clear enough, Mister Mayor?" Berlyn Twick had no qualms about interrupting the Mayor. Auteurs have special rights. "What you ask is absolutely impossible. Turn this limp-witted Quincian nicebody into a Rising Star? I have done at least 4,726 impossible things in my life. The impossible is nothing to me. I eat impossible for breakfast, as you well know.

"But impossibly impossible? Yes, I'm a creative genius. You have said so yourself on more than ten occasions. But I'm a *practical* creative genius. Impossibly impossible? I just don't even bother with it. Waste of time. Makes no sense. None." Berlyn Twick paused to catch her breath and glare more daggers at Glix.

"Even if it were merely impossible or semi-impossible, I have retired from the business of creating Rising Stars. As - you - well - know, Mister Mayor." Berlyn Twick spaced the words w-a-y out for emphasis. "But even supposing I was just a twitch interested in Rising Stars again, the name Tangerine Cream is impossibly impossibly wrong. Wrong doesn't get wronger than that.

"My fans would instantly know that no Rising Star of Berlyn Twick's could possibly be named Tangerine Cream. And to use Tangerine Cream in the same breath as Merrigold Wynter? Mister Mayor! I thought you respected my work. Call me naïve, but I really, honestly did. But this? This ...."

Berlyn Twick seemed to have finally run out of words. Her eyes were over-round and bugged-out, and small froths of spittle bubbled around the corners of her thin-lipped mouth. Glix inspected Berlyn Twick's face as best she could without looking directly at the woman.

The Mayor had introduced her as an "auteur supreme", whatever that was. Evidently an auteur was a Fogwit City word for somebody that creates toobish nonsense and looks as weird as she acts un-nice. Nobody in Quince used skin-toner at all, much less purple skin-toner. And nobody in Quince wore mouse brown berets, either. Fogwit City people were every bit as strange as people in Quince said they were.

Glix snuck a quick peek at the Mayor, who was sitting next to her. A small, bland smile was glued to his face. The toob-woman's tirade seemed to affect him not at all. He sighed a deep, mayor-quality sigh.

"Berlyn, Berlyn, Berlyn. I'm surprised that you underestimate yourself so. You *are* a genius, my dear. There is no doubt about it. None. I have been a fan for years and years. And there is certainly nothing impossibly impossible about the small favor I am asking. Here. Take a look at this."

The Mayor reached inside his pinstriped waistcoat and removed a thick rectangle of folded papers: the current edition of the *Fogwit Morning Lobster*. He gave it a cursory raised-eyebrow glance and passed it across the table to Berlyn Twick. Glix caught a glimpse of a large, bold headline, under which was a picture of Glix herself during her tirade of the night before. The headline read: "Twick's New Tweet."

Glix was just the tiniest bit pleased to see her very own Quincian self in this Fogwit newspaper.

"If you flip to page seven, you'll see that even the ever-so-picky Carriot Glamfass seems to be quite taken with your Tangerine Cream concept." The Mayor winked at Glix. "I believe he says something like 'a true masterstroke of anti-comic showmanship.' Something very close to that. And *Miss Duffy's Toobfarer News* is even better. It appears your Tangerine Cream has already won the hearts of critics and fans alike."

Glix sensed a subtle softening in the strange-looking woman's demeanor, as if it had just gone from being as hard as iron nails to being only as hard as copper rivets.

Berlyn Twick flipped through the *Lobster*, an iron-jawed scowl welded onto her already juttish features. She seemed to be counting something through clenched teeth. Seconds of silence slithered away before she hissed at the Mayor. "*Your* Tangerine Cream, Mister Mayor. Yours. Not mine. *Never* mine. And that's final. Impossibly final. As an impossibly large favor to you, we will do what we can do. But a little bit later.

"Now where is that butterwing you promised? Those new eyebuttons absolutely must be iced on the instant."

19

Only Temporary

"AH, YESS. Ah, yess. Ah, YESSS!" Professor Nardowil's hissed sibilants launched a spray of spittle in Glix's direction through a wide gap between two of his front teeth. She ducked, managing to avoid all but one of the larger droplets. The bullet of yellowish slime she didn't avoid connected with her earlobe where it stayed until she wiped it off with a finger and then wiped the finger on the elegant upholstery of her chair.

Glix glared at the otherwise thin man with the bulbous nose, bulbous paunch and loose-jowled face. "Yeech!" she hissed. "You slobbering blubberoon! Bucket your head when you start 'yessssing' in my direction. I mean, if you could find a bucket deep enough to cover all those chins. Or maybe you just swallowed a squeezebox? What-ever. And take off that ridiculous pink hairnet before somebody decides you're a kissy-dog disguised as a yuck-bubble."

The former Middle Queen clamped both hands over her mouth and flushed. Talk about bad timing; this man was here to make her nice again so she could go home and resume her nice, queenly life. She pretended to smooth out a wrinkle in the tangerine colored morning dress selected for the occasion of the Professor's visit. Perhaps sensing the tension in the room, Cinder relocated himself to one of his mistress' baggy pockets and took a nap.

A corner of the Mayor's drawing room erupted into applause punctuated with several sharp whoops! "You tell him, Schmixie! Attagirl! We may be able to do something with you yet! Where'd you learn that shtick? You ever played Viggas out in the bay?" Berlyn Twick seemed genuinely amused. And just a little perplexed: Professor Nardowil wore no hairnet, pink or otherwise. But he did look a little like a yuck-bubble with that tight tweed suit stretched over his bulbous belly.

Professor Nardowil's mouth opened and closed, but nothing came out. Not even spittle. He turned to glare at the Mayor, who was observing from a nearby chair. "I will not pe inssssulted..." he began, hissily.

The Mayor blinked, rolled his eyes, then wiped his own sprayed forehead with an embroidered hankie. "The girl has a point, Professor. Perhaps an overzealous tongue, but her bucket idea is quite practical. In fact ...." The Mayor gestured to the only burly assistant immediately available. The man departed the room, possibly in search of a bucket.

"Now, Professor, let's get back to business. Evidently, you have reached some sort of determination as to the young lady's problem. Please share it with us."

The Professor was not quite mollified. "Young LADY? Thisssss isss no lady. In any casssse, little can pe done for thisss persssson! The proplem, you ssseee, isss thisss: her esssssenshal character isss clearly inssssstalled in the opversssse phassse. Thisss isss to ssssay, packwardsss. My tessstss indicate the inversssion is a resssent occurrensse. A pranksssy trick? Perhapsss. Perhapsss a crack in the morality nodesss? Perhapsss an infessstassion of ssslurprixesss in the ssspeech ssentersss? Perhapsss ...."

While the Professor was perhapsssing, a tiny translucent spy was listening from a convenient shadow. The spy was a moth the size of a baby's fingernail, its mothy wings marked with a pattern of translucent eyes and ears. Moths of this unusual species had been spying on Glix since before she was born. Of course, spy-moths spied on lots of humans.

But back to the drawing room.

The Mayor had become annoyed with the Professor's perhapsssing. "Yes, yes. Perhaps this, perhaps that. I am paying your sizeable fee so that you can return the poor, afflicted girl to normal. By normal, I mean Quince-normal, of course. As always, a simple pill would be best. Or even a capsule. And right away. As Mayor of this fine city, I naturally have other matters that require my attention." The Mayor's right foot tap-tap-tapped the tile floor to underscore his growing impatience.

The Professor harrumphed, hem-hawed, made important-looking gestures with his hands, and then spoke forcefully. "A pill for thisss, a pill for that. Pah! There isss no pill for thisss condissshion. A sssimple tongue-ectomy isss perhapssss the fassstest sssolusshun..."

Glix became very attentive. A tongue-ectomy just might be a lot like having her tongue removed. As in, cut out. She opened her mouth to speak just as a large hand covered it.

"I am very certain that Glix will wish to use her tongue in the future, if for no other reason than to stick it out at offensive persons from time to time." The Mayor chuckled and removed his hand from Glix's mouth.

Glix began to like the Mayor.

"Very well, then. I have a fresssh and mossst efficassshusss sssquarm. I will write for her a presscriptsshun."

The Mayor turned to Glix: a relieved look occupied his well-formed face. "Squarm therapy is very popular here and Professor Nardowil is Hallah's top squarmist. If you can't pill it, squarm it. That's one of our Fogwit City sayings. I have no doubt that this procedure will work wonders."

Glix was so encouraged by the Mayor's confident tone that she began to imagine a happy reunion with her family and friends in dear, nice old Quince. From her place at the six-sided table she had a fine view out the big picture windows. As she gazed at the billowy clouds, she could almost imagine she actually was back home. The important word here is almost.

The luxury and grandeur of the Mayor's mansion was completely unlike anything in Quince. Everything here was large, everything was fancy. Even the fancy embroidered upholstery had large fancy lace arm-covers held in place by large, fancy pearl-headed pins. All the large fanciness made it just a little hard to think about plain old Quince, but she was trying.

Meanwhile, the Professor went about his preparations. First, he withdrew a glass jar from his vast black satchel. The jar contained a single pink worm the size of a dwarf banana, wrapped in coarse netting with a string attached.

Next, he removed a small vial of bright blue liquid, a small, pointy brush of the sort artists paint tiny things with, and a small glass beaker.

All these items were placed on a corner of the table. Then it was back to the satchel for a tall brown bottle with a Cobnose Fog label. "Yesss, yesss!" exclaimed the Professor with great enthusiasm. "The perfect sssolvent!"

Uncorking the Cobnose Fog bottle, the Professor tilted back his round head and took a great, deep swig, then squinted at the Mayor and held out the bottle. Getting no response, he took one more swig, then pulled the red kerchief from his coat pocket with a grand flourish and dabbed his blubbery lips.

From her high-backed chair in the corner, Berlyn Twick rolled her eyes and snickered. The Mayor only made an impatient gesture.

A momentary gap in the clouds allowed a shaft of bright sunlight to penetrate the many-paned bay window. The bright light danced on the rim of the jar and cast reflections on the somber wood paneling of the walls. One shard of light danced across Glix's eyes, causing her to return from a daydream about her nice life in plain old Quince. For the first time she noticed the jar and its contents.

It is an understatement to say that the fat pink worm instantly captured her full attention. Life in Quince had not prepared her for the odd customs of Fogwit City. Carrying a pet worm around in a jar was just not something that Quincians did.

Fumbling inside his tweed jacket, the Professor withdrew a small sheet of paper. He then painted a series of tiny blue scribbles with the substance in the vial. Glix tried to read them but they were evidently written in a foreign language.

When the sheet was about half filled, he paused and squinted at Glix. Then he squeezed his lips into a pucker, looked up at the ceiling, looked back at Glix and filled the rest of the paper with bright blue brushstrokes.

The Professor squinted at his handiwork and eyed Glix once again. "Ssso! We merely need to feed the sssquarm thisss presss- cripsshun and then we ssshall sssee what we ssshall sssee." A spray of spittle wetted the Mayor's hand and Glix's forehead.

It dawned on Glix that the pink worm must be the squarm. A queasy-uneasy feeling began to blossom in the bottom of her stomach.

Wadding up the paper, the Professor dropped it in the beaker and then doused it with Cobnose Fog. The paper dissolved and the fluid now took on a sickly green cast. He stirred the liquid with his brush, then poured it into the jar containing the squarm.

Almost instantly the net dissolved and the squarm began to spasm, writhe and thrash with great energy. Its thrashing created a greenish froth that smelled quite like stink-apples. A high-pitched, metal-on-metal squeal erupted from the froth, the kind of squeal that makes people want to clamp their hands over their ears. In no more than a single clock tick, everybody in the room had clamped their hands over their ears. Everybody but the Professor, who wore tiny pink buttons in his ears to mute the squeals.

As the horrid squeals faded, the Professor smiled his blub- ber-lipped smile at Glix and nodded. Before she could even blink, a pair of strong hands pinned her arms to her sides.

At the very same moment, the Professor pulled a circular object with two dangling tassels from his satchel and stuffed it into Glix's wide-open mouth. Agile fingers quickly tied the tassels behind her head. Next, he fastened a bib-like affair around her neck, evidently to protect her silk morning dress from becoming unnecessarily soiled. A servant brought in an empty bucket, placed it next to Glix's chair and hastened away bearing a look of chagrin, possibly on Glix's behalf.

The Professor now turned to the jar containing the squarm. In the very next moment, the string that held the squarm was dangling from the Professor's fingers, and the squarm itself was dangling directly over Glix's nose. It was now green, not pink, and had doubled in size. And the stink-apple smell of it was so strong it made her stomach lurch up into her throat.

Glix frantically shook her head, first from side to side, then from up to down and every way in between. She wriggled and squirmed and tried to topple the chair with her feet, but the arms that held her only tightened their grip.

Professor Nardowil tried to reassure her. "There isss no caussse for alarm: Fogwit children are quite used to sssuch procedures. Thiss isss a very experienssed squarm who now knowsss exactly where he mussst go and what he mussst do. Sssoon you will pe a nissse Quince-girl again. You mussst ignore the ssslimynesss and the disssgusssting tassste, of courssse; it isss only temporary."

96

20

Suitable Regime

WITH A BOTTOMLESS shot glass in her mouth, Glix no longer had a way to communicate her very strong reservations about the impending squarming. So she did what girls have done since the species was invented: she screamed. The Mayor, the Professor and Berlyn Twick all scrunched up their faces and gritted their teeth. Glix screamed again.

The Mayor held up his hands in a "whoa" gesture, a perplexed look on his face. "Glix, whatever is the problem? Do you have a cramp or something?"

Glix shook her head and tried to speak, but only a meaningless jumble of frantic sounds came out.

Berlyn Twick spoke. "Uh, Mr Mayor…do you think this might be the Quincian's way of expressing misgivings about her first squarming? Since they apparently don't use modern therapeutic squarming in Quince …."

"Excellent point, friend Berlyn. Excellent point." The Mayor scowled at the Professor. "*Someone* should have explained the procedure to her. And without spraying her with spittle."

The Professor rolled his eyes and shrugged in a way that made his chins flap and roll against each other. Glix couldn't decide whether it was gross or comical, but she sensed she had been given a reprieve from the squarming. Wrong.

"You sssee, thisss..." began the Professor as he dangled the writhing green squarm over Glix's gaping mouth. Glix's eyeballs threatened to leap from their sockets; clearly the horrid man's plan was to drop the thing in her mouth while he explained about therapeutic squarming. His hissy voice droned and down went the squarm; down through the top of the glass, down to the middle of the glass, down through the open bottom, down until it made slimy, wiggly contact with the girl's tongue.

Glix screamed her very loudest, most piercing scream; a scream that made her prior screams seem to be a genteel conversation in sign language by comparison. This exceptional scream from his mistress roused the sodbunny around her neck from his overstuffed sodbunny dreams. In exactly the amount of time it takes an average human to scratch his or her nose, Cinder had spotted the squarm and leaped. The squarm emitted half a squeal: its last.

When the chaos resolved itself, the Professor had stalked angrily out of the room and the slightly befuddled Cinder had crawled under a sofa and refused to come out. He had never eaten a drunken squarm before and now was just a bit drunk himself.

For her part, Glix was just happy to not be held to a chair with a glass tube stuffed in her mouth.

"Well, Glix," began the Mayor in one of those it's-out-of-my-hands tones. "If you continue to refuse a proper squarming, I'm afraid you'll just have to live with your 'speech problem.' I'm sure your friends and family, being nice Quincians, will make the necessary allowances for your, ah, outbursts."

Glix tried very hard, but couldn't quite restrain herself. "That's the stupidest thing I've heard since I've been in Flogtwit. If you really think that, you should get Professor Chin-baggies to squarm some extra brains up your knobby nose. I'd like to see *that*!" Glix blushed, clamped both hands over her mouth and began to cry.

The Mayor sighed. He had endured countless insults during his rough-and-tumble Fogwit political career, but no one had ever referred to his majestic, custom-built nose as "knobby."

"There, there," he soothed, ignoring the insults. "You're probably right, Glix. Your outbursts would quickly grow tiresome in Quince. Of course, if you were to play the part of Tangerine Cream, those very same outbursts would ensure your fame and fortune."

Glix shot the Mayor an unhappy look.

In placating tones he added, "Just until we can solve your speech problem in some other way, of course. I have a very strong suspicion that the answer has something to do with that cinder-egg business at the Fairdilly Fair. If you decide to stay here for a while, we can talk some more about what happened there."

The situation was hopeless: there was no going back to Quince as long as she had her "speech problem." Not to mention the black blotch hiding under her glove. And there was no way she was going to allow herself to be squarmed for even the best of reasons. So maybe pretending to be Tangerine Cream wouldn't be so bad after all. For a little while. Two weeks maximum, she decided.

The Mayor seemed to read Glix's thoughts. "I will send my swiftest butterwing to Quince with an explanatory note for your parents; you may include your own note as well. I'm sure they will be at ease knowing that you are safe and in the care of the Mayor of Fogwit City for a time."

Glix wasn't so sure about that; a complication promptly sprang to mind and leaped off her tongue to join the dialog. "But what about my schooling? Is there an Academy of Niceness in Fogwit City?"

Glix wished she could reel the words back into her mouth and punish them for their hastiness. An Academy of Niceness in Fogwit City? What was she thinking?

A rude caw of laughter escaped from Berlyn Twick's mouth. Under pressure from the Mayor's stern gaze, she compressed her mirth into a snide twist of mouth and a roll of eyes.

The Mayor's voice held no hint of ridicule, for which Glix was most grateful. "You are in luck, Miss Larue. Here in Fogwit City there is no need to have your dramatic training compromised by inefficient methodologies for general learning. With no disrespect to Quincian academic traditions, we do things more expeditiously in Fogwit City. I shall see that you receive a suitable regime of the most potent educational supplements available. You need not fear falling behind." He smiled a comforting the-situation-is-totally-under-control sort of smile.

Glix was not totally comforted. She envisioned a daunting stack of workbooks, catechisms, syllabi, anthologies and so forth on a hundred Fogwittish subjects, not to mention all the usual Quincian subjects. Big mistake to bring up that subject. In fact, her face went gray at the dreary thought.

Again the Mayor seemed to read her mind and his eyes took on a mischievous twinkle. "Just in case you might be applying Quincian assumptions to the term 'educational supplements,' you must reframe your thinking in Fogwit terms. When Fogwits refer to 'educational supplements' they could just as easily use words like 'pill,' 'capsule' or 'lozenge'. I shall have the Superintendent of Public Education see to a suitable regime of supplements tomorrow."

21

Didn't Even Gag

GLIX SIPPED at her tumbler of cold spiceroot tea and decided she did not like Superintendent Flackroy one bit.

First there had been a sort of inquisition, where the man asked her a hundred or more absurd questions and mumbled comments into a silvery metal shoe. At least it looked like a shoe to Glix, who had never seen a Cognitic Panalyzer.

When the questions ran out, the Superintendent pressed some buttons on the shoe, which caused some clickings and whirrings and finally the spewing of a tiny scroll from the end of it. He studied the scroll for a time, mumbled to himself and studied the scroll some more.

Glix found this all very exasperating. Several times she felt the familiar upsurge of an impending verbal blast, but each time the Superintendent would somehow distract her with a question or perhaps even a stupid joke. The verbal volcanoes went back to wherever they hid out.

After far too long, the Superintendent tented his hands under his fashionable chin, cleared his throat and spoke.

"Well, Miss Larue, I can safely characterize your Quincian education as a marvelous blend of sniffle-headed sentimentality and single-minded absurdity larded on an unwholesome foundation of pure nonsense." Superintendent Flackroy shook his head, shrugged and held up his hands in a gesture of pseudo-sad helplessness. Then he leaned toward Glix and frowned. "But there's also a bad side." Mr Flackroy chuckled, winked and sat back in his purple chair to see if Glix had gotten his little joke.

Glix bit her tongue and refused to smile.

"Not funny, eh? No doubt you prefer to hear a kinder assessment of the Quincian Academy of Niceness. Perfectly human, if that's any credit to the species. Well, no matter. You are in Fogwit City now and we must not neglect your proper Fogwit City education, particularly since you are a Rising Star in training. We Fogwits need our Rising Stars and such every bit as much as we need our toilets."

What might that mean? wondered Glix, still biting her tongue and refusing to smile.

The interview with Superintendent Flackroy was taking place in an unoccupied office at Berlyn Twick's rambling Grapeskin Studio in Fogwit City's industrial center. This office was a smallish square of space with a butter yellow ceiling and mouse brown walls. Naked light tubes hung from the ceiling and furnishings were spare: a single tall purple cabinet, a purple desk and two purple chairs fashioned from twisted wood.

The purple desk seemed to please the Superintendent's large feet, for this is where they now rested. More precisely, they rested on a scratched and dented wooden case that sat on the desk. The man leaned back and contemplated Glix as if she were a puzzle of delicious perplexity.

"I suppose we can only do what we can do. Well, then! No doubt you are anxious to be about your new career." Flackroy swung his feet off the desk and opened the wooden case. Glix leaned forward to see countless compartments with glass lids, each labeled in some kind of code. Inside the compartments sat a colorful array of pills, tablets, capsules, caplets and such ranging from ladybug size to giant pillbug size. Some were plain colored, some striped, some polka-dotted, and some looked more like tiny painted eggs than pills.

"We will set the stage with the 'Essential Framework Series.' Fogwit children begin taking these at an early age. You will be play-

102

ing catch-up, so we may have to double certain of the dosages for a while. Now let me see ...."

Superintendent Flackroy began to select items from various compartments and placed them in two bottles. "Those are for today, these are for tomorrow morning," he intoned, rattling the second bottle for emphasis.

A spew of unpleasantries finally worked their way to Glix's voice box. "You think I'm taking anything from an oyster-eyed chin-split? Get serious, squarm-nose! And get a new joke book while you're at it. Or at least suck a box of funny-sticks before you start babbling in my direction!"

Glix bit her tongue, rolled her eyes and shrugged. "Can't help it," she mumbled in her tiniest of mumbles.

"Funny-sticks, eh? Can you point me to a source for those? I haven't seen them in Fogwit City." The Superintendent smiled one of those smiles that people smile when something they expect to happen actually happens. "Not bad, Miss Larue. The Mayor briefed me about your remarkable 'speech problem' and I see he did not exaggerate. Most Fogwit children your age would never dare to address adults so ... so, shall we say, creatively. If they did, they would immediately suffer red bottoms, I assure you."

Glix blushed, squeezed her lips together and pointed at the bottles.

"Certainly you have a right to know what supplements the Mayor has asked me to give you. Well then. These three greenies comprise a marvelous three-volume set: 'Best of *The Fogwit Consumer.*' These will have you shopping with the best of us in no time.

"The twinkles — those with the golden sparkles — contain some timeless pieces from the *Wish & Wager Quarterly* — absolutely essential if you plan on visiting Viggas and returning with your britches. The pair with the yellow dots comprises a fine anthology of highly condensed articles from *Modern Celebrity.*

"The yellow and blue striped tablet is a very popular new item: a clever blend of an ancient story and a tranquilizer, with a delicious coating of bleached greensugar concentrate. The story is called

'*Chicken Little*' and it demonstrates the bad things that can happen to people who believe silly rumors, wild gossip and snuffle-headed nonsense. I must say it is helping to calm the nervous among us who ascribe to the theory that Hallah's sky is falling."

Hanging upside down from the ceiling's crown molding, a spy-moth (this one with a sense of humor), performed a fluttering parody of a falling sky. Glix watched the moth for a moment, frowned, then turned her attention back to the annoying human ostrich.

104

The Superintendent gave Glix one of his looks. Glix, recalling the blue-helmets in the park on her first night in Fogwit City, rolled her eyes and shook her head. This seemed to satisfy Superintendent Flackroy's need for a response.

"Moving right along, 'Unthinkable' is what this black one is called. This newly updated edition contains a list of thoughts and ideas that are deemed unnecessary and are best not thought about: guaranteed to save you a lot of headaches. The idea is similar to what your Quincian authorities hope to accomplish with that fluid that gets dripped into children's ears each night through those tiny funnels, if I understand the concept correctly. What do you call it?"

"Evernice," said Glix. "And the funnels are called Night Funnels."

Was the man ridiculing a cherished Quincian tradition? At first she felt as though she should defend the practice, but before she could formulate a fiery retort, another part of her realized that she had never thought of the practice as something being done to children by "authorities." Hmmm.

This chugging little train of thought was derailed by Superintendent Flackroy's next comment. "On a lighter note," he intoned drily, "this pink one is 'Toobology,' which illuminates — in the simplest of terms — the many benefits of what might be called Fogwit toob-culture."

The Superintendent looked at Glix, frowned, removed another pink capsule from his case and added it to the 'today' bottle. "Now that I think about it, a transplant from toob-deprived Quince probably needs a double dose of this one."

Glix was astonished and amazed. "You mean if I swallow these I'll know everything that's in them? No reading, no studying?"

Superintendent Flackroy spoke just a little huffily. "Well, Miss Larue, what's the point of a taking a pill if it doesn't do its job? Of course, just because you consume a pill doesn't mean that you will instantly be able to recite the encoded content verbatim. That would require numerous identical doses. And if you wanted to be an expert on one particular document you might have to take a hundred doses or more. Even then, the effect dissipates over time if the knowledge is not put to use."

Nothing is ever simple, thought Glix ruefully. Not even simple pillish things. Then another thought occurred to her. "Are these the only topics you have pills for? They don't seem — I don't know how to say this, exactly — they don't seem like the same kinds of things we are taught at the Academy. I mean, what about stuff like..." Glix paused to plumb her mind for recent topics of study at the Quincian Academy of Niceness. "Okay, what about 'Nice Ways to Raise Nicer Goats,' or 'The Algebra of Niceness?' Or 'Practical Courtesy' or 'Documented Hazards of Dreaming?' What about stuff like that?"

Superintendent Flackroy spoke emphatically. "Of *course* we have no pills for such topics. We mostly have pills for topics that facilitate life in Fogwit City: topics that grease the wheels, so to speak. Surely you have been here long enough to know that there would be no use whatever for 'The Algebra of Niceness' in Fogwit City. Someone must want to *buy* these pills after all; the pill makers aren't in this for our health ... er, I mean their health. No matter; there is hardly a need for any sort of mathematics beyond simple arithmetic in modern day Fogwit City."

A bolt of brain lightning seemed to strike the Superintendent. "Silly me!" he exclaimed, slapping the side of his head and mussing his neat amber wave ever so slightly.

"I have forgotten a most essential topic." He studied the case of pills, frowned, then tugged on a pair of concealed handles and lifted the entire tray from the case. Strewn across the bottom in a disorderly manner were dozens of tiny envelopes of various colors.

The Superintendent rummaged through the envelopes, occasionally picking one up, reading the label, then setting it on the table. More than half the envelopes had been displaced before he found the items he was seeking.

"You may thank the Mayor for these very expensive specialty items; he placed no budget limitations on your Fogwit education." Superintendent Flackroy handed Glix two envelopes. "Take one every other day for a week."

Glix read the labels. 'Practical Melodrama: An Overactor's Handbook' said the first. The second was 'Merrigold Wynter: Rising Star of Rising Stars.'

"Thank you thank you thank you!" exclaimed Glix in a blast of girlish enthusiasm. This is very nice of you, Superintendent Flackroy."

The Superintendent smiled, gave Glix a few instructions on proper pill taking, promised to send her an expanded supply in the morning and took his leave.

When she was certain he was gone, Glix trashed all the pills but the ones in the envelopes. She swallowed one of each with the last of her cold tea ... and didn't even gag.

22

In Disguise

"BUT I *CAN'T* walk that way," shouted Glix. "Nobody in Quince would *ever* walk like that. And you are a cruel, snot-dripping, pimple-lipped cod-wicker to make me do it! Besides that, I feel like barfing ... I think it's from those stupid pills. It makes me dizzy having all that gibberish about overacting and stupid Merrigold Wynter spinning around in my head."

Berlyn Twick remained unruffled. "Ah, yes. A pimple-lipped cod-wicker. There is no such thing as a cod-wicker, Miss Cream. Pimple-lipped or otherwise. Where do you get those things?"

Glix had no answer.

"Have I mentioned that your walk is much improved over yesterday? Now, once again: do the Tangerine Cream walk, Miss Cream."

The master of Grapeskin Studio was clever; she only gave Glix one piece of Tangerine Cream to learn at a time. Soon enough the Walk was good enough. Attitude was next.

In the course of getting the Tangerine Cream "tude" down, Glix whined and complained and blurted out a thousand insults. Still, within a week she had learned to hold her head and shoulders just so and to deliver a saucy, raised eyebrow, slightly snarly look. Berlyn Twick insisted this was the proper Tangerine Cream attitude to go with the saucy, bouncing Tangerine Cream walk.

After the tude had been mastered, the next challenge was performing various pantomime vignettes in front of eyebutton-toting butterwings. Unlike the butterwings that hauled glidesacks and delivered scrolls throughout the island of Wyn, the butterwings that flew around pointing eyebuttons mostly where Berlyn Twick wanted them pointed were a snippy bunch.

Like virtually all butterwings, these stood about knee high, had strong, slim frames and pixie-like narrow faces with pointy ears and chins, jaunty up-tilted noses and wide-set black eyes that seemed too big for their faces. Like all butterwings, their skins were covered by a butter yellow layer of tiny feathers that looked like fur but wasn't. And of course they had the marvelous multi-colored crests that made it possible (but not easy) to tell one from the other. In other words, except for their monogrammed red headbands Picters Guild butterwings looked like any other butterwings. But Picters Guild butterwings seemed to have been raised on rude pills.

The Picters Guild butterwings sneered and snickered when Glix made mistakes. Sometimes they mimicked her walk or her tude in a sly and facetious way. But after learning the hard way that butterwings can leave nasty little dung-splats on a person's head, Glix never retaliated. And Berlyn Twick was very protective of her elite butterwings in any case. Whenever Glix complained about their various offenses, Twick would just shrug and say, "butterwings will be butterwings."

Perhaps the biggest challenge to Glix's comfort level was seeing herself on the toobs. With all of Tangerine Cream's snarly sauciness, Glix felt that her real self had been drowned in an unpleasant liquid, even though her face had not changed by so much as one molecule. This bothered Glix quite a bit ... when she had time to think of such things, which mostly she didn't.

But when scroll-letters arrived from her mother, her old Quincian self came up for air. Last night, for example, her mother's latest letter was full of goings-on at the Academy of Niceness, including preparations for the annual Welcome to Lulu Ball, where all the students perform very nice skits having to do with rain, wind, umbrellas, puddles and other things characteristic of Wyn's coming wet-ter-and-colder season. The old Glix — the Queen of Niceness Glix — would have participated in the skits, and as Glix, not as some man-ufactured Tangerine Cream character.

The most surprising news in the scroll was that Twinker's old-er sister Jaynin had been selected by the help-fairies and gone off for training at Miranza Vale. Good riddance, thought Glix, who re-called the years of being teased and pinched and hair-pulled by that very same Jaynin … all on account of her orange hair. So it seemed odd that help-fairies would select a person with a mean streak like Jaynin. How helpful could *that* be?

109

Glix sighed, put that thought aside and went back to wistful thoughts about the Welcome to Lulu Ball, which naturally made her homesick for her home, her hometown and for her old self. Tears were shed.

The next morning she mentioned her concerns to Berlyn Twick. "It bothers me that I'm so … so *invisible* when I'm Tangerine Cream. I'm a Queen of Niceness, but … well, no, I suppose I'm not, actually. Not right now, at least. But I *was* one. And I still …. What I mean …" Glix could not find the right words.

Twick rolled her eyes and made a loud sigh. "Yes, you still think like a Quincian, Miss Cream: particularly, I might add, after you get a letter from your mother. But no matter. Here in Fogwit, we would say that the whole Quincian nonsense about niceness is an act or a wish. That much niceness is not human nature. If it was really so nat-ural, do you think they'd have to put niceness drops in your ears every night?" Berlyn Twick paused and gave Glix one of her special looks.

"It's called Evernice," corrected Glix, weakly.

"Evernice, schmevernice … whatever. It may surprise you, Miss Cream, but I believe it is your peculiar Quincian nature that has al-lowed you to do so well with the Tangerine Cream role. It would have taken me, oh, at least two weeks to get a Fogwit youth to learn what you have learned in a fortnight." Twick paused to see if Glix would pick up the little joke, but she didn't. The word "fortnight" was just not a common word in Quincian vocabularies.

Twick sighed and continued. "Your main problem, Miss Cream, is that you don't appreciate your acting for what it is: acting. You're a natural."

Glix was shocked. Berlyn Twick had never yet said she was doing well. Well, at least not so directly.

"And now to get back to business, Miss Cream, it's time for a test."

"A test of what?" inquired Glix.

"A test of you, of course. Yes, you're able to get into character here in the safety of my studio ... and even in the presence of jaded, rude butterwings. But will you be able to deliver Tangerine Cream when you're out in public? That is another matter entirely!"

"But why would I want to do that? Can't I just be Glix in public?"

"Such innocence does you credit, Miss Cream. And were you an ordinary, reasonably unknown actor you *could* be yourself in public. Not so simple when you're a Rising Star. Rising Stars must be their character whenever they're in public. Take Merrigold Wynter, for example. Her tude and her walk were far different from yours. But no less recognizable to her fans. And part of her glorious star-ness was her ability to project the essence of her character at all times, not just in the studio.

"Merrigold Wynter was a singularity, a nonesuch. Larger than life, idealized. These are terms that go with Rising Star like caviar goes with chopped egg and sour cream."

"I don't think I quite understand," said Glix in a tone that really meant "I'm quite sure I *don't* want to be Tangerine Cream in public."

"I understand your hesitation, Miss Cream. Perfectly natural. But I haven't yet gotten to the fun part. When we go to town today, you'll get to play a most remarkable role."

"But I don't *know* any other roles," whined Glix with an urgency that betrayed wisps of insecurity leaking from the seams of her composure.

"Oh but you *do*, Miss Cream!" Twick's face now displayed the sly grin that Glix had come to recognize as the auteur's now-see-how-clever-I-am look. "You will play Tangerine Cream in disguise!"

23

Memorable

GLIX FROWNED and tugged at her ear. "I don't get it."

"The point of it all will become clear to you when you read the *Fogwit Morning Lobster* tomorrow. And besides, there is a mundane, practical side: our ever-penurious Mayor has finally provided funds for a modest new wardrobe to replace the makeshift garments his house-warden provided to replace whatever horribly unfashionable items disappeared with your backpouch. We must shop. Now let's get you ready."

At the word "shop," Glix made no further protest. But she did wonder if perhaps she shouldn't have trashed all of Superintendent Flackroy's other supplements. Didn't one of his recent deliveries contain one called "Essentials of Modern Shopping for Girls?"

For this excursion to "town," Twick assigned Aneena, Grapeskin's grizzled Head of Wardrobe, the task of dressing Glix as a fashionable, gum-chewing Fogwit teen. Glix put up a minor fuss, but Aneena would hear none of it. "What Her Purpleness wants is what Her Purpleness gets ... it's her castle, after all."

Black was currently in fashion, so black dominated the effect. To disguise her orange locks, Glix was fitted with a fashionable jet-black wig with a fashionable six-foot fake braid wrapped twice around her neck. Next, a selection of spangles, charms and other ornaments were added, including a handsome wrought-copper clasp for the braid. The finishing touch was a fashionable mood-ruby that Aneena affixed to Glix's forehead with spirit gum.

Glix inspected the finished product in the full-length mirror and rolled her eyes, mentally cringing as she recalled that embarrassing experience her first night in Fogwit City. Something about dressing up like one of those sneery gum-smackers at Toob-in-the-Park made her nose twitch in exasperation. At first. Then Tangerine Cream's tude took over. What did she care about a bunch of chatterbox looka-likes? Just under her breath she mumbled, "There's only one Rising Star in Fogwit City, schmuckbabies. And guess what? It isn't you."

"Town" in this case was the fashionable Limewood Canyon district on the upper west side of Fogwit City. Twick and Glix stepped from the long black steam-limo onto a well-kept sidewalk. It was only mid-morning but already crowds of fashionable young Fogwits strutted here and there, mouths busy either in rapid-fire chatter or working wads of the most fashionable colors of chewing gum. Or both.

Glix was more interested in the shops and cafes: unlike the trendy young Fogwits, no two shops were alike. Glix was dazzled by the diversity of design, décor, color, lighting and so forth in the same way a moth is dazzled by a candle flame: that is to say, dangerously.

"The walk, Miss Cream," hissed Twick. "Remember the walk. And the glove; flaunt the glove the way you've practiced. Let it catch light and sparkle."

Outside of the protected environs of Grapeskin Studio where Glix had spent her every waking and sleeping hour since leaving the Mayor's mansion, Glix knew little of Fogwit City and its folk. This excursion was an eye-opener; nothing in Quince was remotely like Limewood Canyon Drive.

But despite the clamor and glamour, Glix was most struck by a feeling of intense loneliness. Until this excursion, she hadn't realized how isolated she had become from people her own age. Yes, there were some youngish people on Twix's staff; she knew their names and interacted with them every day. But it just wasn't the same as having real friends.

A strange thought struck her then. Had her friends in Quince been *real* friends? Or were they just people she knew well enough to speak to every day and share some feelings with? Had Twinker Gidlet actually been her best friend? They had shared all sorts of personal stuff, but could a real friendship come apart so quickly?

In her current state, Glix wasn't at all sure what the answers to these questions were. All she knew for certain was that she felt lonelier than she'd ever felt in her life. She tried to set these feelings aside and enjoy the here-and-now glitter and glitz of Limewood Canyon, but with very limited success. Well, no success, really.

113

After acquiring an extravagant, expensive new wardrobe at Mister Skeet's — an elite shop known for cutting edge apparel for well-heeled young ladies — the pair from Grapeskin Studio crossed the avenue to take lunch at Zest, an elite eatery with a raised courtyard overlooking the trendy bustle of Millicent Square.

It would be memorable.

114

24

Trust Me on That

"MISS TWICK, HOW GOOD to see you again. Your usual table is ready. And is this the ...?"

Berlyn Twick put her finger to her lips and mouthed a silent 'ssshhh.' "Yes it is, Master Twayze," said the auteur in a confidential whisper. "The one and only Tangerine Cream herself. In disguise, of course."

Glix gulped, smiled a saucy smile and performed a saucy Tangerine Cream gesture in Master Twayze's general direction. Then she looked away, perhaps a little too quickly.

The restaurateur was tall and thin in a leggy sort of way. He wore a silky black suit with a silver bow tie, sported a pencil mustache and had black hair that looked painted on his head. In ten seconds, Glix decided his oily elegance was too over the top for her taste.

"But today we are incognito," continued Twick. "We wouldn't want your genteel clientele overwhelmed by the over-insistent butterwings of the paparazzi, now would we?" Glix did not see the wink.

Master Twayze nodded a genteel nod. "As usual, you are considerate to a fault, Miss Twick. I shall personally see to your privacy. This way please."

Prior to arriving at the restaurant, Twick had provided Glix with this instruction: "Once we are seated at my table, we must hunch over to keep our faces in shadow and speak as if we are sharing immensely valuable secrets for our own ears only. Thus, our conversation must be just above a whisper. You may inspect the surroundings, of course, but do so without appearing to do so. Any questions, Miss Cream?"

It all seemed quite absurd to Glix, but it was more than clear that Berlyn Twick knew what she was about ... and also that she was uninterested in further discussions. Glix tried to inject a dose of tude into her non-response, but if that was tude, it was a lukewarm, watered-down edition that hardly deserved the label. She promised herself to get better.

116

They were taken to a corner table on a low platform rising above the courtyard. From this vantage they enjoyed a view across the courtyard to Millicent Square and beyond. Glix could see Viggas Island and the outer rim of Cobnose Bay sparkling in the distance. If this was Berlyn Twick's own special table, she must be very important, thought Glix. No other table had such a commanding position.

A server appeared bearing a silver platter with hot towels, a crystal decanter filled with a sparkling pale gold beverage, fine red-orange caviar, sweet-wafers and assorted condiments. Thereafter, other servers arrived at intervals with platters containing numerous petite portions of this exotic concoction and that.

During the exquisite meal Twick discreetly pointed out a dozen Fogwit celebrities seated at nearby tables. For their part, the celebrities cast gossipy glances at the elevated corner table every few minutes.

"Buzzmanship in action, Miss Cream. All part of the game. You'll see."

A few minutes after the last platter had been removed, a butterwing in a tan and purple Grapeskin Studio uniform flew up and handed a scroll to Berlyn Twick, then flew off. Twick scanned the scroll and nodded to herself.

"All is in readiness, Miss Cream. Time to go. Master Twayze will be walking briskly, so follow him closely and don't lag. I'll pick up the rear."

Master Twayze appeared, bowed low and offered Glix his hand. "I dearly hope you were satisfied with our humble cuisine. And I hope you will dine with us again soon. Any, ahh, friend of the magnificent Berlyn Twick is always welcome at Zest. Please allow me to escort you to the door."

"Quickly now, Miss Cream," whispered Twick. "Remember to keep your head low and appear as though you don't want to be recognized. And don't forget the walk."

Led by the over-gracious Master Twayze, the trio followed an oddly circuitous route through the room, seeming to pass by every diner. What a strange way to be incognito, thought Glix. Nary a diner passed up the opportunity to inspect Twick and her mysterious guest as they strode past looking straight ahead. Master Twayze had a well-waxed smile and a special greeting for everyone in the room and somehow knew each guest by name.

The rose-colored carved glass doors of Zest were set into a graceful arched canopy perhaps twenty feet back from busy Limewood Canyon Drive. The long black steam-limo sat waiting at the curb. The driver, resplendent in his Grapeskin Studio livery, held open the door.

Glix and Twick were halfway to the limo when the dive-bombers appeared. A horde of butterwings with eye-buttons swooped down on the pair, elbowing and hip-bumping each other for the most angular angles and the closest close-ups. Each was after an image worthy of the *Fogwit Morning Lobster*. If not that, one of the several gossip-sheets: *Juicy Secrets* and the *Glitzoid Rag* being the most desirable. If not those, then the *Viggas Eventuator* as a last resort.

Glix ducked and held up her copper-gloved hand to ward off the swarm of butterwings. Another kind of bombardment was not so easy to duck: questions. Voices assaulted her from every direction with questions. They all blended together in a way that felt like a hot question soup was being poured into her ears.

The nice Quincian part of Glix tried very hard to understand what the paparazzi and quote-hawks (she only learned these terms later) wanted from her. And had she understood the questions, that nice part of her would no doubt have tried to answer them. Nicely, of course. And that's even though the questions were prying, too personal and nobody's business but her own. That's just how deep her unnatural niceness went.

Something tugged hard at a finger of her glove. Something else tugged hard at her wig, causing it to tilt on her head, exposing the orange tresses underneath. Another hard tug yanked it from her head completely. The braid was still wrapped around her neck, so the clump of jet-black hair swung back and forth just below her shoulders as she danced this way and that in a futile effort to evade her pursuers. Then something snapped in Glix's brain. Puzzlement and annoyance morphed into an extreme outrage, perhaps fueled by the loneliness she had felt earlier.

Tangerine Cream's arms exploded into a flurry of motion and the winged golden horde winged a hasty retreat to avoid damage to their fragile bones. The Rising Star stood up and surveyed the circle of inquisitors surrounding her. The tude she projected at that moment was strong enough to stop the wagging tongues in mid-question. A weird silence ensued, thick enough with anticipation to scoop up with a pudding spoon.

Into that empty moment Tangerine Cream loosed a radiant ration of rude rhetoric that made her original performance at the Sillydilly Follies toob-show seem about as captivating as legal notices read backward by a half-asleep undertaker.

If the goal were truly to remain incognito, it would probably have been better to have just walked away. And she could have, because a group of black-cowled help-fairies had appeared on the scene and somehow cleared a helpful path to the door of the limo. But Tangerine Cream was on a roll and wasn't about to stop.

By the time Twick dragged her away from the press of the press, Fogwit's new Rising Star was still regaling the reporters and butterwings with delicious unprintables. Well, unprintable in Quince perhaps. Nothing was unprintable in Fogwit City.

Her final act before being hauled into the limo — a rude gesture made by copper-sheathed fingers and flung at everybody in the vicinity — would doubtless appear the next morning in gorgeous full color atop the *Lobster*'s Glitz-O-Rama column.

As the limo chuff-chuffed away from the scene, the normally cool and sardonic Twick wrapped her arms around Glix, planted an exuberant kiss on one very surprised Glixian cheek and exclaimed — with a degree of gusto that flew right off the gusto scale and disappeared into the gustosphere — "Ab-so-lute-ly *splendid*, Miss Cream! You are one fire-breathing, kick-ass buzz-machine! Merrigold Wynter was a kick in the pants, all right, but Merrigold Wynter ain't got nuthin' on you!"

Then she got hold of herself. She gave the stunned Glix her sardonic half-smile and delivered the capper in her more customary style of measured understatement. "Not to put too fine a point on it, Miss Cream, but you are about to become the Rising Star of all Rising Stars. Trust me on that."

120

25

Of Princess Fandessa

BY THE NEXT morning several new realities had set in and Berlyn Twick's think-room sizzled with emotion.

If eyes could really spew fire, Glix's eyes would have burnt Her Purpleness to a speck of ash in an instant. But they could only shoot harmless air-daggers, so her tongue had to do the work.

The purple-skinned object of her wrath had her own smoldering frustrations. They hadn't yet burst into flame but might at any second. For the moment she just rolled her eyes and said, "You seem upset, Miss Cream. Out with it."

"You bum-breathing, slop-slurping, manipulative scab-sucker! How could you put me through that?"

Twick slouched in her director's chair, glowering and picking her teeth with a purple fingernail. As usual, she was unmoved by Glix's outbursts.

"Of *course* I'm manipulative," she growled. "It's the game we're in, after all. I make no apologies for manipulation. What is life but manipulation? No doubt I'm also egocentric and inconsiderate. But what did you call me? A slop-slurping, scab-sucker? My, my, my ... and tsk, tsk, tsk ... and shame, shame, shame.

"Are you aware that all my shameful manipulations and all your, ah, inconveniences at the hands and wings of the press corps yesterday have come to nothing? At least nothing of any value." Twick tossed a copy of the *Fogwit Morning Lobster* in Glix's lap. "Read it and weep, Miss Cream."

Glix scrunched up her face and opened her mouth to rant some more, then gave it up. She picked up the *Lobster* and studied the giant black headline: "Heroic Fangler Sky Saving Mission Set."

Under the headline was a large picture of the Mayor and a bunch of men she didn't recognize standing in front of a model of something the caption called a "cloudship" with a big map of Hallah in the background. Glix looked up at Twick with a perplexed frown.

"We got scooped, Miss Cream. Pure and simple. Your dear friend the Mayor has seriously upstaged us with that silly aerial expedition of his. All we got was a blurb in the Food section about a ruckus in front of Zest yesterday. Didn't even mention your name. We didn't even make the Glitz-O-Rama column! That was all about one of the Viggas Island casino bigshots making a big donation to the Mayor's stupid expedition."

At the mention of Zest, an outrageous thought trickled up from somewhere in Glix's subconscious. "Master Twayze. He knew, didn't he?"

Twick gave Glix one of her sly smiles and punctuated it with a wink. "Bra-vo! Score a point for a certain hyper-innocent former epitome of Quincian niceness. Of course Master Twayze knew. Not only does Master Twayze have a knack for knowing things like that, it's his *business* to know things.

"He also knows every remotely useful-to-know person in Fogwit City. And they all owe him favors. Oh, and he just happens to be a minority partner in Grapeskin Studio. He's quite excited about Fogwit City's latest Rising Star. And if I recall correctly, he used the expression 'unique panache' with reference to your character, Miss Cream.

"Not that anybody else seems to care at the moment," concluded Twick with a sour pucker of lips.

The Purple One looked past Glix to the time-sculpture that graced the far wall of her think-room. The huge silver mallet was almost in position to swing down hard on the eighth goblin, at which time there would be a semi-musical splat and the goblin's squashed head would disappear. Almost eight o'clock.

Struck by a sudden inspiration, Twick leaned toward her Rising Star and snapped her fingers. "Perspective, Miss Cream! Perspective. Vantage point. Sometimes we all need to see things from a different perspective. Get a different point of view. Look at the big picture. And that's exactly what we are going to get this very afternoon. Put on some warm clothes, Miss Cream, and be back here in half an hour."

Glix was baffled. "Uh, Miss Twick ... what about the rehearsal for the..."

"Perspective trumps rehearsals, Miss Cream. At least for one afternoon."

Much later, Glix lay in her bed, almost giddy with new perspectives. Spending two hours flying over and around Fogwit City, Cobnose Bay and Viggas Island in the basket of a twelve-windshark Fogwit Air Tours sightseeing craft can do that ... especially when it's a person's very first experience aloft.

But what made her genuinely, over the top giddy was Javett, the Fogwit Air Tours pilot ... and son of Mr Hipskander, the gawky juggler from Hiphollow. Javett had not only recognized her from the Fairdilly Fair, but he was courteous and gentlemanly in the extreme ... and he insisted on calling her 'Queen.' Twick had rolled her eyes every time he said that or did something gentlemanly, but so what? Glix finally had a friend in Fogwit City. And a tall, handsome one who bowed and even kissed her hand as if she were a princess. But what was he doing in Fogwit City, of all places?

It wasn't only Glix who had gained new perspectives during the aerial tour. Twick had been in her own world the whole time, completely ignoring Javett's nonstop tour guide commentary. Occasionally she would exclaim something to herself or frown or scratch her head or scrawl notes in her everpresent notebook or make gleeful cackling sounds. Glix had never seen her so absorbed in anything.

"I'll be in the Aerie," announced Twick almost offhandedly when the steam-carriage arrived back at Grapeskin. "Probably for at least a couple days, so don't bother me and feel free to do what you want until I emerge. Then we'll see who does the next bit of upstaging. And tell the Propmaster to find me; I've got something interesting for him." Twick spun away and disappeared into the maze of Grapeskin corridors, her mouse brown duster billowing behind her.

When Glix arrived at the Grapeskin commissary for dinner, she found an envelope waiting for her at the corner booth reserved for use only by the auteur and her ward. Twick's almost illegible scrawl spelled out "For Miss Cream" on the envelope. The note inside had more scrawling: "When you've dutifully written your mother and then become perfectly bored, I suggest you check out *Tales of Mariah Castle* from the library. Then tell me if Prince Rupert reminds you of anybody."

Glix ate in silence, maintaining a full-face frown through her entire bowl of redfish stew. She hated the fact that Berlyn Twick somehow knew she'd already written a scroll-letter to her mother and was indeed feeling bored. It was irksome being so predictable and she almost decided to avoid the library and just sit in her room and play Lunkbottom's Revenge all by herself.

By the time her spoon hit the sweetrunket pudding with Quincian chocolate sauce though, the worst of her irritation had abated. By the time she napkinned all remnants of dessert from her lips, she had come to terms with the fact that Twick never did anything at random: everything had a purpose. And usually more than one. And Twick had long since figured out that Glix had a big Curiosity Button and knew exactly how to push it.

That was how she found herself absorbed in the pages of *Tales of Mariah Castle* until very late that night. But it had only taken a few chapters to realize who Twick had hinted at in her note: the gallant mannerisms and speech habits of Prince Rupert and a certain Fogwit Air Tours pilot/tour guide were too similar to be ignored. She wondered when she'd ever have an opportunity to ask Javett if he'd read what was rapidly becoming one of Glix's favorite books. And against her better judgment she couldn't help wondering if she reminded him of Princess Fandessa.

26

Saw His Wink

FIVE DAYS SLIPPED by before Berlyn Twick emerged from the Aerie. Glix barely noticed. She had spent most of that time in the library, browsing the shelves, reading in one of the big comfy chairs and having whispered conversations with Mr Vane, the very old, very bald, very twinkly-eyed librarian.

When Twick had first introduced Glix to the librarian upon her arrival at Grapeskin, she had said, "Miss Tangerine Cream, meet the one and only Mr Lokas Vane, Grapeskin's Keeper of Stories." In the last few days, Glix had seen the truth of it; in his spare moments Mr Vane had regaled her with stories about the long history of Grapeskin Studios and its various owners, and about its theatrical productions and its Rising Stars. Best of all, he wasn't at all shy about poking fun at the current owner and her quirks. He also seemed quite interested in Glix's own story. Because the library had such important functions in the studio, he also had a special sense for when something noteworthy was about to happen. Like now.

Glix was slumped in the chair that was best positioned for butterwing-watching and there was much to watch today. In the past few days, there had been only occasional butterwings bearing messages. Mr Vane would read them, search the stacks for this item or that and then dispatch messenger boys with books, drawings and other materials. Today was different. Today the flow of materials and messenger boys out of the library had come to a standstill, but Mr Vane was kept unusually busy reading and writing messages. All afternoon butterwings in their elegant Grapeskin uniforms had been flying in and out of the library's high windows. After the last one flew away, he caught Glix's eye, winked and beckoned her to his desk.

Then he spoke in his most confidential whisper. "Unless I'm entirely mistaken, Grapeskin is about to go Deep Purple, Miss Cream. That's the shorthand we old-timers use when a monstrous new project takes wing. Total chaos. Those of us with hair want to tear it out by the roots. But just between you and me, Miss Cream, it keeps the dust off my pate. And it's been too long since Grapeskin went Deep Purple."

Glix was about to say something noncommittal, but Mr Vane held up his hand. "Get ready, Miss Cream. Deal-notes have been flying fast and furious and I suggest you steel yourself for some interesting times...and, ah, a new, ah, 'friend.'" He said "friend" in a way that meant anything *but* a friend.

Almost as an afterthought, he added: "Oh, and I am supposed to tell you that you have been invited to the Purple One's think-room for a pre-flight briefing. As in, immediately. Off with you now."

Twick was slumped in her chair, feet perched on her desk, a steaming mug of roasted blickernut tea cradled in her lap. She looked both drained and exuberant at the same time.

"Take a load off, Miss Cream. Vacation's over. Have one of your Quincian chocolates ... and maybe some blickernut tea. You old enough for blickernut tea? Have some anyway."

"Javett," blurted Glix before Twick could say anything else. "I just wanted to say that before we get started. Javett — the Fogwit Air Tours pilot — acts a lot like Prince Rupert."

"Oh. Yes. Javett. Right. Sorry, been preoccupied of late. Almost forgot about that note. I trust Mr Vane has told you that we're about to go Deep Purple?"

Glix gaped.

"I see he did. Mr Vane loves being 'in the know' ... and he is; but it's hardly a secret. While you were being a good library girl, I've been stirring the soup a bit. By the way, you need to work on concealing your shock, Miss Larue. The only shock a Rising Star should ever display has gotta look fake, bogus and overacted.

"But enough on that. We are about to launch a massive — and as yet untitled — toob-production. Mind-bogglingly expensive, cast-of-thousands kind of thing. And we have partners ... always a horrible idea, partners. And even worse, a partner with a condition."

Glix frowned. "You mean, like a disability? Why would that be so bad?"

"No Miss Cream, a different sort of condition. A deal point, if you will. And it's on you, which is why I mention it at this moment, an hour before Mr Bigshot Macaller and his, ah, 'condition', arrive for a brief, on-our-best-behavior kickoff meeting and whirlwind tour of Grapeskin. So prepare yourself to have an understudy. Or in Rising Star parlance, a staralike."

Glix tried very hard to contain her shock. A meeting? In an hour?

"Better, Miss Cream, but you've still got work to do on your shock containment. Please be fully in character at all times for this cameo appearance...it's in the Purple Grotto, by the way. I believe you will find that your inner Tangerine Cream will serve you well in this setting.

"Here's the shtick: you are very busy and only have a few moments before the dress rehearsal of Portia's Revenge begins. You only need to dash in, act saucily, Creamishly charming for a few minutes, then dash out to Set 4, where you'll be briefed by Gliane and the Faz on tomorrow's mission.

"Our guests' whirlwind tour will *not* include Set 4. A suitable outfit and your favorite dresser are waiting for you in your quarters. We can confer briefly about tomorrow's location scouting expedition to Mullver's Rock at 6 AM sharp. Now skedaddle. Please."

• • • • •

Many centuries ago Grapeskin Studio had been an expansive vineyard and the home of a famous winery. When the wine district in the hills above Cobnose Bay had dwindled and become defunct, the vineyard became the home of the Grand Wynderry Circus. Its colorful circulars and posters claimed it was the most extravagant traveling circus and theatre company ever to tour Wyn and the hundreds of smaller islands dotting the Great Wet. And perhaps it was.

This was long before the Fanglers of Gonzotopia invented eyebuttons and toobs. Now, everything was changed. Few remnants of either the winery or the Grand Wynderry Circus remained on the rambling site of the modern Grapeskin Studio. Fires, storms, old age and obsolescence had taken their toll on most of the vintage structures and functions. Still, the Purple Grotto endured.

Glix had only been here once...and only just to look around. Now, she was about to make a grand entrance. The instructions on Twick's note were to arrive a fashionable five minutes late and she did.

Hans, Grapeskin's Chief of Stores who played the role of major-domo when circumstances required it, opened the heavy timber door to the Purple Grotto and announced her with the faintest of bows. "Miss Tangerine Cream, if you will."

Three individuals were seated in posh velvet chairs around a table of thick glass that was once part of a lighthouse lens. A muted purple glow lit the grotto from lights hidden behind the racks of vintage wine bottles. The effect was imposing in an understated way.

All three rose. Twick winked at Glix and made the slightest of nods. Under Glix's glove, the blotch roused itself. A warning, she decided.

Twick spoke first. "Miss Cream, please meet the incomparable Mr Zan Macaller, the owner of Viggas Island's most spectacular hostelry, the Crystal Misthawk. Mr Macaller has agreed to participate in our mold-breaking new production."

"Well, well, well. I finally get to meet a real Rising Star," said a ruddy-skinned man of medium height with a neatly-trimmed red beard. Any warmth in his voice was entirely artificial, thought Glix. Like a painting of a fire as opposed to the actual fire. He seemed powerful, but in a cold, very different way from the Mayor, the only really powerful person she knew. How should she respond to a man like this? Glix had no idea.

But Tangerine Cream did. She took two steps forward and purred a greeting. "The Mayor speaks very highly of that simply gorgeous crystal bird on your roof. And I'll bet he's secretly envious of your marvelous, sleek beard. Ooooh." Seemingly of its own accord, her ungloved right hand reached out and gave the beard a slow, gentle stroke. "Double ooooh ... and my favorite, color, too."

A tiny storm cell of deeper red swept over Mr Macaller's face and disappeared into his tidy mat of gray-streaked red hair. Whatever he had expected of Twick's latest Rising Star, this wasn't it.

129

The real Glix Larue had gone into hiding during this exchange, but somehow was able to watch the Tangerine Cream performance with both awe and detachment. The walk was good, but the tude and dialog were off the charts. Where did this stuff come from?

Then she noticed the girl standing behind Mr Macaller and the sly sneer on her face. Recognition dawned: the girl was the sneery ringleader who had engineered the theft of her coin dispenser on her first night in Fogwit City. Glix was ready to explode at the monstrously unfair outrage of having this person — of all the girls in Flogtwit — about to become her understudy. Her face darkened and her mouth opened to say something, but Berlyn Twick headed her off at the pass.

"Miss Cream, please meet your new understudy, the estimable Miss Zellah Macaller. She will be joining our little community of modern thespians when we all return from our mission to Mullver's Rock. I am absolutely certain you two will get along famously."

Tangerine Cream also headed Glix off at the pass. "Zellah? Oh yes, Zellah. You must be the famous Zellah we've all heard so much about. Your fascination with coin dispensers is truly legendary throughout Fogwit. We've even heard about it up here in Grapeskin." Glix made a can-you-believe-it gesture with her hands, smiled a wide-eyed Tangerine Cream smile that was brimming with tude. After a moment, she extended her hand to the other girl.

Zellah was a study in stone, her sly sneer of seconds ago completely erased. She was every bit as outclassed as her father had been, but she made a tight-lipped smile and shook Tangerine Cream's extended hand.

As if by some prearranged signal, the door opened at that moment. Hans stepped through and bowed. "I beg your indulgence for the interruption, but Stage 4 is requesting the immediate presence of Miss Cream." Only Glix saw his wink.

27

Nut House Tavern

THE SULLEN BUZZ of twenty windmules dropped a couple notches in pitch and the airboat tilted its nose toward land. Finally, thought Glix, her own sullen mood matching the dreary monotonous buzz of the windmules. Sitting in the back of the spacious cabin with her equally sullen new understudy had been an exercise in stiff silence, each combatant trying to size up the other without appearing to be the least bit interested.

So she pretended to be Tangerine Queen moping and tried not to notice that somewhere during the voyage Zellah had decided to imitate her every gesture, large, small and in-between. Was her new staralike trying her hand at being a serious understudy, or was she being churlishly facetious? Probably facetious. But Twick had instructed Glix to pretend as though her grievances with Zellah did not exist ... at least until this critical phase of the project was "put to bed."

Twick had also instructed Glix to leave her sodbunny in the good care of Locas Vane. This wasn't a horrible idea — she trusted the kindly Keeper of Stories to take fine care of Cinder — but at the moment it felt as though she had been forced to abandon her only friend in Flogtwit.

Her Purpleness had never seemed so serious and completely lacking in sympathy for Glix's concerns as during those few minutes of pre-expedition instruction. Even Twick's trademark wry sense of humor had gone missing.

Adding to Glix's list of annoyances, a thick blanket of clouds had obscured her hometown of Quince as they flew over; trying to pick out her family's house and other landmarks from the air was impossible. This was just about the only thing she had been looking forward to, so she was feeling grumblesome. Sighting the snow-crusted tip of Hopover Mountain thrusting proudly through the clouds allayed her grumbles not at all.

There was only one good thing left to look forward to, she thought, brightening a notch. Twick had let on that she had hired Javett to fly Marvis Sashaw, Grapeskin's famous scene designer, to Mullver's Rock in a rented scoutcraft. At least that was *something* ...

A bumpy landing yanked her back to the here and now. They had reached Mullver's Rock.

A flurry of activity was already underway by the time the passengers descended from the cabin. A pair of sturdy roustabouts leaped down from the airboat's sponsons and secured it to anchors in the landing field. Two other airboats were moored on the field, but Glix noted sourly that neither of them seemed to be a two-seater scoutcraft. One was a large utility craft, somewhat worse for wear; the other was a black luxury craft that was almost as large as this one.

She looked away to watch a mule-drawn two-wheeled cart emerge from behind a well-tended outbuilding and stop at Mr Macaller's vessel. The roustabouts now set about unloading heavy sacks and lugging them toward the outriggers that held the windmules in position.

Glix had heard that the feeding of domesticated windmules and windsharks was a messy business, and experienced a moment of ghoulish interest in watching. But before the feeding began, the passengers were hustled away by a man with a black tophat to a waiting black steam-wagon. A blazon on its door said Tophat Blickernut Co.

Soon the wagon was chuff-chuffing up a graded dirt track through low hills planted with acre after acre of neatly tended blickernut trees. They looked old and gnarly, but Glix found that watching the way their spear-shaped, shiny green leaves danced in the light breeze improved her mood and made it easier to ignore the Zellah person sitting next to her.

A bend in the road revealed a cluster of stone outbuildings of various sizes and heights, and beyond them an imposing 3-story lodge made of plastered stone and timber. The place and its luxuriant landscaping looked ancient, but so meticulously maintained that she could almost imagine a troop of mythical wood-wardens lurking just out of sight, ready to leap out with their tidy-wands as soon as the new arrivals went inside.

The steam-wagon came to a stop in front of a broad walkway leading up to the lodge just as a welcoming party appeared on the veranda. Glix recognized them as none other than the Mayor and three of his burly assistants, plus several other persons she'd never seen.

What was the Mayor doing here? wondered Glix. Then something he'd said to her on her first night in Fogwit City finally dragged itself up from her memory: he owned a blickernut plantation on Mullver's Rock. For some odd reason, this memory made the blotch on her palm tingle in a weird way. It wasn't pain, exactly ... it was more like excitement. Like receiving something really special on her birthday.

• • • • •

A mountainous wedge of land roughly fifty miles long, Mullver's Rock deserved to be called an island, but wasn't. A spine of rugged mountains rose from the low cliffs of its narrow southern point to the snow-covered flanks of Istamar Peak, the highest point on its northern verge.

The blunt northern face of the island was, in essence, a cascade of sheer cliffs nearly forty miles across that were kept nearly bare of vegetation by violent lulu storms from the north.

The only practical water access to Mullver's Rock was at Nutbreaker Cove, a small, protected notch in the northeast corner of the island. Here a tiny port community had grown up to serve a busy commerce in hulling and shipping blickernuts. A smattering of warehouses, maintenance facilities and cottages for workers and harbor personnel clung to the vicinity of the pier like the barnacles on its pilings. There was also the Nut House, a tavern where locals and sea-farers often huddled together to slurp clam chowder, imbibe spirits and regale each other with tall tales and bits of news from afar.

Nutbreaker Cove had one other distinction; it was also the place the island's only road began and ended.

At the highland terminus of this road, the Mayor of Fogwit City and his Tophat Lodge staff were currently playing gracious host to the newly arrived scouting expedition from Grapeskin Studio.

134

Meanwhile, at the other end, a much larger group of blue-hel-meted individuals had made its way down the *Lallipop Queen's* gangplank and was now assembled where the road met the long pier in Nutbreaker Cove. Nearby was a mound of camping gear and sup-plies, and also a neat stack of several dozen blue-tarped crates that emitted shrill, eerie noises that most of the Ceruleans ignored. But they did not ignore the ardent harangue being delivered by Midas Blue, the Chief Cerulean. Midas Blue was not a man to be ignored.

From the bridge of the shabby vessel tied alongside the pier, Captain Waterford mopped his brow in relief and took a long pull of Cobnose Fog from his hip flask. Yes, a paying charter for the *Lalli-pop Queen* was a paying charter, particularly in these troubled times. But this group of Fogwit City chicken-littles had stretched his toler-ance for weird nonsense to the limit. Still, he had to admit that they certainly smelled better now that they were all wearing necklaces of some kind of blue flower.

He would later write in his personal logbook that he had never chartered his craft to a stranger collection of earnest innocents, cred-ulous malcontents, sheer rabble and outright nutballs.

The sun was kissing the horizon by the time the Blue Helmets had loaded their crates and provisions onto several hired mule-carts and begun their trek up the steep, pot-holed road that led into the highlands.

Good riddance, thought the Captain as he forced an expression of hearty goodwill onto his grizzled face and waved farewell. At least they were out of his hair for three days while they did whatever they were going to do up on the highlands. He didn't really believe it was some kind of sacrifice to a sky god; the slackwit fool who had proudly made that assertion had been more than half-snockered. Way more than half snockered. Probably just nonsensical bluster from the snarly kjoa wannabe. Anyway, the blue helmet nutcases were no longer his problem. He turned away toward the gangplank and thence to his ultimate destination, the Nut House tavern.

136

28

Her Mind's Throat

PLANTATIONS owned by the Tophat Blickernut Co. covered thousands of acres on the gently sloping highlands east of the north-south range of mountains called The Blade. The road from Nutbreaker Cove passed through these groves and ended in the shadow of the foothills that rose up behind the Tophat Lodge complex.

On the spacious veranda of the Tophat Lodge not a dozen yards from that road, tables were laden with trays of hors d'oeuvres for the famished party from Grapeskin while dinner was being prepared in the kitchens. The guests were nibbling and quaffing with great enthusiasm, with the exception of Glix. She only sampled a bite from this tray or that as she tried to dodge her pesky understudy.

For her part, Zellah was clearly still set on mimicking Tangerine Cream's every facial expression, every gesture and every movement, even the Rising Star's grimace and pucker when she had bitten into a mysterious nugget that turned out to be sea-jelly eggs wrapped in thin slivers of raw eel-flesh.

Zellah had become a noxious insect buzzing around her head … an insect that she had been explicitly forbidden to swat. At what seemed like an opportune moment, Glix dodged behind a heavy timber column, hoping to shake her understudy. She had a minute or two of freedom when a real buzzing sound interrupted her sour thoughts and wishful dodging. Windsharks. Nearby.

Was Javett finally arriving? She forgot about trying to escape the irksome Zellah and darted to the railing at the eastern corner of the veranda. The buzzing rose to an intensity that reminded Glix of the windshark pod races at the Fairdilly Fair. Other curious folk, including Zellah, moved to her spot, but there was nothing to see but the tile roofs of the stone outbuildings poking up through the endless expanse of blickernut trees, their foliage glittering with golden highlights in the sinking afternoon sun. Then she spotted a fast-moving dust cloud just beyond where the road curved away from view, perhaps a hundred yards in the distance.

138

A scoutcraft rounded the bend, flying just inches above the road and trailing a tornado of dust behind it, thanks to the furious beating of windshark wings. It was larger than the single-seat racing pods that can fly 80 miles per hour, so the 2-seat scouter probably wasn't going quite that fast. But whatever its actual speed was, the scouter was now pointed directly at the veranda. The group at the railing gasped almost in unison. The pilot seemed to be waving them away.

Had his windsharks gone wild? Glix had heard stories of windsharks going mad, breaking out of their harnesses and attacking anything in their path with bloody results. Surely that couldn't happen here ...

Sensing doom bearing down on her, Glix ducked behind the column of heavy timber that held up that corner of the veranda's roof. Others lurched backward and crashed into serving tables, sending platters of foodstuffs and bowls of punch flying.

The scouter was now so close that Glix could see the rivets on the nearest windsteed's harness. She started to duck, but the time for ducking was over. Now only luck could save her.

But at the last possible instant, the windsharks and the scouter pivoted sideways in a lightning fast quarter-roll. At the same instant, they veered sharply away, swooshing past the veranda, so close that Glix could have touched the pale underbellies of two windsteeds ... if she'd had the nerve.

Before she could even blink, the craft left the veranda behind in a swirling cloud of dust. Just past the corner of the building it made another maneuver and banked away behind the Lodge, the furious buzzing stretching out behind it like a tree shadow at twilight.

Glix coughed and spat out a mouthful of grit. And then grinned: to her intense satisfaction, Zellah was one of those who had lurched into a table, upending a punchbowl in the process. She was now scowling at her punch-soaked, very expensive clothing. Tsk, tsk, tsk, thought the original Tangerine Cream, not the least bit sympathetic and feeling only a little guilty about it.

139

The airwash from the close fly-by had blown the beret from Berlyn Twick's head, but the Mayor's trademark black top had stayed put. "Brav-o, brav-o! Now *that* is flying!" he boomed with boyish zest. The Mayor underlined his enthusiasm with vigorous hand-clapping. A black-haired young woman standing next to him added hoots and hoo-hahs to her applause and even shouted out Javett's name. Others on the veranda gradually joined in, although with more measured enthusiasm.

Twick scowled a sardonic purple scowl and kept her hands to her sides.

Glix was astounded. Javett had hardly seemed like the show-offy type on the two occasions she'd met him before. But maybe he hadn't done it for her benefit; maybe he was showing off for someone else. The very idea of that seemed to stick in her mind's throat and brought her applause to a sudden stop.

140

29

Daredevil Antics

JAVETT LOOKED FORLORN sitting at the front table during dinner, the table with all the bigwigs. The Mayor had insisted, but he'd never felt more uncomfortable in his life. Still, it was probably the safest place for him under the circumstances.

Although the Mayor had publicly extolled his flying skills more than twice, Javett could see that virtually nobody else in the room thought his stunt flying in front of the lodge was anything but dangerously juvenile behavior. Even Glix and Zellah had glared at him. Talk about backfiring.

Twick threatened to "get his sorry Hiphollow ass fired ... and then some" if he ever did anything to endanger "her people" again. His passenger, the scene designer, had gone Twick one better: he'd just kill him. So Javett was very quiet and kept his eyes mostly on his plate during the entire four-course meal.

After dinner the group moved to a comfortable lounge that sported a toob every bit as large as the one Glix had seen in that Fogwit City park. The elaborate copper funnels on the top made Glix miss her father and feel much more like a little girl called Glixxie than a Rising Star called Tangerine Cream. She blinked away a nostalgic tear.

A short, wide Fangler named Ermius Felkon was introduced, interrupting Glix's moment of melancholy. The rugged-looking Felkon had been named the leader of the Save the Sky Expedition, which was currently being assembled in the old warehouse district out at

Cobnose Flats. He wore drab gray coveralls, but spiced up the maintenance worker look with a yellow "Fangler Powered" long-billed cap and well-stuffed yellow pocket protectors. Glix would have found these costume touches surprising on a "science type" if she hadn't known they had been created by the Purple One in an attempt to modernize the stodgy image of Fanglers and lend credibility to their assertions. She was rolling her eyes when the lights dimmed and Felkon's presentation began.

During the next thirty minutes Glix learned more about the world she lived in than she had learned in all her years of school. And she wasn't alone. Like most people on Hallah, she took her world for granted. And like most people on Hallah, she knew almost nothing about it. Hallah was just Hallah. Like the air she breathed, it was just there, all around her.

She wondered how many people here had known that their "natural" world was actually an artificial construct, a huge, incredibly complicated living machine that had been slowly dying for many years. Centuries, at least. The Keepers that had kept it running for thousands of years were failing … and not even the clever Fangler brainiacs knew exactly why. And the recent spate of skyfalls wasn't the worst of it; if nothing changed, in ten years or less the sky, sun and moons would go black and everyone and everything in Hallah would be dead in days. Every human, every animal and every plant would die and rot like old garbage.

This was hard to swallow … and Glix wasn't alone in her rude awakening. The three Fanglers, the Mayor and Berlyn Twick were the only people in the room who already knew how bad things were. And they'd kept the truth a secret until now. A tiny part of her wondered why.

Fortunately, the Fanglers had a plan: get inside of Hallah's skin and start fixing things … or at least slow down the dying. Fanglers were the closest things to scientists and engineers that Hallah had at this time in its history, so a group of them had come to Wyn from their island of Gonzotopia to persuade powerful people like the Mayor and Mr Macaller to support them. That was the "why" of the Save the Sky Expedition. The "how" was a lot more complicated and it was all too new for Glix to get her mind around.

One thing that stuck in her mind was Bastion 9. She seemed to recall something about Bastions from some class or other at the Academy, but whatever Bastions were, they were too far away to be very important. At least that was the impression she'd been left with. Felkon talked a lot about one Bastion in particular.

"Each of Hallah's twelve Bastions has four access points into Hallah's skin," explained Felkon in his flat, choppy style of speaking. "Two are at sea level and have proven to be impenetrable by any known means. However, we have reason to believe that the upper portals may be more accessible to us. We Fanglers have been studying the Bastions for many years out of pure scientific curiosity, but have never tried to climb a Bastion and reach a high portal. There was no need. Now the need is upon us. Being located approximately ten miles above sea level, the high portals are very hard for humans to get to. Almost impossible, actually. The air is extremely cold and too thin to breathe ... for either humans or windmules. Not a problem, however, for the so-called 'windskates'. They spend their entire lives traveling at such altitudes. Windskates look like this."

The toob now showed drawings of a translucent pancake sort of thing.

"They are commonly called windskates because of their apparent similarity to the sea-skates that inhabit the shallow areas of the Great Wet out near the rim, where sky and water meet. Other than their flat, generally triangular shape, the actual similarity is minimal. Windskates inflate themselves with bubbles of helium that make their bodies somewhat lighter than air. They play an important but poorly understood function in Hallah's ecology and spend their lives trolling the wind currents in Hallah's thin upper atmosphere in great schools, much as schools of whales navigate the Great Wet.

"Windskates can grow to half a mile long and live for hundreds of years, but eventually they die and their incredibly strong and flexible

143

carcasses gradually lose their helium and end up in the sea. The Fangler research station studying Bastion 9 has obtained several of these 'husks' and has discovered objects and materials inside them that strongly suggest windskates regularly visit the high portals." Felkon paused before dropping his bombshell. "We also have evidence that certain non-biological items discovered in these carcasses are 'keys' that permit them access to the portals."

There was a rustle in the room as people sorted through the possible implications of this new information.

Felkon continued. "It is for these and other reasons that we Fanglers are confident that the upper portals will open to us and why we are outfitting a windskate carcass as a high altitude vehicle." The Fangler made a motion and a new image appeared, an artist's rendering of the proposed vehicle being towed through the sky by several teams of windmules. "Ladies and gentlemen, meet the *Wild Blue Wanda*. Perhaps she will save us all. We can hope ...."

Felkon paused, mopped his brow, stared out at his audience and forced a smile. He seemed drained of energy. "Thank you for listening. I know I have said things that are difficult to believe, but ...." The Fangler searched for something else to say but after a few moments he just gestured for the lights.

Erratic applause rippled around the room followed by a thick, tense silence. It lasted for perhaps ten seconds before bedlam erupted: a bedlam of questions.

Glix's head hurt and she wanted to go to bed. She looked longingly at the door and saw hope for an escape from all the adults. Arrol Moon, the rugged looking young woman who had cheered Javett's crazy flying alongside the Mayor, now beckoned to her from the door. For whatever reasons, Arrol Moon had been assigned the job of acting as her 'warden'. Was being summoned by a warden better than being bored by adults?

In the hallway, Glix learned that Arrol Moon was also Zellah's warden. Great. She rolled her eyes, took a deep breath and wrapped herself in her Tangerine Cream persona, realizing for the first time that it almost felt more natural than being a Quincian Queen of Nice-ness had ever felt. Sometimes, at least.

Arrol's tanned face now looked an ashen gray; although she hadn't officially been part of the audience, she had listened from the door. "Ten years? We're all dead in ten years? That's it?" The voice that Glix had earlier thought was husky and strong now seemed any-thing but.

"What are you talking about?" asked Zellah with a sneerish frown and an arched eyebrow. Zellah had left the Fangler's talk very early, telling her father that she had a headache and was going to her room. Glix had watched her leave with mixed feelings. Quincians would nev-er do something as un-nice as leave in the middle of a meeting. Not even a meeting guaranteed to give anybody a real headache. But she also sort of admired Zellah's willfulness — if that was the right word.

Tangerine Cream struck a pose of total superiority and spoke. "Oh! I guess my understudy left before all the good stuff! Our warden is right: according to the Fangler, all of Hallah — you, included — will be dead in a decade. It's not just about some pieces of sky falling."

Zellah ignored this. "My father thinks Fanglers aren't as smart and clever as most people think they are. If they were, they wouldn't have to come around asking for big piles of starglass all the time. I certainly wouldn't believe something just because a *Fangler* said it. If they were really worried about serious things like the sky falling, they wouldn't spend their time creating silly junk like Invisible Spy Rings and three-headed meadowlarks." Her tone had that haughty self-as-surance that some people use as a substitute for actual knowledge.

Perhaps because Arrol spent much of her time caring for Tophat's animals, she knew when a catfight was brewing. "Well ladies, as your warden it's my job to see that you both get tucked in straight away. No dawdling, no catfights. We have a busy day tomorrow. Berlyn Twick has hired me to introduce you to weapons and windsharks, so you don't look totally foolish playing a toob-heroine over the next few months. It's just a beginning, of course. Your training will continue in Fogwit City under Master Few, I'm told."

Arrol Moon was tall for a woman, with luminous eyes the color of ripe pod-peas, coal black hair cut very short, and a wiry, athletic build. There was also something about her — something indefinable — that put her two charges on notice that their warden wouldn't put up with any nonsense.

When she continued, it was in a sort of hissed almost-whisper. "Just between the three of us, I'm going to work your girly butts off tomorrow ... although nothing like what Master Few will put you through.

"If you survive the rigors of your introduction to real physical effort, I've got an idea for a little extra-credit adventure tomorrow night. If you wanna come along with me and our crazy flyboy friend, that is. Maybe you'll be up to it ... or maybe Tangerine Cream's gutsy pose is just a pose ... just more toob-ish nonsense. Either way, I suggest you get a good night's sleep. Breakfast is at 6. Be there on time; I'm sure the Mayor will have something pithy to say."

Glix blinked, Zellah frowned. But both had the good sense to say nothing but goodnight.

Naturally, it took Glix forever to get to sleep. She missed her cuddly sodbunny, for one thing. For another, she couldn't stop thinking about all the awful stuff the Fangler had talked about. Everybody she knew dying horrible deaths as their world went dark? The thought of her little sister Wixit dead made her stomach knot up.

But when she managed to stop thinking about that, something else got her head spinning: Arrol's reference to "our flyboy friend." Who could that be but Javett? Was Arrol the reason he had avoided Glix since his daredevil antics?

30

Quad Practice

BASED ON Arrol's list of clothes for today, the Tangerine Cream personas were getting a vacation. Loose-fitting pants, a baggy long-sleeved shirt tied at the waist with a sash, and supple boots that were more like slippers than boots. No Rising Star would be caught dead in an outfit like this. Glix was almost willing to bet that Zellah would find an excuse for not showing up at breakfast rather than wear this stuff in public. Glix grinned at the thought.

The lounge where the Fangler had given his presentation was now outfitted with a sparse buffet of fruit, pastries, sausages and some bowls of variously colored puddings. But no one was eating yet. One of the Mayor's burly assistants protected the food, directing the desperately hungry to a table with Quincian-made copper beverage dispensers and instructing them to await the Mayor's arrival. Glix filled a mug with something labeled Rock Reserve Mocha and scanned the room.

When she'd left the room last night, Glix had sensed a general mood of stunned shock. This morning the mood was different: resigned, but also re-energized in some strange way. Nobody seemed to be taking the Fangler's death sentence as a given.

The three Fanglers and the Grapeskin contingent were huddled over a detailed relief map of Mullver's Rock. Sashaw, the scene designer, was gesturing to the spine of steep, symmetrical mountains that gave the island its oddly skewed pyramid shape. Twick and the others nodded, watched and made occasional comments.

Javett stood apart looking sheepish, but still paying close attention to the discussion. Since neither Arrol nor Zellah had arrived yet, Glix took the opportunity to study Javett from semi-concealment behind a potted tree-fern next to the beverage table. How was he different from the shy boy at the Fairdilly Fair?

For one thing, he was now one of the taller people in the room. And more man than boy now, with a lean frame, taut muscles and a crisp jawline. The wavy, sand-colored hair, the kind gold-flecked hazel eyes and the unassuming smile were still the same, though.

She looked at other men in the group and her eyes landed on Zellah's father. Compared to Javett, Mr Macaller seemed rigid and harsh. He almost never smiled and he seemed to radiate a dour energy that made his ruddy complexion appear darker than it actually was. The owner of the Crystal Misthawk would be an easy man to dislike, Glix decided. For a fact, she had disliked him from the moment she first saw him in the Purple Grotto.

A bustle from the door interrupted her thoughts. The Mayor and two more of his assistants arrived — fashionably late, as was his long-standing custom — followed by Zellah and an angry-looking Arrol. Conversations dwindled and the Mayor strode directly to the podium.

"Greetings, good saviors of Hallah! I trust you all slept as well as possible under the circumstances?" The Mayor looked fresh and at his bluff-and-hearty best, although few others did. "I apologize for keeping you from breakfast, but Mrs Flagstaff tells me there are a few housekeeping details you need to know. Plus there is one other bit of local news concerning our friends, the Ceruleans."

The Mayor announced that in the interest of fostering public awareness of Hallah's deteriorating condition, he had permitted a sizeable group of Ceruleans to visit a location on Mullver's Rock where atmospheric conditions are favorable for a rite they wished to conduct. A murmur of disapproval rippled through the room; the

Blue Helmets were seen by all present as purveyors of dangerous, unscientific foolishness.

"Yes, I know that the, ah, more thoughtful elements of Wyn and Gonzotopia and so forth find the Blue Helmet approach to halting Hallah's deterioration suspect, at best. Still, as Mayor, I must be fair-handed. So. I have given them leave to camp not far from here where they can be close to the Flue. If you should see a column of blue smoke rising a few miles to the north tonight, you need not be concerned. It is merely another well-intentioned sky-saving strategy at work."

149

The Mayor paused and shot a meaningful glance in the direction of Arrol. "I have also assured their leader — you may know him as Midas Blue — that his group will not be bothered by any scientific observers, spectators, onlookers or even innocent passersby from our party. And in any case, I'm sure we will all be busy going about our own urgencies in relation to the salvation of Hallah. I suspect that is all that needs to be said on the matter."

When Mrs Flagstaff had finished her instructive but humorless pronouncements, Twick described the upcoming "creative intensive" to hash out story, technical and financial issues for the upcoming production. Glix was not exactly looking forward to spending a day with Zellah and Arrol, but she was certain it would to be more interesting than a day of adult talk-talking. She was probably right.

By mid-morning she felt like a sword-bearing sweat machine. Who knew that wooden swords were so heavy? Or that moving them properly was so tricky? Arrol surveyed her two weary charges and called a five-minute break.

The Rising Stars' "overdue physical studies" were taking place in a training room in the basement of the Lodge. Even though the Grapeskin complex had its own training room, it was nothing like this one. The floor in the center was covered in cushioned mats; the walls were lined with machines that looked like elaborate torture devices. Their workout had begun with warm-ups, tumbling and some basic fight-moves, mostly involving footwork. But just before Arrol had shaken her head and called for a break, they had taken up the swords.

"Well," was all Arrol said, arms akimbo. She looked from Glix to Zellah and back again, fixing each of them with a penetrating look. Then shook her head and rolled her eyes. "About as I expected; two soft teenagers with barely the strength to hold up a wooden sword for five minutes, much less fight with it. I am tempted to put sparring gloves on you and let the two of you duke it out just to see who is the softest. Or who'll be the first to cry. But I'm going to resist this temptation ... for the moment. Your real training will begin when you get back to Grapeskin. For now ...."

Zellah interrupted. "This is so-o-o-o stupid. Don't you know anything about modern education? My father owns a company that makes educational supplements for the Department of Public Education. I know there are training capsules for things like archery, so I'm sure my father's people could make something for whatever silly things we need to fake. They already made ... uh, never mind."

Glix became instantly suspicious, but her train of thought was derailed by Arrol's response.

"Why that's an excellent idea, Zellah," exclaimed Arrol. "I will suggest it to Her Purpleness on your behalf. Still, there's a tiny flaw. A pill might be able to tell your muscles how to move, but if those muscles are too weak to make the right motions long enough, all you've done is waste a very expensive pill. Plus, there's no script yet, so nobody knows what stunts you'll have to perform and what moves you'll need to know. So until we have two strong Tangerine Creams and a shooting script, we'll just have to do it the 'old school' way."

Zellah was about to protest, but Arrol held up her hands and cut her off. "But not today. You may relax Miss Macaller. We're done with the physical portion of your evaluation."

Arrol's face was the perfect picture of disgust. "To be blunt, I've seen all I the weakness I can stomach for one day, so we'll continue your education in less strenuous ways." She pointed to a door. "There are some gloves and boots in that closet over there. Find some that fit and meet me on the veranda in five minutes."

Glix found the rest of the day totally fascinating. Zellah was hardly enthusiastic, but made only a dozen or so protests. Glix's favorite time was at the stables where the windsharks and windmules were caged. She had never seen the creatures this close and hadn't ever realized they had legs; three pair that they keep tucked into folds in their belly skin while flying. It was here that she also learned the difference between a windshark and a windmule; besides being thicker in girth, they had longer, wider wings and two extra pairs of them, plus about four feet in extra length. Windmules had been bred for hauling, not speed, and a number of the Tophat windmules would be used to haul the replica of the *Wild Blue Wanda* that Twick planned to use in the Grapeskin production.

151

"What's in those cages? Some kind of special windsharks?" Glix pointed to a bank of cages that were in distinctly better condition than any of the others Arrol had shown them.

"Those, ladies, are the Mayor's steeds and he is quite proud of them. Bred especially for our Mayor by old Master Wyndash, so they're special indeed. He rides them quite a bit when he's up here on the Rock and is an excellent rider. But never in Fogwit City; wouldn't fit his grandiose image. That's our little secret, of course."

It was mid-afternoon when the trio stopped in one corner of a large garage near the main road.

"Well ladies, time to meet your quads." Arrol pointed to a matched pair of stubby, four-wheeled utility vehicles with short cargo beds. You're going to need these for our rescue mission tonight, so pay close attention."

"Rescue mission?" chimed Glix and Zellah in unison?

"It's your chance to prove you really have the stuff to be the daring heroines you're pretending to be. Javett and I are going to raid the Blue Helmets tonight. And I'm inviting you two to join us."

Zellah's eyes narrowed at the idea of a raid on those clueless jerks. Some of her cronies had become Ceruleans and she'd never forgiven them. That was what she said, at least. Was it sheer coincidence that she avoided Glix's eyes when she said that? Glix had her doubts.

She also had her doubts about raiding people like that hapless knob-nosed man she'd tongue-whipped during her first night in Flogtwit. Her Quincian niceness crawled up to her voicebox from wherever it had been hiding: "But didn't the Mayor specifically say that nobody was supposed to go near the Ceruleans tonight?"

Arrol rolled her eyes. "You are *such* a Quincian, Miss Larue. Of *course* the Mayor very publicly prohibited any interference in their rites. Ever hear of 'plausible deniability'? But here's what the Mayor and I know that nobody else knows; they're planning to burn twelve young butterwings that they kidnapped from a wild colony up in Kirpansy Pass. Burn them alive." Arrol's eyes flashed with anger and she said those three words very slowly.

Neither Tangerine Cream interrupted.

"According to our sources down at the Cove, it's some kind of primitivist sacrifice to their sky god. They've dyed the butterwing nymphs blue and are going to douse them in a substance that makes blue smoke; then they'll light the 'sacred' bonfire and burn them right in their cages. The butterwings won't even have a chance to fly away and escape. Well we're going to set them free! Tonight. Are you in or out? If you're in, you'll need to get in some quad practice."

152

31

With a Tomahawk

ARROL SCOWLED from the corner table where she sat with the Tangerine Creams. She was thinking about helpless butterwings being burned alive during tonight's Blackout, the long minutes of total darkness between the setting of Lumo and the rising of Rhomo. Events were getting in the way of her rescue plan.

The instant he returned from his scouting expedition, her daring fellow raider had been sucked into the endless "creative intensive" by the Mayor himself; without Javett, the raid on the Cerulean camp was doomed to failure. Two clueless Tangerines were going to be more hindrance than help. She glowered at the Mayor, then at Javett, not sure which most deserved her ire.

• • • • •

Arrol took them on an indirect route down through the groves of blickernut trees to a position only about a quarter-mile from the Cerulean encampment.

"The pyre is supposed to be lit at Blackout ... less than two hours from now," whispered Arrol to the two Tangerines on their idling quads. It had been a wet, muddy three miles, but at least the rain had slowed. Of course there could be another cloudburst any minute. As she'd learned from experience, that was how the weather was on the Rock.

Only a brighter circle of deep blue-gray in the cloud cover indicated that Lumo was well on its downhill slide. Arrol felt the approach

of Blackout in her bones and wondered to herself why Cruelty prefers
the time between moons for its evil deeds, but said nothing aloud.

The two Tangerines looked utterly miserable and out of place
in their black slickers, black hoods and blackened faces, but she be-
grudged them a dollop of credit for being here at all. They had chosen
to go along with her, whether their heartthrob flyboy was with them
or not. So maybe they had some guts after all.

"Okay Tangerines, listen up. You two stay here while I check out
the situation on foot. If I'm not back in fifteen minutes, turn your
quads around and head back to the Lodge the same way we came.
Clean up and change your clothes where I told you and say nothing
to anybody. And don't worry about outrunning any pursuit on this
end; no Blue Helmet is going to win a footrace with a mad Tangerine
on a quad. Oh, and one other thing. I trust I don't have to tell you to
be absolutely silent. I'd be very surprised if they didn't have guards
posted." She grinned, winked and was gone in the night.

Glix had secretly hoped that the Blue Helmets would be asleep by
now, but from the campfires and the sounds of revelry, a huge party
was underway and nobody was sleeping. Kiss that idea goodbye. She
tried to turn off her mind and wait for Arrol to get back, but her palm
throbbed and she had a bad feeling that wouldn't go away.

The Tangerine silence lasted almost two whole minutes. "I hate
this," Zellah blurted, an angry shiver in her voice. "I don't know what
I was thinking ... I don't even *like* butterwings. They're nosy little
busybodies and their big black eyes are creepy. Maybe we ought to
just go down and join the party. I'll bet they have some good stuff ...."

Zellah let the word hang, perhaps expecting Glix to say something like, "Yeah, I'll bet they *do* have some good stuff. Let's kiss this
stupid raid goodbye and go have some fun." Clearly Zellah didn't
know much about Quincians, even less about Queens of Niceness
and absolutely nothing about Glix Larue.

Glix just spun her head around and gaped at her understudy. She
felt a torrent of insults, slanders and worse fighting their way to her
tongue, but she held them off. Her mind was racing and the blotch

under her glove was sending her some kind of very painful — and entirely incomprehensible — message.

Would Zellah actually *do* something like that? Just walk down to the Ceruleans' camp, join the party and chant mumbo-jumbo along with the rest of those idiots while they watched helpless creatures burn to death? Then calmly find her way back to the Lodge and be Tangerine Cream's understudy again as if nothing unusual had happened?

Before Glix could answer herself, Zellah twisted the throttle of her quad and shot forward down the muddy track they'd been following. The quad slid sideways and nearly crashed into a tree, but Zellah leaned hard to the left, got it straightened out and was already almost out of the grove.

Without another thought, Glix cranked the throttle as far as it would go and launched her own quad after Zellah, her front wheels lurching off the ground and spraying her face with matching pinwheels of cold mud.

Arrol was almost back to where she'd left the two Tangerines. Her heart lurched when she heard the squish and hiss of a steam-quad slip-sliding through mud. Then Zellah burst out of the grove and charged down the grassy slope toward the blue-helmeted revelers. The Tangerines' warden couldn't believe what she was seeing. Then Glix's quad did the same thing.

Two deserters? In one night? What she'd just seen almost wouldn't register in her tired brain. And she certainly didn't know what she could do about it at the moment. Chasing after them would be a disaster, so she just hunkered down and watched the torch-lit chaos unfold. Sometimes opportunities present themselves entirely unannounced, she thought to herself in a moment of optimism. Sometimes ... but probably not tonight.

Glix was gaining on the lead quad, but so what? Zellah's full-throttle clip had brought her into the camp already and she now barreled down on a clot of Ceruleans swathed in rain gear. The spew of moonlit steam behind her added an eerie, dramatic effect. In five seconds there were going to be bodies flying every which way.

The partiers just stood and gawked, dumb as cows. Possibly what they had in their cups helped with their befuddlement, possibly the idea of being run down by a high speed quad was too impossible to comprehend. But at the last second they all lurched, staggered or dove out of the quad's way, cups and contents turning messy somersaults in the air.

Zellah shot past, somehow missing every snockered partier. But drunken blue-hats weren't her only obstacles. She braked hard and jerked the handlebars to the left to avoid the camp table with the punchbowl that had been hidden by the crowd. Sliding sideways now, her quad skidded past the table in a shower of mud. All except for the right rear wheel, which clipped the table's corner with just enough oomph to send the table spinning in one direction, the quad in another. Zellah flew off the seat, hit the ground rolling and came to a stop in an untidy pile of splat-covered blue tarps.

For Glix, a hundred feet behind, this all seemed to be happening in slow motion. She carefully applied the brakes and brought her own quad to a stop in a far less dramatic manner. Ignoring the fascinated bystanders, she vaulted off the seat and sprinted to where Zellah was now staggering to her feet.

"Eeeww! What's that smell?" Zellah's nose puckered and she tried to wipe away some noxious glop that had gotten on her slicker, succeeding only in getting it on her hands as well. "And what are *you* doing here? I didn't ask you to follow me here. You're going to ruin everything, you silly copperhead twit!"

"Copperhead twit?" Glix couldn't believe she was hearing such a lame insult from the wannabe Tangerine Cream. Then she sniffed the air and grinned: butterwing feces. That was exactly what Zellah had all over her hands and her slicker. "Serves you right to have butterwing skrat all over you," she yelled with a sneer of disgust. "You are one puke-slurping, puckernosed, tail-wiping, sneaky pus-clot excuse for a Tangerine Cream understudy, you ...."

Sputtering, furious and having run out of proper Tangerine Creamish unpleasantries to shout, Glix did something she'd never even contemplated before; she lowered her head and launched her body at her understudy's midsection. Zellah's breath escaped with a whoof that even Arrol Moon could hear from her hiding place fifty yards away. Both Tangerines fell into the pile of yucky blue tarps.

Arrol grinned. The strange winds of fate had just handed her the absolute perfect distraction. Time to act. She took a deep breath, raised her eyes to the sky and took off at a dead run back to the Flue.

The two black-caped wannabe kjoas guarding a dozen blue-dyed butterwings in cages had no idea they were about to meet a former Hiphollow Ranger with a tomahawk.

158

32

We Should Talk

"I THINK she's coming around," whispered a voice from a hundred miles up in the sky. "She's still pale from the blood loss and may have a concussion, but I don't see any problem in trying to talk to her."

"Calling Miss Cream. Anybody in there, Miss Cream?"

That was a different voice. Familiar. Getting closer. A closet door opened inside her mind and a handful of memories tumbled out. Her Purpleness. Berlyn Twick. Auteur. Employer. Grapeskin Studio. Mullver's Rock. Arrol. Ceruleans. Butterwings. Understudy. Zellah Macaller. Rage.

Glix's eyes fluttered, blinked twice and opened. Focusing took a little longer, but color seeped back into her face and her voicebox started working. "Did I kill her?"

Twick responded drily. "If you killed someone, Miss Larue, I'm unaware that any corpses have yet appeared. Sorry. But let's talk about nicer things than murder. Like the fact that you're officially on medical leave until we know for sure that your brains aren't totally scrambled. That means your understudy will temporarily be playing Tangerine Cream."

More memory doors opened. "You mean ...?"

"Don't get yourself in a state, Miss Larue. It's only until you're healed up ... and we're weeks from being ready for serious eyebutton work anyway. So just get well and rested up for what is shaping up to be a long and strenuous production. Maybe read a book or two; Mrs

Flagstaff tells me that Tophat Lodge has a remarkable library. If you can remember some of your queenly niceness, perhaps she'll show you around."

The Purple One stood, adjusted her beret and whispered a word to the other woman. Then she patted Glix's cheek and tossed a few words of farewell in the patient's direction. "Please recover quickly, Miss Larue. We need you." Then the door closed.

The other woman remained standing by the bed and Glix struggled to connect a name to the face. She blinked and remembered: Mrs Flagstaff, the lady in charge of the Tophat Lodge. Mrs Flagstaff was probably a decade older than Glix's mother, with gray-streaked blond hair pulled back and gathered in a tight coil at the back of her head. Not exactly pretty, but attractive in a stern, controlled sort of way.

Glix weathered a penetrating gaze from the woman's gray eyes, her taut face bearing an ambiguous expression that made Glix feel like an anesthetized frog calmly being dissected by a bored librarian. A long moment came and went before the woman's eyes and lips collaborated in a knowing half-smile that would have annoyed Glix had she been more fully herself.

"Drink this, Miss Larue," said Mrs Flagstaff with a soft, yet commanding voice. "It is exactly what you need."

Glix's brain still thumped unpleasantly against her skull and dull pain pulsed from multiple locations on the left side of her scalp. And her eyes ached, so she closed them. A straw was placed at her lips and she sipped something slightly fizzy with a pleasant, vaguely familiar aroma that reminded her more of colors than scents. Almost instantly, she slept.

A distant scream that might have been a hunting nighthawk scattered the last remnants of an unpleasant dream. Her eyes blinked open to darkness. Had she slept all day? She blinked again and sat up in the bed ... an unfamiliar bed in an unfamiliar room. Her eyes began to adjust to the dark and she saw a faint rectangle with an orange tint highlighting its rim; the second moon was fading and somewhere in the west a new dawn was being prepared for service.

The oil lamp on the nightstand emitted only a weak cone of amber light under its heavy shade. She barely noticed the moths fluttering around the shade and barely noticed that she was wearing a nightgown. Her urgencies were elsewhere: specifically, where was the bathroom?

Sconces gave the hallway enough illumination for her to find the correct door. A minute later she stood in front of a mirror, alternately staring at her bandaged head and splashing cold water on her face. The chilly water on her skin was a pleasant shock. The realization that her left hand was bare-palm naked was an unpleasant shock; her copper glove had gone missing. She gawked at the dreadful mark on her palm and almost screamed. Almost.

In near panic, she dashed back to her room, turned up the lamp's wick and searched. She didn't have very far to look; the glove sat innocently on the wooden dressing table, with a note under it. It was written with a smooth hand on a small sheet of paper that had the Tophat Lodge logo at the top. It said:

"I trust you are feeling better, Miss Larue. If you are reading this, it is night and I have gone to my quarters. Note that I have taken the liberty of cleaning your remarkable copper glove, as it was quite soiled with what I am told was butterwing dung. Should you wake up desirous of a snack, you will find a tray of victual in the cooler by the door. A suitable breakfast will be delivered first bell when I arrive to check on the state of your injuries."

A squiggle that must have been Mrs Flagstaff's signature appeared at the bottom. Almost reflexively, Glix jammed her naked hand into the glove and exhaled the breath she hadn't realized she'd been holding. She frowned at the glove; having the mark covered up again wasn't providing its usual sense of safety. Someone knew her secret. She felt violated, particularly because it had happened while she was sleeping, when she was defenseless. A messy tangle of unpleasant feelings wrapped themselves around her heart and her brain at the same instant: anger, suspicion, betrayal, frustration, loneliness and a sickly sadness were all there. But they all bowed to a directionless, irrational fear. Fear of what? She couldn't have said.

Her heart was thumping so hard it threatened to hammer its way through her ribcage and she threw herself back on the bed and pounded on it with her fists. She knew she was being stupid and over-dramatic, but at the moment she was powerless to be any other way. A dam broke, releasing a torrent of tears and wracking sobs. Gradually, the tears stopped, the feelings faded and a tentative calm returned. She lay on the bed, not quite asleep, but also not quite awake, her brain still a tangle of half-thoughts, her heart still wrapped in a muck of half-feelings. And she felt hot, almost feverish.

After a time, she sat up, convinced at last that a return to the refuge of sleep was out of the question. She rubbed her eyes, sighed and watched the vague pre-dawn light paint murky glimmers on the vast groves of blickernuts that covered the rolling slopes out beyond the lodge. For no good reason, her throat decided that it was thirsty: the lost-in-the-desert sort of thirsty. She poured herself a glass of water from the pitcher on the nightstand and downed it in a gulp.

This water seemed unusually refreshing and had the effect of cooling her feverish thoughts and feelings in addition to un-parching her throat. There was something odd about the water, but what? The slight effervescence? The faint aromas that reminded her of sassafras, peaches and strawberries? Somewhere in her head were the right memories, but they were still in hiding. Still, memories or not, she was feeling better. Then she began to think about the prospects of an impending meeting with Mrs Flagstaff and decided to get dressed before the woman arrived.

Mrs Flagstaff had struck Glix as aloof and mysterious and for some reason Glix didn't want to be in a nightgown when she arrived. She was done with being a sick-house patient and was feeling an urgent need to get back to Grapeskin Studio and defend her turf against the conniving Zellah.

The wardrobe and the closet were empty, but the bench at the foot of her bed supported a neat stack of folded clothing. Not what she'd arrived with, but the same drab, gray-green pants, shirt and soft boots that she and Zellah had worn for their training session with Arrol. Plus some fresh underthings. What had she expected? Certainly not fashionable Fogwit City things or Tangerine Cream costumes or even nice, practical Quincian things. She sighed and tugged on the clothes.

Now she was hungry. Famished, actually. The cooler Mrs Flagstaff's note had mentioned yielded a tray containing cubes of white cheese, slices of pale green melon and a bowl of tiny brown sausages. Before she could swallow her first mouthful of melon, there was a muffled knock on the door.

A voice whispered: "Glix? Are you awake? It's Arrol. We should talk. Now."

163

164

33

Sick Leave

GLIX OPENED the door to see Arrol with a finger at her lips. "Shssssh," she whispered, looking Glix up and down. "Have to say I didn't expect to find you dressed already. Grab your cloak, stuff the cheese and sausages in a pocket and let's move out; it's time for a special early morning hike. Think of it as a training exercise."

Ten minutes later the Lodge was out of sight and they were trekking a steep, apparently little-used trail that headed north into the mountains. Arrol's long strides had Glix struggling to keep up. Plus, the rising sun was still below the spine of Mullver's Rock and visibility was poor at best. Twice Glix had tried to ask a question, twice she had been rebuffed with a head-shake.

The trail snaked around a thrust of rock to reveal a tiny dell carved into the mountain. Glix followed Arrol as she threaded her way through a thicket of luluberry bushes and emerged into a hidden clearing not a dozen paces back from the trail. Several log stumps were arranged around a fire pit. "Secret hideaway," explained Arrol, with a wink. "Pull up a stump and let's rest a minute. There's still a good ways to go and you're a bit out of shape for trekking."

Glix bit back an acrid comment, nodded and tried to catch her breath.

Arrol unslung her pack and pulled a length of stringy dried meat from one of the side pockets. "Not exactly a luxurious Tophat Lodge breakfast, but with the goodies you stuffed in your pocket it'll get us where we're going. And have a big swig of fizz-juice."

She offered her canteen and Glix took a long pull. "Fizz-juice?"

"That's what I call it. Good stuff for what ails you. The Mayor says it's one of the best reasons for his occasional visits to Mullver's Rock. The stuff we pump out of the brook that feeds the little pond by the landing pad is what Mrs Flagstaff has been giving you. Better than plain water, sure, but nothing like what's at the source. You'll see."

166

"The fizz-juice reminds me of something ... but I can't remember what. It's ...." Glix was frustrated at the nagging feeling that important memories lurked just out of reach."

"You'll remember soon enough. Trust me. Meanwhile, about your famous copper glove and such." Arrol paused to let the implications ripen a moment before continuing. "I took your glove off when I tried to clean you up after we got you back to the lodge ... you weren't exactly in shape to ride the quad back yourself. So I saw the mark. And I've seen pictures of another like it. Burned there by a quantode, if I was told the truth about it. Nothing to be ashamed of, but I guess I can understand why you'd try to hide it; people would wonder ... and talk. Maybe even think you're not normal. Tsk, tsk, tsk."

Glix ignored the sarcasm. "What's a quantode? Anything like a cinder-egg?" Glix was serious.

"What's a cinder-egg? Anything like a quantode?" Arrol chuckled. "Okay, as I understand it, they're the same thing."

"Oh. You said somebody else got burned by a cinder-egg ... I mean a quantode? Really? Someone you know?" Glix was now intrigued; all her other questions were put on hold for the moment.

"Just my sort-of great-granny. But I probably shouldn't have said anything. And I don't really know how it happened anyway. But she's still alive ... a hermit way up in the Rocksaws behind Hiphollow. I used to fly mail and supplies up to her. Then when I came here to look over the animals and such, Javett took over that job."

"Javett? You mean the ... the ...." Glix went stumble-tongued, unable to decide how to describe him.

Arrol guffawed and chucked Glix playfully on the shoulder. "Yes, the Javett that you're all goo-goo eyes over. The boy who is the shyest, youngest windshark daredevil on Wyn. And otherwise known as my cousin. Some sort of a cousin, anyway. I'm an orphan; I was raised by his aunt Glinda — she's Hiphollow's legendary healer — in an ildrit not too far from the one he grew up in. He thinks you're cute, by the way ... ever since he met you at the Fairdilly Fair. Refers to you as 'the Queen' and can hardly believe that you became a Fogwit Rising Star somehow. Didn't figure you for the type: too nice. We Hiphollow folk don't think all that highly of Fogwit culture ... but don't tell him I said any of that."

Glix blushed her very first blush as a Rising Star on sick leave.

168

34

The Truth of It

PRETENDING NOT to notice Glix's blush, Arrol stood up, slung her pack over her shoulder and said, "You look rested enough to walk again. The trail from here's just a narrow little deer trail ... I'm probably the first human to ever use it. So I'll go a little slower the rest of the way and fill you in on what's been happening since you got your skull cracked open.

"Actually, I missed that part, but I got the story from Grond, one of the Mayor's 'watchdogs' in fire-wagons; you probably didn't know they were there. Good thing they were."

Glix found herself admiring how the Mayor never seemed to miss a beat in his management of events. But she said nothing.

"Anyway," continued Arrol, "all the chaos you and your dear friend Zellah caused was the perfect distraction for me. By the way, the butterwings appreciate that you sacrificed all that blood to help their escape."

"Yeah, right. Butterwings are as full of gratitude as cats and not half as cuddly. Can't say I love the snippy ones around Grapeskin, but burning them alive is a little extreme."

Arrol shrugged and said, "Well, maybe I should put in a good word for you. Me and the butterwing clans are tighter than a virgin oyster. Oops, can't believe I said that ... and to a Quincian Queen of Niceness of all people. Sorry."

Glix blushed again ... and she didn't think Arrol was sorry at all.

"Enough of that. Better get going," urged Arrol. "Mrs Flagstaff knows we're taking a hike, but disapproves, of course. And I've got a harvest to manage."

Over the next hour, Glix learned that right after she had tackled Zellah, her understudy had gotten her into a headlock and was making a good effort at throttling her. To add injury to insult, one of Zellah's "former" friends had emerged from the crowd of Ceruleans and whacked her head with a broken table leg. That was how she'd gotten the concussion and the gashes on her scalp that Mrs Flagstaff had stitched up so tidily.

"Grond doesn't have much patience with Ceruleans. And less patience for the kjoa wannabe nonsense that's currently all the rage among Fogwit teeny-boys. Your attacker got roped to a camp table and hung from a tree ... just to get him out of the way, of course. You ask me, Grond was entirely too nice to him. But, given who he turned out to be, Grond's restraint was probably wise. And through all Grond's questioning, this boy continued to insist that hitting you was a mistake. He was trying to hit Zellah, not you ... which sounds just a little unbelievable coming from a boy who turns out to be Zellah's big brother. Particularly when Zellah hasn't been shy about sharing her opinion — not to your face, of course — that you're just a loopwit Quincian skarcher who doesn't deserve to be a Rising Star. Bet you didn't know that, did you?" Arrol looked over her shoulder at Glix, who just rolled her eyes.

"Meanwhile, Bane — the other watchdog — decides that the whole farce has gone on long enough. You've seen him: he's almost as tall as the Mayor and twice as wide. He fetches Midas Blue from his tent, then frog-marches him to the blickernut trees at the edge of the clearing for a 'conference.' Told me he gave Mr Blue 'definite information' about the perils of failing to provide the Mayor with full details of his proposed rite. Seems he left out the part about publicly murdering butterwings on a private wildlife preserve. So Midas Blue was 'sternly instructed' to make amends by immediately releasing his captives, followed by his group's imminent departure.

"Of course, when Bane and Midas Blue arrived at the Flue, the cages were already open and the butterwings had vanished ... along with a jug of the blue dye they'd used on the butterwings. What a mystery, huh? Wonder how that happened?" She grinned at Glix as they trudged the tiny trail, which now clung to the side of a steep, rocky gully.

Glix grinned back. "Hmmm. Why do I get the idea you're leaving out a thing or two? As my official warden, shouldn't you have to tell the entire truth? Like what happened to the two guards? And what are kjoas?"

"You don't know about kjoas?" Arrol gave Glix one of those looks that could mean either "surely you're pulling my leg" or "how is that humanly possible?"

"I suppose Quince isn't plagued by them any more than Hiphollow is, so we're lucky. Real kjoas are young disreputables who dress in black boots and capes and dramatic hats, and form gangs that mostly prey on travelers. Rumor is that some escaped from road-therapy crews or even the Boxton Rock Colony. Probably some are hideabouts from the Fogwit taxers or lost all at Viggas. Some are catchers, some are hermits and some are who-knows-what.

"It's said that most kjoas live in caves and camps way up in the Rocksaws, but some of the young ones venture down by the roads, maybe disguised as jugglers and such from Hiphollow ... or glass-playing gypsies from Sipshilly. Do some stealing and such, but not much harm otherwise. The legend probably toots louder than the reality.

"But in Fogwit, the kjoa look and swagger has become faddish. I suspect Zellah's brother and his buddies are cowardly bullies that like to play at being swashbuckling bravos. To be honest, creeps like that make me wanna spew."

Memories boiled up and would have made Glix's ears steam if such things were possible. "Sure sounds like the boil-buckets that filched my coin dispenser and all my starglass on my first night in Fogwit City. And they did it for a certain snotty female who didn't dare do it herself. That would be the very same rich girl who's now doing everything in her power to filch Tangerine Cream from me. I hope some mysterious person creamed their sorry asses. And you say it was her brother that attacked me? Nice upstanding family, the Macallers." Glix filled Arrol Moon in on the night Glix Larue became Tangerine Cream.

172

"That's truth? That actually happened? Nobody told me that!" Arrol seemed genuinely shocked.

"Maybe that's because I never told anybody until now. You think I'd whine to the Mayor? He saved my life. Or Her Purpleness? She gave me a *new* life. We Quincians are taught that whining is highly un-nice. Besides, with my nasty tongue and living at Grapeskin, it's not like I have lots of friends to talk to. None, actually."

Arrol stopped walking and turned a serious eye to Glix. "Well, you have one now, Glix Larue. And she's a warden, no less."

"Thank you," whispered Glix in a tiny voice. "Thank you, Warden Arrol."

They set off again and for a time, the only sounds were the crunch of boots on the trail and the creaking of rocks expanding in the warmth of the rising sun.

When Glix had bottled up her surge of emotion well enough to speak without a wobbly voice, she popped another question. "So what exactly happened to the wannabe kjoas that were guarding the butterwings? And what happened to Zellah Macaller?"

"I'm certain your charming understudy will be pleased that you asked about her health after you cracked two of her ribs. That much I saw, by the way: very solid tackle. You might not be such a dwingle-doo after all." Arrol grinned and winked again.

"As for the two disreputables, my sources tell me that a hungover member of the cleanup crew found them the next morning. Each was gagged, dyed blue and lashed to a blickernut tree ... and every bit as naked as a wild butterwing. Dunno who would have done such a thing, but it sounds like poetic justice to me."

Glix couldn't contain a chortle. The mental picture of two blue thugs, tied to trees by her new friend was delicious. "You actually did that? How ...."

"Maybe someday I'll tell you about the training Hiphollow Rangers receive. Meanwhile, let's focus on our present adventure. The trail pretty much disappears just up ahead before we turn up into what I call Velvet Cleft. As for an earlier question you never asked, you've been asleep for four days. Everybody else left day before yesterday. When Verla — that's Mrs Flagstaff — judges that you're ready to travel, I get to fly you back to Fogwit City so you can resume your hectic, glamorous life as a Rising Star." Arrol muttered what might have been a sour snicker.

"Yeah, it's really glamorous all right," said Glix with more than a few drops of sarcasm. "You know, it's really strange having fallen into all of this. 'Cause actually, I was just trying to escape a certain piddle-dripping doctor in Quince. I thought he was going to completely unravel my life, and I thought I could go to Hiphollow because I remembered how nice that juggler Mr Hipskander was to me. But I fell asleep while I was stowing away underneath a steam-buggy and ended up in Fogwit City instead. Sounds dumb, doesn't it? But that's the truth of it."

173

174

35

Swallowed Up

LIKE MOST young Quincians, Glix had tromped over the foothills of Hopover Mountain searching for the mythical home of the mythical funnel-fairies and their ilk. So patches of scree on steep slopes were nothing new to her. But she didn't quite feel like a kid any more and the idea of climbing over the jumbled mess that Arrol was pointing at had zero appeal. Of course, there was no way she wasn't going to do it anyway.

Arrol seemed to sense something of Glix's mental meanderings, but was becoming impatient. "Okay, let's do it. Just follow about three paces behind me and do exactly as I do. But if I slip and tumble a few hundred feet down that slope, I expect you'll make an exception. Just rescue me, instead," said Arrol with yet another wink and shoulder-chuck.

When they had clawed their way past the gnarly old rock-maples, the scree was gone and the deer trail, such as it was, resumed. After a couple hundred more yards, it made a hairpin bend and ended at a narrow cleft. It was as if a humongous axe blade had slammed into the mountainside and popped right out again, leaving this narrow wedge. A surprising blast of coolish humid air flowed out of it, washing over their sweaty faces in a way that was both pleasing and mysterious.

"So what do you think about this, Miss Tangerine Cream on medical leave? Bet you didn't expect something like this place. All we've gotta do now is climb up those mossy boulders for about a hundred feet ... then we get to the best part." Arrol was quite pleased with her little surprise.

Glix was enchanted. The walls of the little cleft were coated with thick, spongy moss of such a dark green hue that it was almost black. It absorbed light like a sponge and her eyes needed some time to adjust to the instant gloom. An odd mix of aromas caught her nose's attention: damp, mossy smells, but also other things ... out of place things. And something that was ringing little alarm bells deep inside her mind.

All she could think of to say was, "It's amazing, Arrol. Now what?"

"Just follow me."

They worked their way into the cleft, climbing over and around the mass of slick boulder stew. If Arrol hadn't been there to point it out, Glix would have missed the cave opening completely. In the gloom, it looked like nothing but a jag of deep shadow.

"How did you find this place?" Glix murmured in a hushed, almost whispery voice.

The normally talkative Arrol hesitated, as if she really didn't want to say, for some private reason.

"Is it a secret or something?" asked Glix, who knew a bit about secrets.

"No," said Arrol. "It's just ...." Again she hesitated.

"Okay, I saw it in a dream," she blurted. "When I first came to Mullver's Rock five years ago, I started having dreams. Weird dreams, with strange characters and strange places. I never had dreams like that when I was growing up in Hiphollow. And one dream I had a couple months ago was about this place.

Some shadow-guy led me here in the dream and showed me the cave and the pool. The next morning I decided to see if it was a real place, not just, you know, a dream place. Never had a dream that was so real and so weird. I loaded up a pack and headed out early, just like today. And the strangest thing was, as soon as I got myself on that particular deer trail, I knew I was gonna find this place. Don't ask me how, but I knew it."

"Do you come here often?" wondered Glix out loud.

"This is only my second time up here. Once to find it, once to bring you here. That was the weirdest part of the dream. See, just before the shadow-guy disappeared and the dream fizzled, he tipped this big floppy shadow-hat at me and nodded toward the place where the cave is. My dream-self looked over there and a girl was standing right in front of the cave. She was you: your face, your hair, your size ... the whole package. And dressed just as you are now ... even had bandages on her head."

Arrol paused, stared hard at Glix and shrugged. "That's how I knew I had to bring you up here. You asked, remember? I think there's something you need to do inside that little cave, but I have no idea what it is. I mean, there isn't much in there besides a glow-hole, really."

Glix could find no words to respond ... and not just because of what Arrol just told her. There was a strangeness brewing inside her: on top on an instantly queasy gut, she got a sudden feeling that was like a vise squeezing her brain.

She closed her eyes, took a deep breath and tried to calm herself, but with little success. And the mark on her palm suddenly felt icy cold. What finally helped was listening to what her nose was telling her. Up here deep in the cleft, the smell should have been dank, rank and mossy. Instead, it was cheery and somehow colorful. Tart, sweet, spicy and fruity were terms that sprang to mind ... in short, deliciously mysterious and deliciously almost familiar. And her nose knew they were strongest at the mouth of the cave.

Resolve solidified and she snapped open her eyes. Her warden nodded toward the shadowy opening, shrugged her shoulders and cautioned, "Be careful Miss Larue. The pool is just inside, but it's very slippery in there. I'll be right here if you need me." She handed Glix a flashlight. "And this might come in handy."

The way in was a narrow zig-zag between slabs of rock that required twisting her body to get through. Inside, she found herself on a sort of ledge between the two damp cave walls. Pale pink-orange flickers dusted the walls and ceiling with enough light to make the flashlight irrelevant. The light radiated from an emptiness directly in front of her; one more step and she would fall into a rough, steep-sided hole maybe six feet across. Whatever was on the other side of the hole was lost in blackness untouched by the flickers. She took a deep breath and looked down.

Maybe six feet below the rim was a pool of glowing, effervescent liquid. She couldn't see the bottom, and some sense told her it was deep enough to be dangerous. Glix gulped, pursed her lips and stood peering and listening for a long time. The aromas she had sensed outside were very strong here, almost overpowering. She was drawn by a magnetism — almost a visceral longing — that went far beyond being curious about unlikely aromas from a bubbling pink-orange liquid. Glix just had to climb down into that hole, scoop up a handful of that odd water and trickle it down her throat. Just had to.

The smooth walls of the hole were slick with moisture and a thin golden moss. A couple feet above the water line she could see a narrow ledge about two feet wide. If she positioned her body just right it might offer enough of a perch for checking out the mysterious liquid. Or it might not. She pondered the ledge for long moments before deciding.

Glix aimed the flashlight near the rim, where she spotted a slender groove in the mossy stone. That would have to be her handhold. Turning her back to the hole, she got down on all fours, dug her fingers into the crack, then edged one leg over in search of the ledge. Found it: so far, so good. Now on her belly, she gingerly slid her other leg over and it also found the ledge. Then she tested the perch with her full weight. It held. Excellent.

Next was the tricky part: turning around and getting into a crouch on the ledge. Knees bent, back pressed hard against the wall and wobbling from side to side, she was halfway down when her balance went missing. Her arms flailed in the thick air for something to steady herself against, but found only air. Tumbling forward into the glowing pool, she was swallowed up with barely a splash.

180

36

Quick Enough

HER SKIN BRISTLED at the shock. From jumping into swimming holes around Quince, she knew that the proper thing to do now was kick, struggle back to the surface and gasp for a breath of air. Instead, some strange sense told her to let the water-that-wasn't-really-water-at-all embrace her totally and say what it had to say. Why? She couldn't have put it into words, but somehow she knew that whatever was in this cave had been waiting for her.

She opened her mouth and there was an explosion of her senses that blew open all the closed doors in her memory ... more doors than she'd ever known she had. The blast of images she'd experienced when she held the cinder-egg danced through her consciousness again, but this time they were more orderly, less haphazard. And slower.

She saw the agonized gray face again and now knew it was asking her for help. And that it was somehow ill from the extended ingestion of toxics. The rational, thinking part of her should have seen how silly that idea was, but that part of her was asleep now, so she was free to sense whatever truth was in the vision, unhindered by the shrill demands of logic and reason. The face dissolved into an uneasy thick blackness surging with monstrous feelings that were like mountain-sized waves on the surface of an ocean: confusion, loss, anger, hatred, betrayal and emotions beyond human understanding. She heard these shrieking in the wind and waves of that metaphysical storm. But far below was an unmoving black ocean of loneliness that she somehow knew had been growing and growing and growing for thousands of years. It was an inhuman loneliness that wanted to be human but would always be something else. It was a loneliness so simple, childlike and piteous that she would have cried if she hadn't been drowning.

But she wasn't really drowning, was she? The loneliness dissolved into a scene that emerged from one of the newly opened doors in her memory.

182

• • • • •

Two shadowy figures sit across from each other with a round firepit between them; pink and orange flames flicker up from the firepit. Dream-Glix recognizes the setting as Twisselman Wood and the shadowy figures as the pranksy and herself. Her conversation with the Viceroy now comes back to her in a burst of knowledge-motes. Except that in today's version the dapper pranksy turns to face a different Glix, the one in this drowning dream.

"It is horribly unamusing to confer like this, Miss Larue, but it's how we must play this game for the nonce. And we don't have much time. To get the ball rolling, I will answer two questions you haven't yet had the wit to pose. First, you are not drowning: it is not possible for the human named Glix Larue to drown in quess. So relax on that count. You may recall my calling it 'Blood of Hallah' in our prior conversation? Good, because that's what it is.

"And 'quess' is precisely the answer to your second unposed question: 'what am I not drowning in?' Quess is not water, but it can enfold water. That's exactly how and why the essence of quess is in every molecule of Hallah.

"With that all cleared up, here's the deal. You are now unofficially attuned to quess. Official attunement would be a violation of the First Protocol, but since this is only an unmonitored non-sleeping dream, we're in danger of nothing worse than having our hands slapped with a sledgehammer. Not to worry.

"Your attunement is primitive, but still powerful enough for you to begin to connect more deeply with the essence of Hallah and its creatures. Do so, but try not to get too 'god-like' about it. That will cause problems that we just don't have time for. So be subtle, cool, laid-back ... and don't forget what I told you about dreams. It's all just practice for the last act anyway. And that's about all I can say.

"So enjoy your last moments of un-drowning and get back to work. Our world still needs saving and naturally you humans are laughably off-track on how to save it. Sadly, we eminently knowl-edgeable and wise pranksies are constrained from helping over-much. But just for fun, here's a clue: ask a lady Fangler to tell you about a certain crème-filled sandwich cookie that was once hugely popular in another place at another time."

The Viceroy tips his hat again with a flourish that Dream-Glix decides means that he is pleased with his cleverness.

"Well, then: adieu for the nonce, Glix Larue ... and be sure to keep this little dream meeting just between you and me." With those words, the dream goes black ... except for a sign painted in dribbling pink letters on soggy white paper that says, "End of Dream" accom-panied by a dreamish version of an ancient telephone dialtone.

"But wait! What am I supposed to be doing?" shouts Dream-Glix, finding her dream-voice a little too late. The dialtone crack-les and dissolves into the bloop-bloop-bloop sound of large bubbles bursting in boiling molasses.

• • • • •

When Glix finally dragged her dripping, shivering, undrowned body back into Velvet Cleft, her face wore a perfectly sheepish expression. "Took a little unplanned dip in the fizz-juice. And I'm sorry, Arrol, but I think I drowned your flashlight. I had it when I fell into the pool, but not when I came up for air."

Arrol just shook her head, grinned and gave Glix a huge hug. "Whew! Glad that's over with. Now let's get back to the Lodge; I've got a blickernut harvest to supervise ... you'll dry out quick enough in the sun."

184

37

....

The Moths

GLIX SAT on the veranda and glowered at the steady stream of trucks chuff-chuffing past the Lodge on their way to and from To-phat's freight loading dock at the big warehouse. They'd been going up and down the road from Nutbreaker Cove since first bell and were making her mad. Events had taken her Rising Stardom away from her and she was ready to reclaim it, but she needed to get back to Fogwit City to do so. Grrrrr!

Her bandages were off and the 64 stitches in her scalp (she had counted them three times with the help of two mirrors) were almost ready to come out. Yesterday they'd stopped itching. Now her only remaining itch was to be away from Mullver's Rock and back at Grapeskin. Mrs Flagstaff had even said she could go back as soon as transportation to Wyn was available. And that was the problem.

Arrol couldn't fly her back to Fogwit City on account of the mad-dening blickernut harvest. In addition to several dozen youths re-cruited from Sipshilly for the season, Glix's warden/friend was re-sponsible for three colonies of expert butterwings that harvested the premium sun-ripened scarlet "cherries" at the tops of trees. These expert butterwings were skilled and diligent workers, but the colo-nies often quarreled with each other and occasionally fought. In such cases, Arrol, the most butterwing-savvy human on Mullver's Rock, would have to soothe the tensions and coax them back to work. But

Arrol didn't mind: it made her job interesting and she liked the chal-
lenges. Fine for Arrol, but no help to Glix.

Earlier in the morning Glix had killed some time by exploring
the vicinity of the Lodge. She'd started by wandering around the gardens, where the most interesting thing was a fountain with three ugly
stone gargoyles that spewed streams of water from nostrils the size
of goose eggs. There was also a small hedge-maze that took several
minutes to solve.

186

A few patches of late-blooming flowers boosted her spirits for a
few more minutes before boredom took her to the big barn where a
crew was working a steam-press that squeezed lamp oil from wag-
onloads of whip-cane stalks hauled up from the Rock's coastal low-
lands. Then she'd wandered the empty corridors of the mostly-de-
serted Lodge in search of interesting rooms. Nearly everything was
locked, but at least she'd developed a sense of the Lodge's geography,
which was something. Or so she told herself.

By mid-morning, she was on the veranda watching trucks go.
This made her mad at herself as well as everybody and everything
else. Then she remembered something about a library.

As Berlyn Twick had implied, the Tophat Lodge library was a
pleasant surprise, although it didn't seem that way at first. The main
room was mostly devoted to blickernuts, which Glix found only slightly more interesting than if it had been mostly devoted to shoelaces.

A smidgen more interesting was the tiny alcove devoted to the
history of Mullver's Rock and Tophat Lodge. Right away, Glix learned
several new things. According to *Fortunes of Four Islands*, Mullver's
Rock had been unoccupied by humans for thousands of years. With
no nearby Wynian settlement and because of the treacherous currents
of Mullover Passage, the island had found no favor with long-estab-
lished commercial centers at Sipshilly and Fogwit City.

The first human settlers arrived from the Loopskelter Archipelago in the far north only 1,100 years ago, give or take. A tiny fishing
community had been established at Karabash Inlet [now known as
Nutbreaker Cove], but it had never been prosperous. Several hun-

dred years later, a well-to-do Sipshilly rancher established Buckleburn Ranch, a cattle-raising operation that had prospered for a time.

Glix gulped at the thought of so many awful brutes all in one
place, but she also knew that her distaste for bovines was a Quincian
prejudice due to the infamous stampede. Other Wynians were just
fine with the stupid things.

Fortunes of Four Islands had nothing more to say about Mullver's Rock, so Glix switched to what she hoped was a more promising
volume: *Varmin's History of Greater Wyn*. Almost immediately she
was treated to an eye-opening tidbit: after Buckleburn Ranch had
withered away, the property had become the site of the original help-
fairy colony on Wyn. A group of some hundreds of help-fairies had
acquired the defunct Buckleburn property about 500 years ago and
planted the first blickernut groves, which lasted 57 years before suc-
cumbing to Minion's Blight.

By that time, however, the help-fairies had tired of blickernut
culture and were already beginning their migration to Miranza Vale,
where they developed a large natural cave system into what they
now call the "grottoes." Around this time they also established Wyn's
eight Waystations during a flurry of "helpful enterprise" spanning
several decades.

Glix went on to read about another cattle operation after the
help-fairies left, then a failed vineyard followed by a succession of
blickernut plantations. The last historical entry was the purchase of
the extensive blickernut acreage and all facilities nearly a hundred
and fifty years ago.

Boring, grumped Glix to herself, deciding that it was time to
stretch her legs. Or take a nap, or fill up her fizz-water bottle.

Then she noticed the moths.

38

Warning Buzzer

WEIRD, SHE THOUGHT. Why would a small cloud of moths be fluttering around one small area of a bookshelf? They were completely ignoring the only light in the room, a pendant lamp over the alcove's single chair where she currently sat. Not exactly moth-like behavior, or so it seemed to Glix.

Some drab and mundane things can become marginally intriguing when one is hopelessly bored, but do moths ever qualify? Glix thought so at this moment. Still chair-bound, she watched them intently for a minute or two but couldn't see anything at all remarkable about the area they were clustered around. Since it was still too early for lunch, she investigated.

On closer inspection, these moths were seriously unusual in appearance. Although they were nearly transparent, their wings and bodies bore a pale gray-green tint, very much like the color of the mold that grows on cheese that should have been eaten a year ago. Their size wasn't remarkable — she had seen much larger moths before — but never moths with wings shaped exactly like question marks. And the wings themselves had unusual markings: realistic-looking eyes with eyelids, eyelashes and what might be eyebrows. One of her rediscovered memories popped into place: the Viceroy had wings like this. Could these moth wings be a coincidence ... or was there a pranksy connection here?

An irrational thought struck her: maybe they were friendly. She held out her copper-gloved hand, palm up, but nothing happened ... except that the mark hidden under the glove smiled at her. At least that was how her mind's eye saw it. More like a grin than a smile, actually. One of the moths fluttered to her palm. Its wings moved in lazy back and forth sweeps that were almost hypnotic. Then another joined it on her palm. Then three more. As Glix watched, the open eyes on their wings slowly closed. Was that a message? She closed her eyes and waited to see what happened.

A highly detailed image of a spacious, richly appointed room snapped open before her mind's eye: a wealthy man's room from the look of it. In the center of the scene was a large, heavy table of polished wood the color of dark-roasted blickernuts. It had intricately carved legs and bronze feet that resembled the clawed feet of a large raptor, each grasping a ball of black stone. A wainscoting of similar dark wood covered the lower portion of the wall behind the table; above it, the wall appeared to be a faded fresco of a dramatic skyscape. Beneath the table, the polished rock-maple floor was covered with an intricately-figured rug in muted dark hues.

The view rotated slowly in her mind, revealing additional features. First was a tall cabinet of matching wood with glass doors and glass shelves, each shelf containing a row of identical black tophats. As the rotation continued, a mysterious item was revealed. It was a large rectangle hung over a portion of the fresco depicting a bank of dramatic cumulus clouds. At first, Glix thought it was a painting but it wasn't an image of anything at all familiar. Maybe it was some kind of sculpture?

In the center of the rectangle was a metallic dome of some sort with a number of pie-shaped openings. She counted seven. All seven openings began to pulse with a crimson glow that cast a mysterious hot light into the otherwise sedate room. The rectangular area outside the dome structure seemed to be a sheet of flat dark metal inset with a regular pattern of symbols and small gemstones arranged in a

190

ring around the dome. Perhaps it was a machine of some sort instead of a sculpture?

Centered on the top of the dome was a smaller geometric shape, also made of polished metal. Glix counted seven sides — a heptagon, if she remembered her geometry correctly. Inside the heptagon was another incomprehensible symbol. As she pondered this, the symbol blurred, faded and was replaced by the image of a human head peering through tendrils of dark mist that reminded her of the creepy dancing ghost-snakes she'd seen at the Fairdilly Fair.

A battered helmet covered much of the scarred, rough-shaven face and wide eye-slits bracketed a beak-like ridge of metal that protected an unseen nose. A large knife was clamped between ragged, discolored teeth that were a perfect "before" picture for a dental advertisement.

Then the image in the heptagon suddenly expanded to fill the entire rectangle. The black eye-slits came alive; luminous red spots darted from side to side as if seeking an intruder. There was a sniffle, then a low growl and a slight shift in the jaw that caused the edge of the blade to gleam in the murky light. A name emerged unbidden from her explosion of cinder-egg images: Lozar the Sentry. She knew it was the right name to go with this face, but had no idea how she knew.

The darting eyes stopped and stared directly at her, boring into her soul; a hiss and a puff of rank-smelling steam escaped from a gaping hole where an incisor should have been. "You there with the orange rag-mop. The seventh window awaits you. Why do you skulk?" The voice was raspy, harsh and impatient. "Display the sigil and you may pass beyond and test the portents. Otherwise, begone! Lozar has more than a single portal to monitor and no time for timid skulkers!"

Glix shuddered involuntarily and pressed her eyelids tightly together as if this might squeeze the wild strangeness out of the moment. The sigil? What was the sigil?

That mysterious question was interrupted by a sound: the latch of the library door, followed by a familiar clump-clump of footsteps. Glix's eyes popped open, the image vanished. She knew Mrs Flagstaff's footsteps by now and was certain the woman was looking for her. But she was still transfixed by the mysterious moths and wanted the magic to remain. The moths thought otherwise. As one, the entire group that had colonized her palm suddenly took flight and disappeared into the shadows behind the shelves of old folios.

Glix was busily scratching her gloved palm when Mrs Flagstaff spoke. "Ahh, there your are Miss Larue. Should you be interested in lunch, the cook has set out a light collation of fruit and sausages in the small refectory." Glix could sense the woman's eyes scanning the alcove and spotting the open book on the chair. "I see you have been educating yourself on the history of this lonely rock. Have you found anything to interest you?"

Mrs Flagstaff's demeanor was usually bland and always courteous, but Glix couldn't escape the feeling that this was mostly a pose to disguise her basically suspicious nature. Had she seen the strange moths?

Still scratching her palm, Glix responded: "Thank you, Mrs Flagstaff. Lunch would be nice right about now. And would you by any chance have any sort of ointment for itches? The scar on my hand has been itching like I've been ant-bit lately." Glix had found that appealing to Mrs Flagstaff's strong nursing instincts was a good way of distracting the woman from more penetrating queries.

Mrs Flagstaff nodded. "As it happens, Baedelli's Bacon Balm works nicely to quell itching. Of course, regular washing with soap and water is also surprisingly effective." She gave Glix one of her raised-eyebrow looks and added, "Then again, you might just be allergic to wearing a clean glove after so many months of that filthy one."

Glix had to work very, very hard to stifle a pent-up stream of verbal abuse. But she ignored the barb and asked a question with all the bland innocence she could muster. "Did you know that help-fairies used to live in this place, Mrs Flagstaff? That's what the book said and it kind of surprised me."

"As it happens, Miss Larue, that information was part of my training. You may be even more surprised to learn that I, myself, was once a help-fairy. In fact, I retired from service just two years ago." Mrs Flagstaff's smile was entirely too sweet.

Glix hoped Mrs Flagstaff didn't notice her wince ... or the twitch in her shoulders. Something about that revelation — and about the way the woman said it — triggered the silent warning buzzer under her glove.

194

39

Up Anchor

GLIX WAS BACK on the veranda. The moths, the vision and the words of Lozar the Sentry had spun her brain into a cyclone of craziness and she was trying to pretend that none of it had happened. Pretending out here was much easier than pretending during lunch with the ex-help-fairy watching her every move.

It was mid-afternoon and the comings and goings of trucks had slowed, with more now departing than arriving. She wrinkled her nose for the umpteenth time; her hand smelled like it had spent the last month making mud balls out of bacon grease. But at least the stink of Baedelli's Bacon Balm distracted her from the strangeness of the morning. Then something else distracted her.

A canary yellow vehicle that looked like a boat with wheels chuff-chuffed up the road and parked directly in front of the veranda.

A man with a yellow briefcase stepped out, walked briskly up the walkway, took the steps two at a time and bowed in front of the only person on the veranda. "Glix Larue, I presume. Quincian Queen of Niceness, Rising Star and now ...."

The man paused his speech to study Glix intently. Glix, slightly annoyed that he seemed to know so much about her, studied him right back.

He wore a tidy gray suit, a starched white shirt, a yellow cravat, a gray bowler hat with a yellow band and shiny yellow shoes that matched the hue of his vehicle. His hands were hidden by black leather gloves. As Glix looked him up and down, his narrow face formed into a wry frown; he was probably not used to being scrutinized like this by someone her age. Then a tiny smile tweaked the corners of his somewhat bugged-out eyes, which looked even more bugged-out due to his large, black-framed spectacles.

Glix stood up, adopted a jaunty Tangerine Cream pose and held out her hand. "You were saying, good sir?"

"Oh. Yes. I fear I became distracted by your remarkable countenance. I was about to say that you seem bored and most anxious to be away from this hotbed of stimulating activity. Or so I surmise from your languid posture. Vonson Rakow at your service, Miss Larue. I am here to ferry you back to Fogwit City with all speed ... just as soon as I service our esteemed Mayor's hats."

Mr Rakow bowed again, gave the girl's hand a tidy shake and smiled. Glix just gaped, slack-jawed with astonishment. "Leave? You mean now? Right now?" Her Tangerine Cream tude deflated quicker than a balloon at a porcupine's birthday party.

"If, by 'now' you mean within the next hour, the answer is 'yes indeed'. We must depart just as soon as I inform Mrs Flagstaff of the Mayor's wishes in this regard and service the good gentleman's fine collection of exquisite tophats. I might suggest that you pack whatever you need for a two-day voyage upon the Great Wet. Oh, and he asked that I give you this note."

What an odd character, thought Glix, liking the man despite his crisp manner. When the hat repairman had disappeared inside, Glix broke the seal on the envelope and read the note. The message, typed on the Mayor's personal stationery, said:

> "Dear Miss Larue,
>
> Mrs Flagstaff tells me that your recovery has proceeded splendidly and that you are again fit to travel. I am sorry to interrupt your holiday, but your presence is required in Fogwit City immediately. Please accompany Mr Rakow with all due haste.

196

Despite her years, the Sandbar Savant *is a fine, seawor-
thy vessel and Mr Rakow is a trusted colleague of many
years acquaintance.*

*Please extend my apologies to Arrol Moon for having to
cut your training short. She thinks highly of you and will
doubtless understand. And I'm certain Mrs Flagstaff will
assist you with your preparations.*

Most sincerely,

*Thomas Jefferson XIII
Mayor, Fogwit City, Wyn"*

Mrs Flagstaff was every bit as surprised by the news of Glix's imminent departure as Glix had been. But she and Mr Rakow were acquainted — he had been doing his monthly hat servicing since before
her arrival — and she could find nothing askew with the Mayor's letter. So while Glix tearfully jotted a note to Arrol Moon, Mrs Flagstaff
helpfully packed up Glix's clothes as well as some warmer outerwear
suitable for sea travel.

Before Glix truly realized she was escaping her boredom, Mr
Rakow was closing the passenger door of his curious conveyance. A
minute later, Mrs Flagstaff and the Tophat Lodge were out of sight.

Then things got interesting: the bland Vonson Rakow of the veranda was a complete maniac behind the wheel. For the entire twenty miles of steep, narrow, potholed road, Rakow swerved, zigged and
zagged around the steady stream of slow moving steam-trucks carrying full loads of raw blickernuts from Tophat to the processing plant
at Nutbreaker Cove. Glix gritted her teeth, held the dash-bar with a
white-knuckled grip and resolved to say nothing, lest she distract the
goggle-eyed maniac. For his part, Mr Rakow concentrated on driving
and also remained silent.

The ebbing sun was painting luminous tangerine highlights under dappled smatters of cloud before the town and the port became
visible. With the end in sight, Glix relaxed … prematurely. Rakow
swerved around a steam-truck and skidded onto a barely visible dirt
track skirting the Cove on the south side. He jammed his foot to the

floorboard, slowing only when they skidded onto a rough, muddy track halfway to Cogburn Point. The carriage slid to a stop on a hard, sandy beach about twenty feet from the lapping water of the Cove.

"Don't go away, Miss Larue. We're almost there. If all goes well, this will only take a moment."

Glix closed her eyes and savored a brief moment of safety. As Rakow exited the car and went around to the storage compartment in back, she surveyed the dusky expanse of water for whatever watercraft was coming to meet them. So far she had noted exactly two ships. A steam-freighter tied up to the single pier in Nutbreaker Cove was likely taking on a load of dried blickernuts. Lights on its rigging illuminated tiny moving specks that must have been the crew.

A smaller vessel lay at anchor perhaps two hundred yards from their current position. Its hull and superstructure were painted a dark color and, unlike the freighter, it had no lights at all. Glix couldn't repress a shudder: it looked sinister. Was that the *Sandbar Savant*? Just then Rakow opened his door and got in.

"Well, Miss Larue, now comes the fun part," said the driver. "I'm told you can swim, but should anything unplanned occur between here and our destination, there is a flotation pad under the seat."

"This is really a boat?"

"Well it's supposed to act like one if I do a few more things correctly." Rakow repositioned several levers, triggering a chorus of mechanical groans that ended in a resounding clunk-thunk. Rakow winced, shrugged and stepped on the throttle pedal; the vehicle lurched forward across the sand and into the Great Wet. To Glix's great surprise, the carriage slid gracefully into the dark water with barely a splash. The gurgly hiss of a small bow wave and a faint chuff-chuffing were the only sounds. Five minutes later the craft entered a hole in the side of the dark ship and stopped at an internal dock, a dimly lit cave inside the ship.

"I told you this was the fun part," said Rakow, wiping invisible perspiration from his brow. He opened his door and climbed out. "Hope you're hungry."

Seamen in dark gray uniforms tied the carriage-boat to cleats. Another person opened the passenger door and reached in a hand to help Glix out. "Welcome to the *Caveat Empress*, Miss Larue. I just wanted to say a proper good-bye."

"Arrol? Arrol Moon?" screamed Glix as she leaped out of the vehicle and wrapped her arms around her warden/friend. "How did you get here?"

"Fast personal windshark ... what else? Gotta leave after dinner. Still a couple days of harvest to go."

199

"What did you just call this ship? The Mayor's note said I was supposed to be on the *Sandbar Savant*."

"The *Sandbar Savant* left port an hour ago. No doubt the Mayor lied, probably for Mrs Flagstaff's benefit. But he's a politician. I'm sure it's against all the rules for a politician to tell the truth more than half the time. Maximum. Bet that's true even in your hometown of Quince, the very capital of Nice. Come on, there's an up-anchor meal being served in Captain Barlett's quarters and we're invited."

200

40

Moon Again

THE *CAVEAT EMPRESS* skimmed over the Great Wet, its black hydrofoils kissing the surface with sleek metal lips. Its roughly semicircular course would loop west past the Rock, then south around the island of Wyn to get them to Fogwit City in less than a day. Inside the captain's suite, Glix, Arrol, Captain Barlett and Vonson Rakow sat at a round table of waxed boatwood and exchanged pleasantries. Except for that table, untidy stacks of this and that occupied every visible surface. The Captain looked anything but happy about hosting this unscheduled meal.

A uniformed crewmember brought in a large, steaming tureen and filled their bowls with a dark fish stew, adding a garnish of garlicky croutons. Glix felt half-starved, but also taken over by a fey, almost surreal mood. In the bowl before her, fragrant toast-islands rose from a murky sea that smelled of redfish, clams, sea-pepper and charred wrackweed. "Do you wish fresh-grated cheese, Miss?" inquired the crewmember, breaking the spell. Glix blinked, nodded and watched snowflakes of white cheese flutter down over her toast-islands.

"Dive in, please," urged Captain Barlett when the server had gone. "Apparently Miss Moon will be returning to her blickernut urgencies immediately after she and her steed have been refueled. So on behalf of the Fangler Guild, I should like to express our collective gratitude for certain items obtained from Mr Midas Blue during the recent Cerulean foray to Mullver's Rock. And thank you for being our aerial courier service, Miss Moon; you are most generous with your time. Analysts are already hard at work with the materials."

"You are entirely welcome, Captain. The Mayor didn't know what to make of the items, but knew that the Fanglers certainly would figure it out."

Glix looked at Arrol. What would she have gotten from Midas Blue? Arrol ignored her gaze and focused on her bowl. Glix decided it was a signal to keep quiet.

As the four ate in silence, Glix made a sideways inspection of the Captain. She saw a short, stocky woman in her later middle years who managed to look frumpy and rumpled even in her freshly pressed gray uniform. Untidy swirls of iron-gray hair sticking out from under an official-looking short-billed gray cap added to the frump effect. To Glix she seemed to be a weird composite of Berlyn Twick and the pill man — Mr Flackroy — which was odd because neither of them were at all frumpy.

When the bowls were being removed, Glix finally asked a question that she'd been wondering about. "Are you a Fangler, Captain Barlett?"

"Indeed I am, Miss Larue. The Fangler Guild would hardly allow a vessel in its fleet to be captained by a non-Fangler. We're funny that way."

The captain paused, waiting for a response, but Glix said nothing; she was still trying to imagine what a sky-cult person like Midas Blue would have that could possibly interest the Fanglers, who were all about science and technical stuff.

"Well then," said Captain Barlett, injecting a distracting squiggle into Glix's line of thought. "Miss Moon is about to leave us and we have yet to learn exactly why the Mayor of Fogwit City called us away from a critical research mission to ferry a young toob-person at top speed back to Fogwit. Do either of you have any idea?"

Glix had no idea at all and said so. Arrol Moon shook her head.

Captain Barlett frowned. "No idea at all? Really? Not some crisis to do with that purple woman's toob nonsense? A much-needed Rising Star hair-bob, perhaps? Or an overdue tidying of the fingernails?" The captain made an exaggerated sound of disgust that almost made Glix snicker. "Our world is falling apart and you Fogwits just keep snaggering your piffle-headed flapdoodle."

The room fell silent. Glix bit her tongue and squeezed her lips together. A spew of unpleasantries was all set to punish the Captain for her snide comments, particularly the unflattering reference to Berlyn Twick, but she held them back. "I'm not a Fogwit," she said in a small voice.

Arrol broke in. "Excuse me, Captain, but that is correct. Miss Larue is actually from Quince, where she was a Queen of Niceness ... of all things. She was kidnapped by kjoas during a class outing to survey the destruction of the Longfunnel Inn by a fragment from the first skyfall. Luckily for her, she has a surprisingly sharp tongue for a Quincian and upbraided her captors relentlessly, using language they never expected from a Quincian. So they decided to abandon her. At first they were going to brutally abuse her and leave her at Waystation Two. But when an opportunity presented itself to tie her to the undercarriage of a Quincian steam-buggy, they did so and went on their way.

"By sheerest chance, the buggy contained copper goods bound for Fogwit City. Once in Fogwit she managed to extricate herself and made her way to a park where a public toob exposition was taking place. Shocked by the sheer fogwittedness of the folk and their rude customs — and also by the fact that an embarrassing moment of hers at the Fairdilly Fair had been displayed on the toob for all to see — she treated the crowd to a dangerously fearless harangue. According to all accounts, it stirred the Fogwits into an evil frenzy. The crowd was about to tear her and her sodbunny apart when the Mayor stepped in and rescued her.

"So I think you'll find that Miss Larue has no great love for Fogwits, Captain ... or even her current job as the Purple One's latest Rising Star.

"Being an unassuming Quincian by nature, Glix would never have told you her story, but since no one has ever called me unassuming, I thought it might clear up the matter of her Fogwittish sympathies."

Before the Captain could respond, Arrol wiped her mouth with a napkin and continued. "Now, I think I'd better head back to the ranch. Thank you for your fine Fangler hospitality, Captain Barlett. And my compliments to the galley slaves: best Loopskelter chowder I've ever had."

204

Glix squelched a grin ... and realized that despite the outrageous fibs in Arrol's tall tale, one thing was exactly true; she really didn't much care about being Tangerine Cream. At least at this moment.

Apparently mollified, the Captain nodded. "Fly carefully, Miss Moon. We've recently seen forays of Blues quite far afield from the Vale."

Arrol made a salute and turned to go. "One last favor, Captain. May I borrow Miss Larue for a moment? She's never met my steed."

As they departed, Glix saw Mr Rakow whispering something in the Captain's ear.

• • • • •

Arrol was barely visible in her night-colored flightsuit. She sat in the saddle-rigging on a gray torpedo named Jock. In her windshark ignorance, Glix thought Jock's spindly bird-like legs looked unsteady as it waited on the foredeck of the sleek Fangler vessel. Or maybe it was just anxious to be back in the air.

Arrol flashed Glix a parting grin. "Don't worry about the Fanglers; they're good guys ... even Captain Barlett. And they know all about you ... even the sigil under your glove and how you got it. Naturally, she knew you weren't a Fogwit and knew my story was eighty percent nonsense. They were testing you, watching your reactions, trying to figure out what you're made of. Learn from them, Glix. There's far more to the Fanglers than most Wynians know. They have the longest memories on the planet ... and they feel vastly underappreciated."

Arrol winked down at Glix from her perch on the windshark. Then, at some unseen signal, Jock's wings came alive. The creature shot straight up just high enough to clear the ship's superstructure, made a tight u-turn, then buzzed away toward the tall mass of moon-lit shadow that was Mullver's Rock. Glix ran to the stern and watched her friend's form merge with the night, wondering if she would ever cross paths with Arrol Moon again.

205

206

41

Cleared for It

"THAT, MISS LARUE, is a Septriq Divinator," said Vonson Rakow, pointing. "Alas, few remain, and the technology for creating them is long lost. Even maintaining them is difficult these days. We know the whereabouts of five, and it's my job to keep them functioning as well as possible. Unfortunately, we can no longer get past the gatekeeper."

It was the thing in Glix's moth-vision … except different. Something clicked in her head. "There's one of these in Tophat Lodge somewhere, isn't there?" said Glix. "In a room with a bunch of hats like the Mayor's." Her guts and her brain were churning, but in a good way. "I saw it in a dream."

"Possibly you did. There *is* one in the Mayor's private study … along with his collection of tophats. We believe the gatekeeper is looking for you. Possibly you can enter the world of the seventh window and …."

Glix looked at him, waiting.

"We really don't know what you might find or discover or learn, Miss Larue. The gatekeeper — perhaps you saw its avatar: a rough, untidy fellow with a metal helmet and a blade in his teeth …."

Glix blurted. "Yeah, yeah! That's the guy that came out of that thing in the middle. Blowzar or something? Beady red eyes?" Rakow nodded. "So my vision was real! Wow!"

"So it would seem, Miss Larue. Lozar the Sentry is how the gatekeeper currently represents itself. But things are changing; it never required a sigil for entry until about week ago. Always just a password, but now nobody's password works. And we're not absolutely certain we know what it means by 'sigil'. Of course we have our suspicions." He glanced at Glix's copper-gloved hand in a meaningful way.

"How about we have a nice cup of tea while I explain some things that may fill in a few gaps in your understanding. Then perhaps you'll agree to have a go at Septriq. I'll be right back with the tea."

Glix watched Rakow depart, deciding she preferred the version of the man in the blue lab coat over the one with the gray suit and yellow shoes. With no hat, she could see that his thick mat of brown hair was streaked with gray; he was older than she'd originally thought. And more relaxed.

While her host was fetching tea, Glix tried to relax, too. Didn't work. Part of the problem was the room. It reminded her a little of the shops where her father worked on his toob-funnels and other more mysterious copper things back in Quince. She remembered the workbenches with special lights and big magnifiers that her father would use to make his eyes look like monster eyes when she was a little girl. Her shrieks and giggles from those times were so clear in her brain that they might have happened yesterday.

Where her father worked had lots of technical things: odd-shaped boxes with dials and knobs, clamps, probes, and all manner of tools for putting things together and taking them apart. This Fangler room had different kinds of equipment, but what was most different about this room was that it also had books. Shelves were packed with them, some very old looking, with ragged leather bindings and spines so faded that you could hardly tell their original color. There was also comfortable furniture. The rooms her father worked in only had wooden stools with padded seats.

In one corner between two banks of shelving was a tiny copper sink with three shiny metal spouts coming out of the wall above it: one with a blue handle, one with a red handle and one with a polished copper handle.

208

A few feet away loomed the Septriq Divinator. Two utilitarian chairs were tucked under a narrow desk with a flattish box fitted with various buttons, knobs and levers, a feature she hadn't noticed in her vision.

The door opened; Rakow had returned with a tray bearing a blue china teapot, blue cups and saucers, and a dish of petite pastries. Her stomach gurgled at the sight. When she was munching and sipping tea, Rakow talked.

"May I call you Glix, Miss Larue? Captain Barlett is elsewhere and all this formality is getting to me. We Fanglers are hardly formal types. We even use words like 'fart' in polite company when occasions warrant." Rakow grinned his slightly bug-eyed, black-framed grin.

Glix felt a brief rosy flush, then grinned back. Finally an adult besides Berlyn Twick and Arrol that she could talk normally with.

"Well," she began with a bit of Tangerine Cream tude and a sassy half-smile, "If we were in Fogwit City I would have to insist that you call me Miss Cream. I am the official Rising Star, after all. But since I'm in this mysterious room with a mysterious Fangler, I suppose plain old Glix will have to do."

"Well said, Miss Cream! Er ... um ... plain old Glix. You do have a knack for dealing with we ancients. Possibly you are what even more ancient ancients call an 'old soul'. I suspect your knack will continue to serve you well.

"Now back to business; time is short. First, you should know that amongst our various faults, we Fanglers are compulsive detectives. We want to know everything about everything. So when a certain Quincian Middle Queen appeared in Fogwit City one night and was instantly transformed into a Rising Star with the full protection and support of the immensely powerful Mayor of Fogwit City, we became curious.

"We sent out agents to discreetly interview numerous attendees of the Fairdilly Fair, including the poor old Wickelwharf proctor accused of the cinder-egg theft. We watched eyebutton recordings that did not end up in Twick's 'Sillydilly Follies'. We interviewed your schoolmates and your former best friend Twinker Gidlet — and her mother, of course — and believe we have a reasonable hypothesis about how and why the infamous — and very clever, I might add — copper glove fad at the Academy of Niceness came into being.

Glix frowned, feeling invaded and exposed, but said nothing.

"Judicious conversations with your family revealed the date of the first incidence of your unusual, ah, speaking behavior and how your outbursts began to separate you from your friends and family in many ways, large and small. Of course we interviewed your family doctor and examined his records in detail. You may or may not be pleased to learn that he has never quite gotten over being called a 'piddlehead dunce' over and over." Rakow winked an admiring wink.

"Somewhere during this research we began to suspect pranksy complicity in your sudden malady."

Rakow paused, surveyed the ashen-faced Glix and said, "A deep breath or two would be good right now; this is no time for hyperventilation. In fact, perhaps a brisk draught of what we call 'Fangler Tonic' would be in order." He went to a cooler and brought out two capped brown bottles and a pair of chilled tumblers that he filled with a sparkling rose-colored liquid.

"Drink up, Glix." The Fangler tilted his glass and downed the contents in a gulp.

As Glix put her glass to her lips, Rakow loosed a medium quality belch: "Bra-a-a-a-p" was how it sounded.

The very surprised Queen of Niceness spewed her first mouthful of Fangler Tonic all over the few uneaten pastries. Then they both laughed until their sides hurt ... and Glix only barely resisted throwing her arms around him in a huge hug.

"Sorry, Mr Rakow. Guess I'm not used to adults who aren't my father belching in 'polite company'." She wiped up the mess with a napkin and spewlessly downed the rest of her drink.

"This is some kind of quess thing, isn't it? Like the fizz-juice at Tophat Lodge, only tastier." She felt her awareness sharpen almost instantly. She shook her head, blinked and noticed that the forgotten invisible spy ring on her finger had suddenly become visible; it was now a fuzzy blob of swirly pink-orange on her right index finger. She blinked again but said nothing.

Rakow smiled. "Well, thanks for sharing your familiarity with the Blood of Hallah. It'll make my storytelling task a little easier.

"So. I don't know what you know — or think you know — about pranksies, but we Fanglers are persuaded that they have reasons for everything they do. Just because they sometimes act in ways that appear whimsical does not mean they act aimlessly. Of late, we have begun to suspect that they're a sort of safety feature designed into our planet's operating system by the intelligence that engineered the deep systems that keep things working in here.

"And in case you're curious, our artificial planet — which was originally built as the ultimate Transpoint Station — has been in existence for 3,794 years so far. And it's only been in the last thousand or so that things have been noticeably falling apart.

"Anyway, we suspect the pranksies are more actively meddling in the affairs of humans than they have in the recent past, at least. And for reasons beyond our understanding.

"One thing we do understand is that the mark made on your palm by the quantode — cinder-egg in the popular parlance — connects you to Hallah's deep systems in some important and still mysterious way. So far as we know, no other living person on Hallah has this connection. In the distant past, however, such 'sigils' were evidently commonplace among the Technicals."

The Fangler closed his eyes, rubbed his neck and took a deep breath. "Sorry. I'm getting a little far afield. Technohistory — and mysterious gadgets like the Septriq Divinator — are my specialty ... and why I'm aboard. And that brings us back to your sigil. You see, in addition to replacing the batteries in the Mayor's hats, I perform routine maintenance on his Septriq unit. And just between you and we Fanglers, I also check the activity monitors. Because of the password problem, the only activity since my last visit was your mysterious vision, which to the machine, was not a vision at all. Let me show you something." He handed Glix a folded sheet of paper.

Glix frowned; Rakow's scribbles were hard to read, but in a few seconds the words of Lozar the Sentry fell into place: "You there with the orange rag-mop. The seventh window awaits you. Why do you skulk? Display the sigil and you may pass beyond and test the portents. Otherwise, begone! Lozar has more than a single portal to monitor and no time for timid skulkers!"

Glix sighed: things were getting too weird.

"Your face suggests that Lozar's words strike a familiar chord. If you're ready to give it a go, I'll explain how it works ... the basics, at least. So far as I know, nobody with a sigil has ever tried to access a Septriq portal."

Glix took a deep breath. "Yeah, I guess," she half-mumbled. "But could I have another round of Fangler Tonic first?"

"I can do better than that. The real stuff — straight, no chaser — comes out of that copper tap in the corner. You've been cleared for it."

42

Up the Metal Stairs

"SO THE SKULKER returns," growled Lozar the Sentry. His image was sharper, clearer here than it had been in the dream ... and much uglier. The web of pink scars on his cheek pulsed, almost as though writhing worms lay just under the leathery pocked skin. But that was nothing compared to the withering tunnels of heat radiating from the red coals in his eye-sockets. Glix shuddered, then caught herself: this thing was just playing a part; that's what Rakow had said. He'd also advised that a bit of Tangerine Cream tude couldn't hurt in dealing with truculent avatars. But she hesitated, unsure what to do.

"We figgered yer fer a lime-eyed yellow-gut, but now yer come back an thinkin' yer ready to take the plunge. That it, eh? Yer don' look so ready to me. Yer truly ready, yer'd show me yer sweet little sigil and we'd see whatchur made of." Lozar leered and made a gross snuffling noise that sounded like wild pigs in a feeding frenzy.

"Lozar, Lozar, Lozar! I am just so-o-o-o intimidated. Not. What are we going to *do* with you? Are you tired, worn out, run down? Or are the wimpy little scars on your cheek itching horribly, poor thing? And you with no way to scratch them? Well! I know just the thing: a tube of Baedelli's Bacon Balm. I guarantee that'll fix you up. You'll stink, but smelling like smoked pig is surely better than that horrid itching."

Glix paused, studying the face. The beady eyes still glared, but it hadn't spoken yet. Perhaps it was waiting. She pressed what she hoped was her advantage, bringing her hands to eye level and making a show of pulling off the copper glove. She did it slowly, and oozing tude, provocatively showed only the backs of her hands.

As the glove came off, the sigil on her palm came alive. Really alive. Entirely of its own accord, her sigil-bearing palm slammed against her forehead. Powerful invisible connections began to form between her self and ... and what? No time to wonder; Glix's core self was swept into a vortex of pink-orange motes, swallowed up, torn into a trillion particles. For a timeless instant, she was a scatter of disconnected dots. Then just as instantly, her self was reassembled ... with a little something extra.

Lozar the Sentry was gone; the heptagon in the center where Glix had first seen him in her vision was empty. She found herself at the Septriq Divinator's control board, feeling more vital and alive than ever in her life. The only sound was Rakow's steady breathing in the chair next to her. The Fangler said nothing, but she could feel the intensity of his presence.

The framed Domat now filled her field of view, its seven windows slowly pulsing with a bland, colorless light that barely illuminated their pie shapes. Her left hand moved over the tot-wheel for the first of her seven spins. The ball spun in its socket and the portals responded, becoming a fast-moving wheel of pie-shaped blazes of random color. A ratchety sound kept pace with the spinning wheel of color. Gradually the sound and the wheel of color slowed, the lights blinking out at random until no windows remained lit: only the vague colorless light illuminated the portals.

Glix frowned. This wasn't how it was supposed to work; one of the portals was supposed to remain lit, indicating the attribute that the portents would be probing: health, spirit, power, joy, abundance, love or luck. Rakow shifted impatiently in his chair as he thumbed pages in a thick, ancient book in search of an interpretation.

A gentle chuckle erupted from the vicinity of the Domat, along with a crackle that might have been electrical sparks; a harsh stench of ozone tarnished the air. In the center heptagon, an image began to form.

"Oh, hello dear." It was the face of an old woman: round and plump, with rosy dimpled cheeks, clear gray eyes and a voice that was like all the best friends and all the doting grandparents in the world rolled up into one and aged to kindly perfection. "It's so sweet of you to pay me a visit. I see you have finally found your way through the door and given the tot a tidy little twirl."

"Who are *you*?" blurted Glix with zero tude and even less grace.

215

"Why, I'm Lady Crocus, dear. I'm your Oracle, of course. Well, for today at least. I'm here to help you understand your portents ... and I do hope you'll forgive me if I'm just a touch rusty at this."

"I'm very pleased to meet you, Lady Crocus," said Glix with as much cheery innocence as she could muster. "Septriq is a brand new experience for me and I need all the help I can get. Thank you very much for your kindness."

"You're most welcome, dear. Because of my work with the sky you know, I retired from active Oracle duty, oh, just eons ago. But with all the little problems we've been having in here, the, ah, customary Oracles are currently, ah, indisposed. And besides, I've heard so much about you I just wanted to meet you. They tell me you are a rising starboard thespian in that foggy place. Is that right? And your name is Lemonade Crumpet? That's a very novel name I should think ... although just between us girls I would have thought Lime Tart would play better with your eyes. But I don't much keep in touch with styles and fads these days."

Lady Crocus blinked her eyes and puckered her cheeks in a parody of kindly interest flecked with puzzlement.

Glix herself was more than a little puzzled and not at all sure what she should be saying to this dotty Oracle. Starboard thespian? Lemonade Crumpet? What's *that* about?

The ozone smell had become very strong. Rakow jabbed her leg with his pencil and nodded toward a note he held out of the oracle's view. "Septriq hacked. Serious trouble. End session now!!!!"

Before Glix could do anything at all, Lady Crocus batted her eyes and asked Glix a question. "Do you know that nice man, Mr Blue, dear?"

"You mean Midas Blue, the Cerulean guy with blue hair and a blue beard ... and blue skin dye too, if I remember."

"Oh, that's not dye, dear. That's his actual skin color. He's quite unique that way ... I don't think any of the others on Florkin's Folly were that color. But I believe that is his name, yes. He is quite wise, don't you think? And so respectful of the sky. You should really meet him. I believe he ... has ... an understanding of things. You two would get on famously, I'm very sure of that."

"Uh, thank you Lady Crocus. I will certainly try to meet him. But could I ask you a question about Septriq?"

"Why of course, dear."

"What does it mean when I spin the little ball and it all ends up the same way it started?"

Rakow coughed and jabbed Glix again. The ozone smell was overpowering now. Glix's eyes stung and her lungs burned more with every breath.

Lady Crocus's face seemed to be softening, as though an artist were smudging it with a finger. "Oh, don't trouble yourself about that, dear. I'll have you brought inside where your portents are nicer."

Glix's forehead felt like a blob of mush being sucked toward the heptagon by an invisible black hole. Her skull felt like a monstrous pimple being squeezed by a humongous giant. Her mind's eyeballs stretched like rubber eggs and her vision blurred. Lady Crocus's face was now a fleshy whirlpool framed by thousands of writhing gray snakes. Desperate to do something, Glix pressed her hands on her forehead, hoping to keep her core self from being sucked away, but it made no difference at all. She was helpless.

"Just relax, dear," said a distant warbling voice. "The transfer has already started ... it'll be just a little longer now. You see we're having a little trouble with the ...."

216

A burst of blinding pink-orange light filled every corner of Glix's awareness. At the same instant, a deafening hash of white noise filled the room. Glix blinked open her eyes but saw nothing, heard nothing, sensed nothing. Then her body went limp and slumped to the floor like a human noodle.

Wisps of acrid smoke curled out from behind the Septriq Divinator's frame to form lazy gray curlicues in the caustic air. In the heptagon, the face of Lady Crocus was gone and only dull black remained.

Glix barely felt Rakow's hands under her arms as he dragged her out of the room, up the metal stairs and out into the crisp night.

218

43

Tearful Pet

DAWN BASTED the *Caveat Empress* with a marinade of watery orange light. Inside the infirmary, a sedated Glix slept off her narrow escape from Lady Crocus's psychic vacuum cleaner. Inside the observatory, excited Fanglers rubbed sleep out of their eyes, slurped triple-strength blickernut tea and readied their telescopes.

As a celestial observatory, this one was a total failure; not a single star had ever been spotted, and only a single planet. The *Caveat Empress* Fanglers were astronomers in the same way a gnat with binoculars would be if it were floating in the middle of a ping-pong ball. The Fangler floating observatory focused its telescopes at Hallah's sky looking for tiny gaps where pieces had been detached to fall away and become flaming skyfalls. They also searched the nearly invisible seams for new places where the sky might be in danger of coming apart. With a million square miles of sky to look at, it was a semi-hopeless task.

But yesterday, Arrol Moon had brought them a cheat-sheet in the form of mysterious coded charts filched from Midas Blue. If the analysts were correct, Blue's charts were maps and a schedule of some sort; possibly for detaching pieces of Hallah's sky and letting them plummet through the atmosphere to wreak havoc on the surface. Today, if clouds stayed away from certain parts of the sky, the astronomers might see the dismantling in process. And if they did, a whole new can of worms would be opened; who exactly or what was doing the dismantling and why weren't Hallah's Keepers keeping it from happening?

• • • • •

"Time to wake up, Miss Larue," said a voice. "We're almost in port."

Glix's brain came awake but her eyes refused to open; they felt glued shut. "My eyes won't open."

"Hmmm, I see," said a different voice. "A bit of crusty gunk there. You must have picked up some kind of inflammation. Let me clean that up for you."

Someone dabbed her eyelids with a soft, damp cloth. "There. That should do it. You can open them now."

Her eyelids felt like rocks had been glued to their undersides, but at least they opened. She quickly shut them again. Everything was way too bright, too orange and too fuzzy. "Owww. The light is really bright."

"Let me take a quick look, Miss Larue. Just try to relax. I'll put in some drops that should take away the pain."

The drops went in and the eyelids slammed shut again.

"We'll let the drops do their work for a while and then I'll want you to do something for me, okay?"

"Okay," said Glix, not liking this at all. She should be getting ready to get off the boat and get back to work.

A few moments later, the person behind the voice put something in her hand. It had a handle. "I'd like you to slowly open your eyes just enough to look at them in the mirror. Then tell me if you see anything unusual."

She slowly opened both eyes; the gritty sensation was mostly gone, but both were totally bloodshot. Ugh. And that was the good news; the bad news was that they weren't her eyes. While she'd slept, someone had switched her familiar green eyes for some alien orange ones.

"The colored parts are orange; they used to be green. What's that about? And everything is still much too bright."

"Well, Miss Larue," I don't really have an answer for you. "You'll need to see a specialist in Fogwit City. But for the moment, try on these dark glasses and tell me if that helps the brightness."

Glix had never worn glasses, so having things hanging over her ears and perched on her nose felt weird. But looking at the world was no longer painful. "Much better, thank you. Can I go now?"

The Glix that walked down the *Caveat Empress'* gangway looked almost exactly like the Vonson Rakow who had appeared on the To-phat Lodge veranda. Same gray suit and hat, same black gloves, same yellow shoes and briefcase. And a brown wig, even. "A wig?" she had said to the person who had fitted it to her head. "You have a costume shop on this boat?"

The wig-fitter chuckled. "We Fanglers amuse ourselves by performing historical costume dramas on long voyages," he said. Glix was certain she was being tweedled with, but kept the thought to herself. She just wanted to be away from here.

Two gray-uniformed crewmembers accompanied her down the plank and ushered her into the back seat of a canary yellow town car waiting on the pier. It bore a Fangler insignia and had dark-tinted windows. She had expected one of the Mayor's black vehicles, but had to chuckle at herself; how often did anything she expected actually happen? Almost never.

The door was barely closed when she heard a familiar voice. "Welcome back, Miss Cream!" exclaimed her back seatmate. "Nice outfit! If I didn't know better, I'd say you were the twin brother of a certain Fangler hat repairman of my acquaintance. That'll probably fool the blue-hats on bicycles that have been circling our wagons. A whole flotilla of the idiots are already camped out at Pier 6 where the *Sandbar Savant* is due to dock at around midnight. And plenty of Fogwit mediots and newswings are right there with 'em."

Glix tried to conjure up some Tangerine Cream tude for an in-character response, but failed. She just threw her arms around the Purple One, knocking her sunglasses to the floor in the process.

Then she backed off. "Sorry Miss Twick. I guess I'm kind of happy to be back. Things have been kind of weird lately."

Twick was staring at Glix's eyes. "Been eating too many oranges, Miss Cream? Galloping goblins! But seriously, what happened to your eyes? Can you see?"

"As long as I'm wearing the sunglasses; too bright otherwise. But it's dark enough in here so I don't need them. The med on the ship said I've got some kind of inflammation or something and need to see a specialist."

"Of course, of course. I'll have Fogwit's best at Grapeskin in no time. Meanwhile, you just gave me a delicious idea! We'll get Creative to design some outrageous Tangerine Cream shades and build the whole look into your shtick! Color me blown away, Miss Cream! You're not back five minutes and the chemistry is going full-tilt boogie again!

Twick stared at her Rising Star. "Wel-come *back*, Miss Cream. You've been missed. You probably don't know it yet, but the blue hat whack jobs have decided that Tangerine Cream is the new Great Evil. Evidently, their sky-goddess hates you. Crockpuss or something. But who cares? The magic's working better than ever, Miss Cream. You're still a kickass buzz machine."

Glix retrieved her shades and grinned. "So I still have a job? I mean, what about Zellah?"

"Of *course* you still have a job, Miss Cream. There is no other Tangerine Cream but Glix Larue. As for your understudy ..." Twick paused, rolled her eyes and pretended to stroke an invisible goatee. "Now how do I say this as inoffensively as possible? Hmmm. Your understudy — as sweet as she is — is her father's daughter.

"Sad to say, but — and this is just between you and me — Zellah's becoming the official Tangerine Cream understudy may just have an eentsy-teentsy bit to do with politics, Miss Cream. Which, as everybody not from Quince or Hiphollow knows, is all about money. Well, and lies and deceit and bullshit and subterfuge. Do you think the Mayor actually wrote that fetch-letter? Nah. But he actually signed it and Tophat Lodge's resident help-fairy spy thinks he wrote it. That's all that matters in the end, eh? Getting what needs to be gotten. Right?"

Glix's Quincian niceness mentally shuddered at Twick's last assertion, but was drowned out by a bigger anxiety. The word "Crockpuss" had gotten her heart boxing with her ribcage again. Crockpuss had to be Lady Crocus. Glix was tempted to tell Berlyn Twick about her encounter with the Septriq Divinator, but at the moment the whole thing seemed unbelievable and hazy ... even to her. So she didn't. Instead, she asked Twick to fill her in on the latest at Grapeskin.

223

"Well, in some ways you're lucky, Miss Cream. Most of what you missed was your favorite Grapeskinner wrangling with our backers, who have balked at the cost of every little thing ... the Mullver's Rock location shoot, the fabulous windskate prop and all the other fun stuff. It is just s-o-o-o-o irksome dealing with grandiose schemers who refuse to open their wallets; the stupid Save the Sky Expedition is over budget and behind schedule with lulu fast approaching. And it's sucking off all the money, leaving us to hop and scuttle and beg for the dregs. So I've had to scale things w-a-a-a-y back. And we're now going to do it as a serial."

Twick made a sour sound and an exasperated hand flurry.

"Still, as of two days ago, the deal is done ... which was why I had to get you back here in a hurry. Our first episode is supposed to hit the big toobs two days before the expedition departs. Time to put your shades back on and get to work."

The yellow town car was passing through Twick's private gate at Grapeskin Studio before Glix cranked up the nerve to ask the question she knew she was going to pay for, so she kept her tone light. Or tried to. "Uh, Miss Twick, what happened to that crazy pilot ... Javett? Did you kill him like you said you were going to?"

Twick pretended to sputter in shock and then cawed a sardonic laugh. "I wondered when that topic would come up, Miss Hopelessly Smitten. Nope, didn't kill him. Didn't even get a chance. He got called back to the Hiphollow Rangers right after we returned from

Mullver's Rock. Best to just forget about him; windshark jockeys are not the sort for a Rising Star to get involved with. Disasters just waiting to happen. Trust me on that." Twick winked and strode off in the direction of her aerie.

Glix tossed her head with what she hoped was a Tangerine Creamy tude and a careless smile, but Twick was gone. Grumbling under her breath, she went to look up Mr Vane at the library to fetch back her sodbunny and have a tearful pet reunion.

44

Dropped Back

ALMOST immediately after dinner, she fell asleep with Cinder wrapped around her neck. The dream that followed was anything but comforting.

• • • • •

Dream-Glix stands in a pale blue land that is featureless save for a purple hill far in the distance and a hat sitting on a purple rock a few feet away. There is no sun or moon, but none is needed: the sky is an inverted bowl of glowing monstrous crocus flowers (the term "of Biblical Proportion" might be an apt descriptor of their size). A path goes straight and true toward a familiar golden tower visible behind the purple hill. Something in the tower seems to call to the dreamer's sigil, so she ignores the hat and sets off along the path. The sigil seems to nod.

Arriving at the hill, the dreamer realizes it is taller than she had thought. So tall, in fact, that its height temporarily hides the golden tower from view.

The dreamer is not discouraged; she knows it's only a trick of perspective. But as she passes around the hill, the golden tower is not where it should be. In fact, the scene is now identical to the scene at the beginning. Except for a signpole.

Near the top of the pole, three destinations are indicated by small, arrow-shaped signs. They are attached to a glossy cylinder painted with a helix of alternating pink and orange stripes. It appears to be rotating, but since the signs aren't moving, it obviously can't be. One arrow points straight ahead along the path toward the golden tower behind the hill. In plain black lettering are the words "Crystal Misthawk." The other two signs point off into the empty landscape, but in opposite directions. The lettering on both of these signs is the same: "Waffletown." Dream-Glix furrows her dream-brow: no roads lead toward Waffletown. Not even a trail or a footpath in either direction.

Equal parts perplexed and determined, Dream-Glix sets off for the Crystal Misthawk. She's certain it can't be far, now that she knows exactly where she's going. (Yes, this is dream-logic, which makes no sense at all to people who are awake. Please cut Dream-Glix a little slack.)

Along the way, Dream-Glix notices that the drab landscape is now dotted with wilting crocus flowers and that a light rain of fresh, dewy ones has begun. Eventually she arrives at the purple hill and is disappointed to discover that the Crystal Misthawk is not around the hill where it ought to be. The signpole is still there, but it has lost its signs and is now half buried. What Dream-Glix finds more interesting is that the wide-brimmed hat she had ignored earlier now rests at a jaunty angle atop the signpole.

She studies it a moment, rubs her chin in a thoughtful way and says in an exaggerated stage whisper, "Hmmm, I wonder if there's a Viceroy under this hat. Let's take a look." She reaches for it, but the hat and the pole bend away to dodge her outreached fingers.

In an eyeblink, the hat and the signpole have become the Viceroy of Twisselman Wood. Dream-Glix is only surprised by the absence of Twisselman Wood. "Pull up a mushroom and take a load off, Glix Larue," says the pranksy, who looks exactly as he did when she met him in Twisselman Wood. In another eyeblink her surroundings have transmogrified into the pranksy's office. "And please wipe that silly bogglement off your face. Bogglement rarely, if ever, becomes the unproud possessor of a genuine quantode sigil."

"Is this still a dream?" muses Dream-Glix in the pranksy's direction.

226

"*Of course not! It's a squeam. Ask a silly question, get a silly answer.*" The pranksy reaches into the pocket of his snakeskin long-coat and removes a string of slender white toothpicks, joined end to end by invisible threads. He dangles them in front of the dreamer. "*Take your pick,*" says the Viceroy.

From the greenish gloom Glix hears groans and mutterings from the pranksy peanut gallery: "*Oh Viceroy, you are s-o-o-o-o pick-of-the-litter;*" and, "*Keep his picks away from your schnozz if you nose what's good for you, Miss Tangelo.*"

Dream-Glix grins in spite of herself. Pranksies are so weird. But refreshingly weird, at least.

The Viceroy turns his head to the side and issues a terse instruction to the peanut gallery in an incomprehensible language.

"*Now, to business,*" he says, collapsing the string of toothpicks and tucking it back in his pocket. "*Our sources tell us that you have had the good fortune to become acquainted with the estimable Lady Crocus via a Septriq muse-channel. She's the sweet one, isn't she? The very dplsjrrsmx of kindness and fresh-from-the-oven green-sugared scones.*"

Dream-Glix is about to say she doesn't know what dplsjrrsmx means, but the Viceroy makes a tiny shake of his head and a tinier lip-zipping motion that might appear to a distant observer as a mere wiping of his lips. Was someone spying on them?

"*We also hear that your eyes suffered some abuse during the affair, possibly due to actions of your own. No matter. Fortunately for you, we pranksies have concocted a proprietary moth-serum that works wonders for nearly any form of oculescence. Several applications of one drop in each. Now get some sleep; some intense times await you. Twisselman Wood Illusitorium, over and out.*"

· · · · ·

When Glix woke sometime after midnight, she remembered nothing of the dream. So when she switched on the bedside lamp, she was surprised to see a dark green dropper-bottle with a moth shape molded into its surface. That certainly hadn't been there when she'd gone to sleep. But it was here now, so she squeezed a drop into each eye and dropped back to sleep.

45

Involve Boys

THE DREAM WAS right about her eyes. They returned to their normal color and sensitivity in two days. Twick canceled the appointment with the eye specialist, but insisted that the new Tangerine Cream Signature Shades would be worn at all times anyway as a new feature of the Tangerine Cream persona.

The dream was also right about "intense times." Glix's next month broke all previous intensity records.

A team of Scripters spewed a steady stream of paper at the small army of setmakers, propsters, painters, costumers and whatnots that Twick had brought to Grapeskin Studio. The result was a nonstop blur of frantic activity. Somehow in all this chaos a dozen scenes were pantomimed in the dialog-free, archly overacted style that was the current rage in Fogwit dramatic circles.

Between the intense scening and the even more intense physical training, Glix could not decide whether she was more exhausted or more exhilarated. And wonder of wonders, it seemed the local butterwings were nicer to her than they had been before. Even more wondrous: the butterwings treated her understudy worse than ever; maybe Arrol had put in a bad word or two about her.

Still, conflicts with Zellah had been minimal. She hadn't complained about being made up and wigged to look exactly like Glix and even seemed to enjoy wearing the exotic new Tangerine Cream Signature Shades at all times. Her understudy had been on her best behavior, a fact that made Glix both suspicious and edgy. Zellah was up to something nasty. But what could Glix do about it? Zip.

"Time for a little break," Twick announced to the assembled crew on Stage Two one morning. "As much as I'd like to continue scening forever, we're done for a few days. So just cool your heels people, stay where a butterwing can find you and get re-energized for the next round. Dismissed."

"With me, ladies," she said to her two Tangerine Creams as all the others departed. They followed the Purple One to a corner of the windskate interior set where she stopped and gave them long, cool looks topped with her special crooked-mouth smile. "Nice work ladies," she finally said. "Very nice. And thank you for keeping your claws on a leash; things work best when you're being your sweet, lovey-dovey selves. So thank you again.

"You've now got two days off; don't waste 'em too much. Memorize the Overactor's Codec, pester butterwings, write letters to your mothers, go off into corners with boys who aren't windshark jockeys ... or whatever. Have a nice couple days and get back here alive." Then she was gone.

Glix and Zellah stood together in a ripe silence that went stale almost immediately. Zellah finally broke it with a single word. "Here," she said, handing Glix a gilded envelope. "My father is having a private party for the big supporters of the Expedition and he thinks the Tangerine Creams should be there. It's going to be at the top of the Crystal Misthawk, so I'm sure it'll be a memorable experience for a Quincian nicebody." Zellah made no attempt to conceal her sarcasm. "The Purple One's invited, too, so maybe you can ride over with her. Bye."

As she watched Zellah depart, Glix tried to decipher whatever unpleasant thing her sigil was trying to tell her, but failed. It just triggered random unsettling feelings that made no immediate sense. Then she scowled at nothing in particular, stuffed the envelope into a pocket of her work-skirt and went off to her rooms.

The in-box outside her door had something in it today ... and not a scroll-letter from her mother. If her guess was right, this was another piece of musical fan mail from her anonymous admirer. At least it had the same wrapping as the other three. "What do you think, Cinder?" she mumbled as she sat down, tore open the paper and untied the string around the box. "Another little locket with an ear-tab in it? I'd bet good starglass on that. How about you?" Cinder made no sound, not even a fiffle.

She had guessed right ... not exactly a recordbreaking surprise since the package had been identical to the other three she'd received since returning to Grapeskin. Inside the tiny heart-shaped glass locket was a tinier ear-tab attached to a fine gold chain. Seconds after she stuck it in her right ear, a disguised voice uttered the words, "For the true Tangerine Cream, a brief rhapsody for harmonica." The rest was the single voice of a simple, ancient instrument.

To her ear it was a heart-wrenching set of musical landscapes painted in majestic shades of gray: seabirds on a lonely shore, a stroll in a soft sulu rain shower, pine branches whispering in a gentle breeze. The music turned on a tap of saltwater somewhere inside her head that refused to stop even after the sounds had ended in a long mournful warble.

For a while she just sat with her eyes closed. After a time she went through another round of wondering who this person could be. Javett? Not likely the sort of thing a daredevil Hiphollow Ranger would do. But if not Javett, who? Certainly not anybody at Grapeskin. He would have betrayed himself by now. Not knowing was exasperating, but a good kind of exasperating.

Reinvigorated, she started a letter to her mother three times but nothing she wrote was coming out right. Writing letters to her mother was an exacting artform and she just wasn't in the mood to get it right. So she wrapped Cinder around her neck and headed to the commissary for a snack. Except that she wasn't really hungry, so she took a few detours and eventually found herself in the library. Mr Vane was busy cataloging scripts, so she decided to catch up on the last week or so of the *Fogwit Morning Lobster*.

The headlines were either about the Save the Sky Expedition or the Ceruleans. Nothing else. The most provocative of the batch was "**FOGWIT CITY DOOMED: Blue Predicts Skyfall Disaster.**" That was from about a week ago. Today's headline was: "**CERULEANS FLEE CITY: Blue Followers Trek to Songwater.**" Glix got increasingly icky feelings as she read the story, particularly the part about Midas Blue receiving messages from Crocus, Goddess of the Sky, by somehow "reading" the patterns of blue crocus flowers tossed into a large bowl of still water. A feeling of wooziness came over her as Septriq memories rose up from their shallow grave, but she squeezed her eyes shut and managed to bury them again.

She waved good-bye to Mr Vane, left the library and wandered into the Purple Garden. Cinder always liked this spot, which was about the only heavily landscaped place on the entire lot, so she let him chase butterflies and sniff around for edibles. The morning fog had thinned and although threatening clouds were brandishing sluggish gray fists down in the south, rain was still just a prediction. Glix sat in a goblin chair carved from a single purple-stained windwillow log, closed her eyes and felt bored; having no friends here was getting old. An image of Arrol's face came to her mind, but it didn't stay long before it morphed into Javett's.

He is just s-o-o-o-o cute! she said to herself with an invisible grin. And he likes me. Javett never seemed very far back in her mind these days and evidently it showed: no wonder Arrol and Twick had teased her. But some part of her doubted she would ever see him again.

She also wondered if she'd ever meet her mystery musician even once. Good thing she hadn't told anybody about her anonymous musical love letters. There would never be an end to the teasing ... even worse than being teased about her growing boobs, which had been happening a lot lately.

A particular worry would be her rich, obnoxious understudy hearing about her secret ear-tab fan mail. Especially where the disguised voice always starts out with "For the true Tangerine Cream

232

...." Zellah would not like that at all. Not worth all the headaches that would trigger.

Glix grinned at herself, amazed at how complicated relationships were ... even when they involve boys you barely know or don't know at all.

234

46

Thank You, Politics

WHEN THE boy-thoughts finally faded, her stomach pointed her toward the commissary. It was nearly empty today. In fact, only one other person was presently dining: Mr Vonson Rakow. Glix wouldn't have been more surprised if it had been the Quincian Grand Funnelmaster sitting there. What was Rakow doing at Grapeskin? She fetched a tray and scowled at all the perfectly good stuff she should probably eat. She put a selection of fresh greens in a bowl, but just wasn't in a mood to eat what she should eat. And since no one was looking, she filled up a soup bowl with sweetrunket pudding, whipped cream and chocolate shreds. Cinder could eat the greens.

Someone *was* looking. Rakow was watching her between bites of a hamburger the size of Mullver's Rock. When he saw what she'd selected he winked and made a gesture Glix interpreted as an invitation.

"Good afternoon, Miss Larue ... or Miss Whipped Cream, I should probably say." He looked meaningfully at the huge snowcap on top of her bowl. Between attacks on his hamburger, he had been reading the "CERULEANS FLEE CITY" story in the *Lobster*. "I hope your eyes are better and that you've fully recovered from your adventure." He leaned forward and whispered: "By the way, we Fanglers appreciate how well you got, er, Lady Crocus to volunteer information about her favorite fanboy, Midas Blue. His sudden appearance on the scene has been quite puzzling to us, but she dropped an interesting tidbit, thanks to you: Florkin's Folly."

"If I did anything, I don't remember: all that is still a blank to me."

He leaned forward, delighted to have somebody he could trust with a juicy bit of Fangler detective work. "It seems that the late Florkin's Folly was a tiny island in the Great Wet, way south of anything else. It took some detective work to figure out that it was actually blasted into oblivion by a skyfall we didn't even know about. Predated the one at Fairdilly Commons by at least six months. And after giving the Songwater area a thorough once-over, we have a sneaky suspicion that Midas Blue was shipwrecked there several years ago; we found wreckage there of a kind of dinghy that only Florkin lobstermen used. We also think he became the blue ghost that haunted the old Songwater ruins for a couple years. The muckberry pickers sure think so, at least. Anyway, the mysterious Mr Blue is a work-in-progress mystery for us. You should probably steer clear of Ceruleans, though: you're their new Empress of Evil. Word to the wise."

Rakow sat up straight just long enough to get his mouth around another huge bite of hamburger, which gave Glix a chance to spoon a not-so-dainty bite of sweetrunket pudding into her mouth.

When he'd sent his bite on its merry way, Rakow looked around and stage-whispered. "By the way, Fanglers don't publicly name that particular device that you did such a nice job destroying on the ship. Kind of a secret."

Glix grinned and whispered back. "You think I destroyed it? Really? I don't know how I could have ... after the gatekeeper guy all I remember is waking up and feeling like my eyes got blasted by a light bomb. They're back to normal, but Miss Twick insists that we wear these everywhere."

"Very, ah, unique frames," he said, making a polite almost-sneer. "A smidgen too decorative for Fangler tastes, but I'm sure it will be a trend-setter among Fogwits and an excellent moneymaker."

"What a surprise to see you here, Mr Rakow. I didn't know anybody at Grapeskin would need a tophat serviced. Done any belching in public lately? Oh, and please meet my sodbunny, Cinder. He's never met a real Fangler before. And he doesn't like hamburgers, so your huge lunch is safe." She sort of wanted to ask Rakow what he'd seen in that room with the Divinator, but she equally sort of didn't.

"Well, there must be some tophats in your Wardrobe Department, but probably none that would need my help. As for public belching, I fear not; I'm always on my best behavior in Fogwit City on account of the Belch Police." Rakow bent over and pretended to search for any Belch Police that might be hiding under the table. "I think I'm safe," he said.

237

Glix laughed; silliness in an adult was a rare treat and she appreciated it.

"Actually, Miss Larue, I'm here to maintain Grapeskin's various items of Fangler equipment during production. I stop by every week or so, but usually keep to the little Fangler workshop tucked away in the back of the Prophouse; if I walk around I'm constantly pestered by the gaffer and best boy to tweak things they could easily tweak for themselves. With everyone gone today, I figured it would be safe to eat in public. And I surely didn't expect to see you here today."

"I live here, I guess. I really don't have anywhere else to go and the Purple One is in her aerie ... no one dares to interrupt her when she's in the aerie."

"Well, if that envelope sticking out of your pocket is what I think it is, you're going to what I'm assured will be a highly select party at the Crystal Misthawk tomorrow night."

Glix had forgotten the unopened envelope. "Oh. Yeah. Can't say I really want to, though."

"That would make two of us," said the Fangler.

"You're going?"

"Alas, I have been appointed the temporary Fangler in Residence for Fogwit City. All the other Guild members here are busy with meaningful projects. Since Mr Macaller and his colleagues have contributed mightily to the Save the Sky Expedition, I will be the official Fangler Guild representative. To my chagrin, I'm the perfect choice; I know next to nothing about the status of the project, so I can persuasively claim ignorance if asked any pointed questions." Rakow grinned.

"Plausible deniability, right?" mumbled Glix through a sweet and creamy mouthful of pudding that qualified as the highpoint of her day so far.

Rakow cocked his head and peered across the table. "I think that's what the politicos call it, yes." He took a long time to chew the last bite of his hamburger, which he washed down with a long swig of something in a metal cool-bottle. He winked at Glix, then belched quietly into his napkin. "Oops," said the Fangler with a wink.

Glix laughed into her own napkin and wished she had a belch of her own handy. Then she recognized a colorful aroma. "That wouldn't be fumes of Fangler Tonic you're belching, would it? How about a deal: I promise not to report you to the Belch Police if you share a bottle or two of that stuff. Next to the 'real stuff', Fangler Tonic was the best thing about my experience with the thing I maybe destroyed but can't mention by name."

"Well, Miss Whipping Cream, I'll pretend you're not trying to blackmail Fogwit City's official Fangler in Residence and will arrange for a supply to be delivered to your quarters this afternoon. Meanwhile, I must attend to some off-site un-Guild business posthaste." He made an exaggerated grimace and put a finger to his lips. "Can you keep a secret? I play spockhorn, mandolero and sometimes even mouth-organ in an ancient music ensemble ... and I'm late for a practice session. Not very Fanglerish, I know. Until tomorrow then." Rakow tipped his hat, winked and hurried away.

Glix watched him and tried to match his voice with her mysterious musical admirer. There didn't seem to be a match, even disguised. And even if Rakow were a musician as he said, he couldn't possibly be the person who sent her the ear-tabs. Could he? Not with him being so old ... at least thirty, she guessed. Some nice Quincian part of her told her to just stop this un-nice line of self-flattering thought in its tracks. Easier thought than done.

238

Although she completely ignored the Overactors Codec (a real handbook), that afternoon, Glix wrote a long overdue seven-scroll letter to her mother. Unlike her weekly hi-how-are-you-I'm-fine-gotta-go notes, this one contained all sorts of chatty trifles about costumes and about the daily swordplay and martial arts training and about how hard it is not to laugh when making outrageously melodramatic gestures in front of Picters Guild butterwings with eyebuttons and about how those butterwings sometimes hold their eyebuttons in their mouths so they can make scary faces and rude gestures at the actors when the director isn't looking.

239

She also mentioned spending a couple days on Mullver's Rock with the crew in search of locations and how disappointed she was not to see Quince from the sky on her way there from Fogwit City. Since she'd previously complained to her mother about being lonely, she made sure to mention her new friend, Arrol Moon, and a Fangler named Vonson Rakow who had become at least a sort-of friend.

The best gossip-fodder, she saved for last. The son of that nice juggler — Mr Hipskander from Hiphollow, the man who had gifted her daughters with sodbunnies named Nugget and Cinder — was actually a daredevil windshark jockey. Who would have thought? She'd talked to him at the Mayor's lodge on Mullver's Rock and he was very courteous ... not at all like Fogwit boys his age. And terribly shy.

Knowing what to leave out, she was spared writing about having her head split open and being unconscious with a serious concussion for four days. Not to mention almost being blinded while interacting with the Goddess of the Sky. She also left out anything to do with mysterious musical fan mail, which might sound ominous and dangerously un-Quincian to her mother. While Glix sometimes thought about resuming her nice Quincian life, as long as she was subject to uncontrollable bursts of un-niceness, she knew it would be a bad idea. Besides, nothing truly interesting had ever happened in Quince.

When the letter was done, Glix slipped it into a scroll-tube, affixed postage, dropped it into the out-box on the wall outside her quarters and flipped up the flag.

The in-box flag was up again. No mystery love-music this time, just a terse note from Twick instructing her that preparations for to-morrow night's party would begin at 6 AM. Evidently Mr Macaller had found Twick's idea of having two identical Tangerine Creams at his party amusing. Her Purpleness, of course, had definite ideas about how the event should be played. Glix sighed and mumbled to Cinder: "So much for two days off. Thank you, politics."

47

Neither Brain nor Sigil

A BLANKET of mottled mauve settled over Fogwit City, blotting up the last traces of daylight and turning the glass top floor of the Crystal Misthawk into a sparkling mauve mirror. Ace newspod pilot, Miss Carlisha Grable, circled the building, absorbing the surreal effect of the colors and saying a silent appreciation for beauty in all its forms.

Her passenger, Carriott Glamfass, society reporter for the *Fogwit Morning Lobster* and Fogwit City's most illustrious celebritarian, completely ignored the dusky beauty. Instead, he fumed, gnashed his perfect teeth and cursed the fates: the biggest celebrity gala in years would be taking place without him. All he could do was snoop like a common spy. "No reporters," was what Macaller's press secretary had said. "As in, not even you, Carrio." The fact that she'd smiled and made a helpless shrug was no consolation.

So he pointed his eyebutton-scope into the glassed-in Hall of Moons that capped Viggas Island's tallest, gaudiest tower and captured what there was to capture. He had already recorded some establishing imagery of the hemispherical glass dome that covered a portion of the roof, so as soon as the glass misthawk sculpture's inner lighting came on he would have the setup for his report.

Well and good, but he was too early for any celebrity sightings and he knew it; the only live bodies present were uniformed staff scurrying around doing last-minutey staff things. On each loop around the building, he noted the huge model of the *Wild Blue Wan-*

da — the vast windskate carcass that was being transformed into the high altitude transport aircraft for the Save the Sky Expedition to Bastion 9. But Glamfass could hardly have cared less; it was just a dead hulk with no personality quirks, no untidy secrets, no foibles or missteps or foot-in-mouthings to be exposed to the world. In short, it was big, dead and boring.

Glamfass scowled at the magnified image in his scope and pulled his eye away. Then he scowled at the queasy roil in his belly, shook a handful of pills out of a bottle, gulped them down and snapped terse instructions to the pilot through the talk-tube. "We're still too early. Get over to the flats for a quick look at the real *Wild Blue Wanda* while we're waiting. Maybe it will deflate or explode or something and we'll get a scoop. Quickly now, Miss Grable ... this waiting and hesitation does you no credit!"

"Yes sir, Mr Glamfass. I'm on it, sir!" exclaimed the pilot. The buzz of windshark wings ratcheted up a notch and the newspod dropped like a barrel plunging over a waterfall. It made a tight bank around the Misthawk's western face, streaked past nearby smaller casinos and flattened out over the stream of vehicles wending their way along the Corniche, the 25-mile road skirting the bay between the city and the glittering "island of winners."

Miss Grable heard a satisfying retching sound as the *Lobster*'s snottiest, rudest reporter vomited his lunch into a bag. "Hope that wasn't too sudden for you, Mr Glamfass," she added with all the innocence she could muster. "Oh, look! Isn't that the Mayor's black limo down there? Oh wow! Look at all the Ceruleans still straggling along the old road to Songwater. Amazing!"

Glamfass was too busy emptying his guts to look. He was still making dry-heave noises when the newspod settled into a hover just outside the north gate and a couple hundred feet above the road. A high fence of woven bamboo protected the complex from the curious; tonight, the newscraft was in that category. A signal light from the guard tower homed in on the newspod and flashed a coded message that meant "perimeter clearance 100 feet." The pilot signaled back and repositioned the craft to the nearest legal spot where the real *Wild Blue Wanda* was clearly visible. "Is this close enough for you, Mr Glamfass?"

The green-faced reporter mumbled something that might have been "yes" and watched as the perimeter lighting along the top of the fence flickered to life. The Cerulean graffiti that had appeared on the fence in the vicinity of the North Gate also flicked into view. Glamfass had been outside this complex only two weeks ago to interview Midas Blue. It had been the final Cerulean protest against the Expedition before their mass departure for the abandoned townsite of Songwater by Muckberry Cove. But the graffiti had grown even with most of them gone. To Glamfass, Midas Blue was a power-hungry whack-job wearing blue skin dye, but one who seemed to sincerely believe his own ludicrous claptrap. To Glamfass, sincere beliefs counted for something: not much, but something.

"Wow," said the pilot with a low whistle. "It's huge! You could play lawnball on top of it. Do you think anything that huge could actually fly, Mr Glamfass?"

"I, for one, will believe it when I see it," sniffed Glamfass, who was starting to recapture his aplomb. "I'm sure it will be endlessly talked about tonight. Our inside source has positioned several fresh farspeaks, so we should be able to hear a good deal if we can stay in range. You'll keep us close, won't you Miss Grable?"

"Yes sir, Mr Glamfass. Wherever you want to be, we'll be."

"Speaking of which, I see that the Misthawk's eyes are lit now; can you take us back up there, Miss Grable? Gently, please? Our busy little newswings here are anxious to be buzzing the windows and annoying the guests with their antics."

"Yes sir, Mr Glamfass," said the ace pilot, working hard to keep the smile out of her voice.

• • • • •

From backstage inside the Hall of Moons, Glix peered through the slit in the curtains and felt like throwing up. Wasn't this supposed to be a small party? She had never had to play Tangerine Cream — actually speaking lines and not just pantomiming — before a live audience. To make it much worse, their little company had had almost no rehearsal time. Exactly this morning, in fact.

Twick and Mr Macaller had cooked up this silly little dramatic confection last night and the Purple One had sprung it on them this morning. Zellah shrugged and tried to pretend surprise, but it was obvious that her father had told her about it last night. Surprise was not an issue with Jimjim and Tonton, who would be playing blue sky-demons. As long-time Grapeskin veterans, nothing could surprise them any more. Rakow had frowned when he'd been drafted to play his part, but he was being a good sport and only had a tiny part to play anyway. Glix was by far the most nervous of the cast.

But it wasn't just because of this stupid skit. Something horrible was looming. Her brain knew it, her sigil knew it. But exactly what sort of horror was it? Neither brain, nor sigil would say.

48

....

Inexorable Power

BEYOND THE CURTAIN Mr Macaller's guests were doing what elite party-goers do before formalities begin: small-talking, critiquing each others' attire, nibbling hors d'oeuvres and wandering around with drinks in their hands. A number were also going gaga over the minutely detailed model of the *Wild Blue Wanda*. Near the podium, the Mayor, Zan Macaller and Vonson Rakow were huddled in intense conversation.

Backstage, Zellah was joking around with the two male players and making an occasional snide glance in Glix's direction. Glix ignored the three of them and went off to a more or less quiet corner. Maybe her uneasiness was something to do with the Ceruleans. There had been some Grapeskin scuttlebutt this morning about fresh hate graffiti aimed at Tangerine Cream that had appeared last night on the walls enclosing the studio complex. Maybe that had been what her sigil's warning was about?

She didn't think so. More likely it had something to do with her second dream last night, the one about Zellah's brother. She hadn't thought about that jerk since Arrol said he'd been the one who'd tried to splatter her brains all over the Blue Helmet camp. Well, in her dream he was way more splattered than she had been; but Glix hadn't done the splattering. She was just being a nice Quincian and trying to collect all the pieces of him that had gone missing. By the time her alarm went off she had assembled a tidy pile containing bloody fingers and toes, an ear, a lower jaw, several mashed-up internal organs she couldn't identify and a mushy oval blob about the size of an egg. There was also a black leather boat-brimmed hat.

Glix pushed the dream-image back into its closet. The nasty thug would doubtless be here tonight and would probably be part of whatever nasty scheme Zellah was cooking up. But after a month of intensive martial arts training, she wasn't feeling particularly threatened by a poser kjoa or two. Master Few had taught her a number of what he called "practical, large-muscle moves." He'd even said she had talent as well as quickness. Of course Master Few had also told her not to feel over-confident, as her level of skill was quite rudimentary. Still ...

"Positions, people!" whispered Virgil Voss, the Grapeskin assistant director who was handling this little scene instead of Her Purpleness, who was sitting next to the Mayor in the front row.

Glix moved back from the curtain, slashed at an imaginary foe with her sword for a few seconds and found her place on stage; the other cast members did more or less the same thing.

Beyond the curtain, the Hall of Moons settled into a low murmur. Glix recognized Zellah's father introducing himself, greeted the audience and telling a joke. After a polite ripple of laughter he introduced the guest of honor.

From backstage, Glix recognized Vonson Rakow's voice. She knew the basic outlines of his script, the beginning of which was loaded with obligatories and gracious thank-yous to the people who had contributed much starglass to the Save the Sky Expedition. The cue would be coming up in a couple minutes. Meanwhile, she wished she had some Fangler's Tonic to calm her sigil, which was acting stranger than ever. And for the first time, it smelled. At that thought, her mind's nose dialed into the waftosphere and caught whiffs of imaginary fragrances: ripe apricots, freshly torn in half; the pink-white flesh of a juicy strawberry with a bite out of it; cinnamon-peppermint frosting on a bubblegum flavored orange snap ....

Somehow, thinking about quess had shifted Glix's senses into overdrive. Now, even muffled by the heavy curtain, she could hear each tiny articulation of Rakow's voice with intense clarity as his speech zeroed in on the cue-word.

"... the devilish problems faced by the people of Hallah ..."

A blue sky-demon leaped from the wings brandishing a short zigzag sword that glowed with an eerie blue light and crackled with lightning bolt energy. The audience gasped in unison.

In two giant bounds the demon had one arm wrapped around the Fangler's neck, while the other pressed his lightning-sword against Rakow's throat. The sky-demon's wide-eyed glare spun to the audience and a spew of unintelligible syllables burst from his blue-lipped mouth, its foot long fangs dripping blue ichor that smoked wherever it landed. The creature's mane of steel-tipped blue spikes sparkled with tiny lights as it made wild gestures at the audience with its sword. Then it thrust the zig-zag blade toward the crystal dome and bellowed an incomprehensible command. The room shook with rolling thunder and the dome crackled with dazzling blue sparks.

In the front row, a tiny crooked smile turned up the corners of Twick's mouth. Would Midas Blue regard this little show as blasphemy? Probably. And wouldn't *that* be fun, she thought.

Now the demon seemed to take notice of the miniature *Wild Blue Wanda* suspended in the air near the glass wall. His face took on a look of savage rage and his sword arm made frenzied gestures in the direction of the model, as if he were hacking it to bits. Another blast of thunder rocked the room; the model crackled with vivid blue light and purple smoke curled up from its underside.

Backstage, Voss gave Glix her cue: the original Tangerine Cream somersaulted into the scene from the left wing. Haughty of face and arms-akimbo, she contemplated the sky-demon as if it were a naughty boy-child and she was its superhero governess. She tilted her elaborate shades down and looked over her nose with a sly sneer. "Where have your manners gone, sky-boy? I'd wager this entire hotel that you weren't raised in Quince." She turned a quick look at the audience and made an exaggerated wink.

A murmur of chuckles rippled through the crowd of Fogwit movers and shakers.

"Eeeww. Who did your hair? A cake decorator? And the fang-dribbles? Really! Couldn't hold the blue pee-pee, sweetie? That is just so-o-o-o undemonly." Tangerine Cream drew her sword from its sheath and leaped at the sky-demon with a hero-girl semblance of a battle cry: "Prepare to die, you sorry excuse for a pus-wart!"

The blue man-beast dropped his captive and took a mighty swing at the girl in the orange-and-cream striped bodysuit. Glix danced aside, her copper glove, woven copper belt and copper cone-bra glittering copperishly in the footlights. The sky-demon's stroke hewed only air, but it recovered in time to parry her quick sword thrust at its torso. The swordplay now waged fast and furious, harsh clangs of steel-on-steel echoing off the glass walls and ceiling.

Into the fray leaped a second sky-demon. Tangerine Cream made a gesture of dramatic outrage and screamed a challenge. Then the two sky-demons were upon her and the swordplay became a blur. Glix was pressed hard parrying their thunderbolt swords and retreated toward the edge of the stage. Then she stumbled.

Both sky-demons swung their blades at the falling heroine with sword strokes mighty enough to hack an ox in two. Sword clanged against sword to an explosion of blue sparks. A cloud of orange smoke enveloped the players and the orchestra played a dramatic crescendo of horns, cymbals and kettledrums.

Then it all stopped; a sudden wind blew away the smoke, the music and the lights. Silence and darkness settled over the Hall of Moons. Seconds of blackness passed before spotlights faded up on a frozen scene. The two thunderbolts were stuck in the stage, their demonic wielders bent over, straining to pull them free. Behind them stood two identical Tangerine Creams in triumphant poses, their swords held high and poised for death-strokes to the sky-demons' necks. Bombastic chords welled up to fill the hall as the four characters took bows to hearty applause, then danced behind the curtain.

Servers were filling the guests' champagne glasses when Rakow stepped back to the podium and waited for the room to become quiet. He mopped his brow with a yellow handkerchief, then rubbed his neck where the sky-demon had collared him. "Well that was a close call. I had no idea when I mentioned 'devilish problems' that I would be inviting such instant reprisals. Fortunately, as we have just seen, Hallah is not without heroes willing to do battle with our problems. Our delightful Tangerine Creams are two of them."

Rakow paused as another spontaneous round of applause came and went. "Before I give the podium back to your host, the intrepid Zan Macaller, I would like to propose a toast to a whole room full of heroes. You. The ladies and gentlemen of Fogwit City who have supported ...."

Several members of the audience had lost interest in Rakow's toast and were pointing toward a blazing object now visible in the crystal dome over the room. As Rakow looked up, a blast of world-class thunder shook the building followed by a noise like huge glass eggs being struck by mallets. The dome burst into a million shards and rained down upon the best and brightest of Fogwit City.

A minute back in time, Glix had found a quiet backstage corner and collapsed in a heap, her glazed eyes open and staring. Something had begun to invade her mind while she'd stood motionless in the final tableau with her sword raised over the blue sky-demon. She knew she had to escape to somewhere quiet and fight it off. She barely heard the blast and was protected from the rain of glass by the heavy curtains and the structure housing the fly loft and its pulleys, ropes, backdrops, scrims, lighting and whatnot.

What she had no protection from was the now familiar face of Lady Crocus. The smooth words of a kindly old woman crooned above the shriek of a mental tornado that was trying to suck Glix into oblivion. "Come, come, dear. Open your eyes and just relax. Let me bring you inside where it's much nicer. I've just baked greensugar scones, you know. Don't they smell just yummy?"

The mention of greensugar scones triggered an un-memory that had somehow entered her brain through the pranksy eyedrops: a highly informative backgrounder on the true nature of Hallah's enemy. And much more, including the fact that Glix was not entirely helpless against the inexorable power of the entity disguised as Lady Crocus. She had allies.

49

....

No Sound

VONSON RAKOW WATCHED from the shelter of the proscenium arch. Half his attention alternated between the growing orange blob in the sky and the chaos unfolding in the ballroom. The other half listened to his hat.

The local Fangler office had just relayed a message from the observatory on the *Caveat Empress*: a new piece of Hallah's inner shell had become dislodged and was plummeting toward the surface. According to current projections, it would make landfall somewhere within a 20-mile radius of Fogwit City in less than ten minutes.

Then came his instructions: "Get the Larue girl and get up to the roof ... a rescue craft will be there in two minutes."

Rakow scanned the room. While he had been listening to his hat, the Mayor's assistants and Misthawk security people had taken control of the panicked crowd. Only a few injured stragglers remained and those were being helped to the elevators.

Backstage was empty of people, too. Had Glix escaped with the other members of Twick's group? Someone was curled up on the floor by the back wall. From the costume, it had to be Glix; he just couldn't picture Zellah like that. Ever. Tangerine Cream's hands were pressed over her eyes, her mouth was open and she appeared to be in the middle of a seizure. Rakow sniffed the air. Ozone.

His mind went back to the Septriq Divinator and the face of the old woman who had called herself Lady Crocus. While Glix had been lying blind in the *Caveat Empress* infirmary, the other Fanglers had grilled Rakow for information on what he had observed. Eventually a consensus hypothesis had evolved: Lady Crocus was a personification of the Prime Keeper, the intelligence in charge of Hallah's continued functioning as a habitable planetoid.

For unknown reasons it had hijacked the Divinator in an effort to communicate directly with Glix — possibly with hostile intent. But why?

Somehow, the strange Quincian girl had defended herself and survived. It had been Rakow's job to delve into the girl's side of the experience, but the proper opportunity hadn't yet presented itself; now it might be too late.

As he jogged over to the slumped form, Rakow's head was full of questions. Did the ozone smell mean that the Lady Crocus oracle was somehow communicating with Glix again? Even without the Septriq machinery? Was Glix in danger? From the look of her, she was. He removed a flask from his jacket and gently shook a quivering shoulder. "Glix. Vonson Rakow here. I've got some of the real stuff here and I think you need it."

Without waiting for an answer, he trickled a few drops of undiluted quess into her open mouth. Glix swallowed, gasped and opened her mouth again. "More," she rasped, grabbing the flask out of Rakow's hand and emptying it in two gulps. Almost immediately, her body relaxed and her eyes popped open, a fierce orange gaze radiating a strange heat that wasn't really heat.

Rakow helped her to her feet, but she shook him off. "I'm okay now. She's trying to bomb Viggas Island with pieces of sky ... and she can steer them now. Gotta get to the roof or we're all dead in two minutes. Jove, my rebel Keeper contact says maybe they can divert it, but ...."

Glix left the sentence hanging and dashed for the fire door that led to the stairwell. Rakow did his best to keep up.

She was halfway up the stairs to the roof when the door at the top opened. A shadowy figure stood there, holding it open and gesturing.

"Hurry," said the voice, needlessly. "The Fangler pilot says there's not much time. Nice costume, Miss Cream. Very superhero."

Neat black suit, tidy hair: it was one of the musicians in the orchestra, Glix decided. Both voice and face were somehow familiar, but there was no time to try to sort out such stuff. "Thank you," was all she said as she charged through the doorway.

At the top of the stairwell was an area set ten feet below the roof. Known as the mech level, most of it was crammed with metal sheds hiding machinery that hummed, whirred, whined and occasionally clunked. The actual roof was up another flight of metal stairs, which Glix took three at a time while mumbling numbers: "three, two, one. Sheebuz! ... they were right ... to the second!"

Another blast shook the building as the fireball shed flaming pieces of itself. As fireworks go, it was spectacular only in its deadliness: no rainbows of bright sparks or multicolored fountains. Just lazy arcs of burning sky that would wreak havoc wherever they landed. Was this dispersed destruction better than if the rebels hadn't somehow caused it to break apart? Glix had no idea. She felt sick just thinking about it.

Her next message from Jove said they'd failed; the Prime Keeper had somehow been able to keep about a third of the fragment from breaking apart. Still heading straight for the Crystal Misthawk it had retained enough mass to destroy Glix, Rakow, the musician, the building and maybe the whole island. But maybe there was a way she could ....

The message was interrupted by a looming figure. In her quesssight, she could see the smiling, victorious face of Lady Crocus painted in flames as the brilliant remnant the size of a bus roof shot down at them at — a number struggled to appear in her brain — 738 feet per second (roughly 500 miles per hour for those of us who prefer to think in those units). Then she felt hands.

"She's in a trance, Zirk," said Rakow's voice. "Now's not the time to talk to her. Help me get her to the shuttle and we might still make it off before impact." Glix slapped the hands away and took her eyes off the fireball for a second to glare at Rakow and the musician.

"Leave me! Get on the shuttle and get out of here. A lot of people are going to need your help tonight, but I'm not one of them; I have all the help I need from the rebels. Go-go-go!"

Rakow's information from the *Caveat Empress* had mentioned nothing about rebels, but that didn't mean it might not be true. It would be just the sort of information they would label Top Secret anyway. And Glix might be right to send them away. After all, she had survived a duel with Lady Crocus once already. Still, he hesitated. Abandoning a child to a fiery death was just not in him. The young musician tugged at him. "Come on Von, she's right. We're not in her league," he said. "I think we just have to trust her."

The Fangler's eyes pleaded with whatever mysterious power was behind the girl's orange gaze. "Keep her safe," he whispered and then let the musician lead them to the sleek Fangler pod and its buzzing windsharks.

"Thanks for the 'real stuff,'" she shouted at the backs of the fleeing figures. "I needed that!"

"Thirty seconds to impact," said the rebel codestream inside her head. She sensed there was going to be more, but the face of Lady Crocus abruptly displaced it, reappearing in the looming fireball as a distorted, yawking face from a childhood nightmare.

The face now wore a frumpy, drooping beret-like hat woven from tiny skulls painted to look like blue crocus blossoms. Between her crusty blue-painted lips was a half-eaten piece of some kind of crumbly pastry. Bits of it were stuck to the garish lips, others were buried in saliva oozing down her lumpy chin.

The vortex was still trying to pull Glix to wherever, but it was weaker now. She heard a garbled stream of words that might have been, "I'm eating your greensugar scone for you, dear. Can't you just taste it? We could still be such good friends here, you and I. Be sure to stop by if you're ever in Waffletown ...."

Waffletown? Where had she heard that recently? Well, it didn't matter now. Time for that later ... if there ever was a later. Glix suddenly hated that face for its pathetic, needy loneliness and the destruction it was causing. On purpose. Gods shouldn't be like that. With great effort, she pulled herself away from that idea and focused on the eyes in that sagging face.

The rebels had temporarily hijacked the whites of the Prime Keeper's eyes, which now contained urgent instructions for Glix: "Distract her ... now or never," was the message.

Her gut told her she was already too late, but Glix mentally blurted the first thing that came to mind. "Lady Crocus, what's happening to you? You look just awful. Did Midas Blue's people do your make-up today? You really should fire their sorry asses. Grapeskin's ...." Glix stopped herself, sensing Lady Crocus' awareness focus on her more intently now. Maybe it was a bad idea to mention names of the good guys.

"You know about grape skins, don't you? We eat a lot of grapes down here, you know, and a lot of really smart people say the skins are really, really good for wiping off blue lipstick. Particularly the green ones; the purple ones, you know, sometimes stain ...."

Glix's monologue was cut off by another explosion. Ten seconds before projected impact, the rebels succeeded, sort of. The main sky fragment bearing down on the Crystal Misthawk had come apart in a burst of shoebox-sized pieces of high-energy shrapnel.

Some landed in Cobnose Bay, creating tall, sizzling waterspouts but doing little damage. Others blew holes in the Corniche roadway or blasted cars and their occupants into flaming, messy wreckage.

The official Fangler damage report would later say that exactly thirteen pieces impacted the *Wild Blue Wanda*, causing 97 percent destruction of the Save the Sky Expedition's vessel. The mission to enter Hallah's shell from Bastion 9 was over before it ever got off the ground.

One piece hit dead center on the Crystal Misthawk's roof. The blast flung Glix into the railing around the mech level. Dazed and breathless, she didn't see the piece that blew the Misthawk light sculpture off its mounts and sent it tumbling 33 stories to the street below. Or the piece that blew apart the Hall of Moons. Or the piece that sent the Fangler pod to a flaming doom. Or even the one that turned the mech level below her into its own fireball and singed all the hair off her head.

When her eyes opened next she saw a roof enveloped in flames and smoke, but no flaming missile and no Lady Crocus. That's something, she thought before a fit of coughing took over. Idly, she wondered if it would be the flames or the smoke that killed her first. She chuckled at that and coughed again; how many times can you get killed, after all? Then she noticed that there was no sound to go with what she was seeing, not even a dim crackle of flames. The shadow was silent, too.

Eat Steel

AT FIRST the silent shadow seemed to be aimlessly dodging the patches of flames. Then she noticed that something in the air above her had caught its attention. Darting through the smoke and flames above the shadow were five butterwings with eyebuttons ... mostly pointed at her.

Had to be newswings: there was a sort of frenetic quality to their actions that the smooth Picters Guild butterwings at Grapeskin didn't display. Of course for pure laid-back demeanor in the course of duties, you couldn't do better than the postals. She made a rueful grin, aimed mostly at herself.

A part of her knew that if she was musing abstractly about the various natures of butterwings while this building was going up in flames, her brain was not functioning up to par. But she waved her gloved hand at the newswings and gave them a bit of somewhat battered and bruised Tangerine Cream tude.

"Tangerine? Is that you?"

Glix swung her attention toward the voice. It was the musician. Hadn't she shooed him away with Rakow? His name escaped her at the moment, but she gave him a quick once-over. He didn't look much better than she felt ... and his left pant leg was on fire. She pointed at it.

"We need to get to the edge of the roof," said the musician as he smothered the flames with the charred remains of his black jacket.

"There's a newspod from the *Lobster* hovering just off the far corner of the building where the misthawk used to be. They're waiting for us, but I don't know for how long. I don't think their windsharks have been fire-trained and the pilot's having trouble keeping them from bolting. But Glamfass is inside and those are his newswings hovering around you.

I promised him a juicy Tangerine Cream exclusive — my father says he's the type who'd slit his children's throats for an exclusive — so let me help you up. I know the way by now."

Glix allowed her wobbly self to be half-dragged across a roof that was rapidly becoming a solid mass of flame. Somehow she trusted that the musician actually did know how to get through it.

When she saw the newspod hovering in space ten feet from the lip of the building, her first thought was to wonder how two more people were going to fit inside that tiny thing. Of course, the truly Tangerine Cream thing to do would be to stand on the skids and hang onto the railing as the thing flew to wherever a safe place was. Maybe waving her sword defiantly at the sky while she was at it? Too bad she didn't have some of the real stuff handy.

At that thought, her sigil began to act up ... in a new way this time. It seemed to be acting like some kind of energy vacuum cleaner, sucking vagrant energy from all around her and pumping it into every cell in her body. Inside her head, something came through on the quess channel from the rebels behind the sky: do it. That was it: do it.

Was she dreaming? She thought not. A gesture like that made a kind of sense. There was a hidden war going on and she was now part of it, whether she wanted to be or not. Somehow Midas Blue was on Lady Crocus' side of things, although she couldn't see what anybody had to gain by helping to destroy the world they all had to live in. So maybe a defiant Tangerine Cream might help slow the migration of believers to Songwater.

While she was thinking these things the musician was having a shouted conversation with Glamfass. He turned to Glix and blinked. Where had the half-dead girl with the scorched hair gone? She still had the scorched hair, but the person standing there was now a larger-than-life Tangerine Cream. The energy radiating from her outshined the flames behind her at the moment. At least that's how it seemed to him.

"Let's go," she shouted. "Right now. The wind's about to shift and we'll all be fried. Get inside, Mr Musician. Tangerine Cream will ride the rails."

Inside the newspod Glix could see the reporter's eyes bugging out. He'd heard it all and she could almost read his thoughts. Was she joking? Nobody did stunts like that. Certainly none of Berlyn Twick's minions ever did. But he was just a reporter about to get the story of the century. Why argue? Even if she fell off and got splattered all over the pavement it was still the story of the century. No way to lose. And his newswings' eyebuttons would capture every bit of it … as they were already doing.

On cue, the wind shifted. A wall of flames forced Glix and the musician to the very edge. Ace pilot Grable was on the edge of exhaustion, her uniform soaked with sweat from trying to keep her windsharks hovering. The creatures lurched and bucked against their harnesses as the pilot inched them close enough to the building for a rescue. She knew they could bolt any second, but she wasn't about to tell anybody that.

The pod bobbed up and down and side-to-side, a motion guaranteed to make the reporter retch if it kept up. Not that that would be such a bad thing, mused Miss Grable to herself. But the steeds could freak any second and she was too young to die in such an unprofessional manner. Couldn't handle her steeds, was what the other pilots would say. No way that was going to happen. "Do it now or we're all barbecue!" she bawled. "Five seconds until we're leaving."

Glamfass reached out his hand to the musician, who, like Rakow a little earlier, finally abandoned the idea of gallant hesitation. When he was inside, Tangerine Cream stepped onto the skids, grabbed the rail with her gloved hand, drew her sword with the other and brandished it at the sky … accompanied by a properly wild-eyed-heroine expression for the butterwings and their eyebuttons. The overloaded pod lurched away from the dying Crystal Misthawk and wobbled toward the nearest place with no smoke or flames that wasn't in Cobnose Bay.

At that moment, Glix felt more alive than any time in her life. Unable to keep her energy bottled up for very long, she bellowed "Eat steel, Lady Crocus!" at the top of her lungs. Had she known that would be the headline of the *Lobster's* special skyfall edition in the morning, she might have restrained herself. Or not.

51

Or Something

LITERALLY and figuratively, the escape from the inferno was the high point of her long night. Everything that followed was one low point after another. Nothing had prepared her for such carnage. She and the musician worked all night with rescue crews, pulling people from wrecked cars and helping evacuate the parts of the Misthawk that hadn't yet been taken over by flames. They both sensed there were many unsaid things between them, but by unspoken agreement deferred all unnecessary conversation until later. It was a good thing.

Glix expected that Rakow would show up, but he didn't. That didn't seem like him, but maybe he was helping save the *Wild Blue Wanda*; she could see the towering flames across the water at the Fangler complex on Cobnose Flats and realized they must be having as rough a time of it as they were here in Viggas. So she put him out of her mind and focused on the horrors in front of her; the young musician worked efficiently alongside her. Occasionally she would glance in his direction and catch him studying her face, but mostly she pretended not to notice.

By dawn, a stiff onshore breeze was blowing the pall of acrid smoke inland and replacing it with a salty freshness that briefly re-energized the crews, volunteer and professional alike. Emergency teams had made temporary repairs to the Corniche and traffic was moving again. Until then, all aid from Fogwit City proper had to come in by boat or air.

Glix and the musician had just finished escorting a group of Mist-hawk employees from the basement kitchens to a staging area near the water and were taking a momentary break. At about the time Glix spotted the *Caveat Empress* anchored offshore, a tall, grave-faced man in formal attire approached at a fast walk. As he stopped in front of them, she noticed the jeweled Crystal Misthawk pin on his lapel. The man bowed and introduced himself in a cultured voice of quiet authority.

"I am Gelph, you are the illustrious Tangerine Cream and I see you are already acquainted with Master Zirkon. Forgive me for interrupting, but I have news that requires his urgent attention."

Before Glix could even acknowledge the man's words, he took the musician by the elbow and escorted him some yards away for a whispered conversation.

After a time, the musician nodded and returned to Glix. "Please excuse me, uh ... Miss Tangerine Cream, I guess. I'm really not sure what to call you. Uncle Gelph informs me that I am needed elsewhere for a time, but I trust we'll meet again. I'm Zellah's brother, by the way: Zirkon Macaller, but most people call me Zirk. Not to put too fine a point on it, but working with you tonight has been an, uh, unexpected experience. You're a nonesuch ... no matter what my little sister says."

There was a painful smile on his face as he made a small bow and was led away by the impatient older man. After about ten paces, he stopped and jogged back to the exhausted, gape-jawed Tangerine Cream. He removed a somewhat worse for wear package from the pouch he wore at his back. "With my deepest apologies ... this is long overdue."

Glix took the package, still vastly confused. "Uh, thank you." Then she blurted the question she'd wanted to ask all night: "Why did you come back after I sent you away? Particularly, you being who you are ...." It didn't come out so well, but at least it was out.

"May I think about my answer for a while? Thanks." With another bow, Zellah's big brother turned away and soon disappeared around the burned out shell of the Crystal Misthawk.

The air was still thick with the buzz of windshark wings and the ground was still thick with emergency crews plowing through the wreckage looking for survivors, but now Glix barely noticed. Her eyes stayed glued but unfocused on the spot where Zirk Macaller and his uncle had disappeared. She felt empty. Inside her brain, practical thoughts wandered the barren landscape of her mind making tinny sounds through tiny bullhorns as they vied for her attention.

"Open the package," said one. "Get something to eat," said another. A whole chorus of them simultaneously shouted, "What happened to Twick-Zellah-The Mayor-Rakow?"

Only the name "Zellah" triggered a response that brought her back to the present, more or less. What *had* happened to Zellah? Certainly she had escaped to safety somehow. Twelve hours ago Glix had been wondering what sort of nasty little scheme Zellah had planned to spring on her after the skit. Now, everything was changed.

She had done battle with an entity that, when she thought about it in a certain way, maybe only existed in her own mind. Maybe she was the insane one; maybe Lady Crocus and the rebel Keepers were things she'd made up. At the moment, they all seemed very remote from this reality of destruction.

Maybe the skyfalls were just the sort of falling-apart things that happened to every made thing. She remembered the Copper Cora doll she'd had when she was small. It had been made by the Quincian coppersmiths and it was beautiful. It had eyes that blinked and joints that moved and she had loved it to pieces. Literally. First, a tubular leg had bent after she stepped on it. Then she'd spilled sweetrunket pudding on it, gumming up the neck joints. Then something else had happened and an arm had fallen off. And then the other. She remembered crying and begging her father to fix it.

She also remembered his gentle head-shake, his sad smile and his huge sigh. "Sorry, Glixxie. I know you love Cora, but sooner or later, everything put together comes apart. The Fanglers have a word for it: entropy."

Was that what was happening to Hallah? Was it just a world-sized Cora?

"Groy-yoy-yoing," announced her stomach, interrupting morose thoughts of entropy and insanity with something she could actually do something about. She scanned the area and noticed that big white tents had been set up on the wide lawn that separated the ruined Crystal Misthawk from the beach. From the aromas catching her nose, a kitchen was in there somewhere.

Glix wandered off in that direction, occasionally aware of the odd looks cast in her direction. A part of her wanted to scowl and snap something sharp and nasty, but the energy she had been living on for the last twelve hours was gone. So she said nothing.

Alone, empty and exhausted, she trudged along in her shabby Tangerine Cream superhero costume, her scorched head wrapped in a once-white sheet it acquired sometime during the lost night. A memory from another lost night bubbled up from somewhere: wobbly soup-straws. That had been how her legs had felt the night she escaped from Quince after pedaling that bicycle for hours and hours. A tiny smile flicked through the gray mask of exhaustion: that was exactly how they felt now. She would wobble her soup-straws to the tents, sit down somewhere and beg something to eat. Then she would think about how to find her way back to Grapeskin. Or something.

"Excuse me, Miss Larue," said a gruff female voice behind her. "Might we have a word?"

"Or something" had spoken.

52

Sickened

BREAKFAST was not in a tent. And Captain Barlett was not a smid-gen happier than the last time Glix had dined in her cabin. This time, Glix understood completely.

"It will do you good to eat something, Miss Larue," said the Captain.

The bowl of Fangler chowder sat untouched in front of Glix, ex-cept for the occasional tear that rolled off her cheeks and made tiny spatter-volcanoes in the murky surface. How had he not survived? Glix could just not conceive of the idea that a hugely smart, hugely competent, hugely human adult she called a friend could die. It just wasn't right. She had sent Rakow away and now he was dead. Was it her fault?

The Captain spoke, breaking the painful silence. "There was nothing you could have done, Miss Larue," she said gently. "Your friend and his pilot were killed instantly ... a fragment traveling at that speed is like a bomb. Their pod virtually exploded; there was nothing anyone could have done. But there may be something you can do now. You see, your friend's last transmission mentioned that you had said something on the roof about 'rebels'.

"This was surprising information to us, but it might help explain some of the mysteries our telescopes have spotted. Is there anything you care to tell us about these so-called rebels ... and about your conversations with Lady Crocus? As you must know, the *Wild Blue Wanda* is destroyed and now it seems we might be at war with our planet ..."

Glix had been staring at her bowl during the Captain's speech, but now brought her eyes up to meet the sad eyes across the table. She saw pain there, too. Clearly, Vonson Rakow had been a favorite and she was feeling the loss, too. "He was close to you, wasn't he?"

The Captain's face softened. "You didn't know, did you? Your friend Vonson was my son."

Blood rushed to Glix's cheeks. Should she have guessed the connection? She didn't know how. But for some reason this failure made her feel small and disconnected ... from everything and everybody. And there were other feelings she just couldn't put into words. "I don't know what to say, Captain. I am just so ...."

"There's no need to say anything, Miss Larue. Vonson and Jace — his pilot — may be the first Fangler casualties in this new war, but they won't be the last. Vonson had taken a real liking to you ... and he thought there was much more to you than meets the eye."

Glix could think of nothing to say, but she was very glad that there was no one else in the room to watch her burst into tears and sob for a solid ten minutes. Captain Barlett took off her hat, closed her eyes, rubbed her temples and allowed herself the luxury of a few silent tears as well.

When the moment seemed right, the Captain spoke again. "As I told you earlier, Ms Larue, we Fanglers have agreed to get you secretly back to Grapeskin. The ever-impatient Berlyn Twick has reluctantly agreed that staying off the Fogwit streets in daylight is probably for the best, so we'll keep you aboard until after midnight. Then a cargo carriage will meet us and take you to Grapeskin's 'back gate'. With any luck, this should keep the *Lobster* newswings and Midas Blue's minions guessing. And you'll be in disguise, of course.

"So now you should sleep. Later — and if you're willing — you and I can perhaps share a few items of mutual interest. I suspect that there's as much you'd like to know from us as we'd like to know from you. And perhaps you'll help us strike a small blow in the service of artful confusion."

• • • • •

The "back gate" to Grapeskin Studio was not in the back and it was not a gate. It was in the Orange Door.

Sandwiched between a dingy hardware emporium and a neat and tidy dispensary for pills and tonics was the venerable Orange Door Tavern. The "all hours" pub and eatery had become famous for its Lost Opportunity fare: cheap, fast, overspiced and of dubious nutritional value, including 47 varieties of pizza.

On any given night when "normal" Fogwits were tucked into their beds, the Orange Door was filled to overflowing with blurbists, scene picters, aspiring street magicians, insomniacs, conspirators of all stripes, plumbers returning from emergency stoppages, toob technicians, fun-girls, fun-boys, slumming dandies and persons of artful nondescription. And that's not even counting the wannabes and the freelance newswings on the prowl for any manner of saleable gossip.

At three minutes past midnight, the Orange Door was its usual jumble of sounds and stenches when the front door opened. Into the common room lurched a remarkable young woman. Of middling size — except for an astounding out-thrust bosom — she was swathed in a dirty blue floor-length robe and sported a standard-issue Cerulean blue helmet. A length of heavy chain trailed behind her, making an unpleasant rattle-clatter noise and clearing a trail through the peanut hulls that blanketed the floor like a plague of scuttle-bugs somehow frozen in mid-scuttle.

Covering her eyes and nose was a hammered copper band with four protruding lenses; her hands were swathed in dirty white gauze and held a small wooden crate tied with a blue ribbon.

The young woman walked stiffly down the main corridor toward the bar in the back, apparently struggling with the weight of the crate. Patrons and orange-scarved servers alike gave her a wide berth, instinctively avoiding her strangeness. The usual babble faded to a rustle of whispers and by the time the woman had hefted her package to the counter, the room was pin-drop silent.

Grapple, the burly barkeep frowned down at the bizarre young woman and her special delivery parcel. He said nothing, but cocked his head and deepened his frown. As he scratched his head in apparent puzzlement, a voice from the far end of the room shouted "Bomb! It's a bomb from Midas Blue!"

In seconds the room had come to life with an unharmonious bomb-chorus. Grapple bellowed, "No, it's not a bomb!" but his voice was lost in the chaos of patrons trying to escape through the Orange Door. No one noticed the buxom Cerulean drop to her knees and crawl behind the bar, through the curtain and into the kitchen just in time to see the cooking crew fleeing through a back door into the alley. She made a quick dash past the pizza ovens to a walk-in cooler for kegs of ale where there was a trapdoor just where is was supposed to be under a rubber mat. Then down a ladder and into a dank tunnel.

"Well if it isn't Tangerine Cream disguised as a blue cow with a metal tail," sneered the Purple One as she unlocked the metal grate at the Grapeskin end of the tunnel from the Orange Door across the road. "Very creative. I'm certain that every single eyeball in the Orange Door was on you. I don't know what those Fanglers are drinking, but I've gotta get some. Welcome home, Miss Larue. I understand that you have had way too many eventful moments over the last day or so and I wanna hear everything. But let's both get some sleep first."

Glix just stared at her employer. Berlyn Twick looked exactly like she always did: same outfit, same look, same everything. Somehow she had come away from the Crystal Misthawk disaster without even a scratch. "It's good to be back, Miss Twick. Did everyone else get out okay?"

"If by 'everyone else' you mean your fellow Grapeskins and not, by latest count, 5,742 dead Fogwits and one dead *Wild Blue Wanda*, then yes. We're okay. Shell-shocked, but okay. Except for Midas Blue's growing band of mush-headed idiots that are trudging for

Muckberry Cove in greater numbers than before the attack. Go figure." Twick sucked in a deep breath to control her rising anger.

"Even your dear friend Zellah is just fine, although her father is in serious condition after a 50-foot Crystal Misthawk light sculpture dropped on him from 33 stories up. He's not going to be walking anytime soon. And you already know we lost Vonson Rakow who, in my humble opinion, was possibly the best and brightest of the latest generation of Fanglers."

Twick paused when she saw the tears well up in Glix's eyes. "Von was my friend, too, Miss Larue. We'll all miss him a great deal. But let's leave such sad topics for later and get some sleep."

They walked in silence as far as the commissary. "I'll say good-night here, Miss Larue. Perhaps you'd be so kind as to meet me for lunch in the Purple Grotto?"

• • • • •

A half-empty bottle of chilled Fangler Tonic sat on the edge of the tub, next to the unopened package from Zirk Macaller. Glix lay submersed to her chin in steamy water, the latest ear-tab from her secret admirer filling her ear with a slow, mournful melody played on some sort of low-pitched woodwind that she would later learn was a shakuhachi. After a few minutes the sad woodwind was replaced with shimmering arpeggios that gradually rose in pitch until they were mere tinkles, like tiny glass bells. Glix could not help but feel this was a memorial to Vonson Rakow. When the sound died away it seemed as if faint echoes lingered just out of reach until the disguised voice broke the spell. This time, it was at the end of the music. "For the true Tangerine Cream, a requiem for a lost friend."

Glix blinked away tears. Zirk Macaller. Could it be anyone else? Not too likely. She downed the last of the Fangler Tonic and steeled herself to open the package. Under the plain white wrapper was a plain white box. On it were the words, "Returned, with interest."

Just as she'd guessed, it was her coin-dispenser, the pride and joy of a much different Glix, one that felt years younger. Innocent, naïve, foolish. She rubbed her smooth scalp. And one whose hair

269

hadn't been burned off. She turned the coin-dispenser over in her hands and inspected it closely. Each cylinder was completely full: 30 coins in each, 150 coins in all; it certainly hadn't been that way when it had been stolen. In fact, it had been mostly empty.

Suddenly suspicious, she pressed a lever and dispensed a 1,000 Mark starglass coin. An icky feeling rose up in her gut as she dispensed a coin from each of the other four cylinders. Instead of 1, 10, 50, 100 and 500 Mark coins, each was another 1,000 Mark coin. If her next guess was correct, she was holding a small fortune in her hands. The thought of it sickened her.

53

Out That Way

A MILD early lulu rainstorm had lubricated the grounds in the pre-dawn hours. A dramatic streak of sunshine broke through a hole in the clouds to shine on the door leading down to the Purple Grotto. Maybe that's a good sign, thought Glix. Then her heart fell. Hans was at the door, playing the role of major-domo, something he only did when bigwigs were about.

"The Mayor is crashing your quiet lunch with Her Purpleness," he whispered. "Be sharp." That was definitely not a good sign; for starters she wished she had worn something sharper than a standard-issue purple Grapeskin jumpsuit.

The Mayor stood, bowed and appeared not to notice her casual attire. "Well if it isn't Fogwit City's latest hero disguised as a script-girl. Good to see you safe and sound, Miss Larue. I am sorry to have missed your performance at the Orange Door last night. That's two front-page stories in two days. Most remarkable."

"All in a day's work for a Rising Star, Mr Mayor," said Tangerine Cream, shrugging with jaunty nonchalance. Her tude had somehow arrived right on time from wherever such things come. "And I didn't even need hair to do it." She stopped in front of the Mayor and thrust out her hand. "I'm glad to see you looking so well after the attack on the Crystal Misthawk. I was hardly expecting to see you so soon."

The Mayor smiled his broad, mayorly smile. "Ah, yes. As it happens, you will be seeing even more of me in two days time. Your employer has given her not entirely enthusiastic consent for you to accompany me on a bit of, ah, mayoral business, at the behest of the Council of Notables."

Glix looked at Twick, who was clearly irked by this turn of events. "Not entirely enthusiastic? An outrage of understatement, Mr Mayor. I detest the idea. Perhaps you would explain to my heroic, irreplaceable Rising Star exactly why her presence is required for your, ah, mayoral business?" She snapped off the words.

Unruffled, the Mayor explained. "An invitation has arrived from Miranza Vale. The, ah, heroism and helpful repute our Tangerine Cream earned during our recent disaster has piqued the curiosity of the Grand Mother herself...who would like to meet your Rising Star in the flesh. In the interest of maintaining our excellent relations with the help-fairies — and since the Notables have certain unfinished business with them — we will be taking a quick little, ah, 'diplomatic excursion' to the grottoes before lulu descends upon us with full force."

Even though help-fairies were mysterious and somewhat forbidding creatures, the idea of escaping Fogwit City for even a day suddenly seemed very appealing. For one thing, she wouldn't have to think about Zirk Macaller and how to give the wealth in the coin-changer back to him. For another....

The Mayor's voice brought her back to the moment. "Now, to business. We will be taking my traveling carriage and your sodbunny may accompany you. I recommend conservative attire — preferably black — and for the sake of the weather, the extravagantly expensive cloak we acquired for you at Mister Skeet's. As our preparations are still being made, our exact departure time is still in flux; details will be sent by messenger this evening. Meanwhile, you two enjoy your lunch."

With that, the Mayor departed.

Berlyn Twick bit back a sharp comment. Instead, she turned to Glix and spoke in a concerned voice that took the girl by surprise. "As you may or may not know, Miss Larue, I am not, shall we say, a huge fan of the winged busybodies that infest our island. I am even a less huge fan of their Grand Mother … if that's even possible."

Twick cocked her head and adopted the expression Glix now thought of as her Most Serious Face. "Be very careful around her, Miss Larue. Since you are now an actor of some experience, I suggest that you keep your Tangerine Cream character under wraps and play the role of clueless Quincian nicebody around her. And be very modest about your heroism.

"The Grand Mother is humorless, quick to anger and is rumored to have dark powers and little compunction about using them against those she imagines might thwart her. She is also rumored to have a highly paranoid imagination. There's also the matter of your sigil. I am without-a-doubt certain that she knows far more about sigils and quantodes and quess than you do. Should the subject come up, be the grossed-out, disfigured Quincian and speak only when spoken to. Word to the wise."

Twick scowled and stood up. "If you'll forgive me Miss Larue, I'm suddenly not hungry. Our catching-up conversation can easily wait until you return. I'll send Hans in to join you; he'll be only too happy to eat my lunch and regale you with tiresome tales. Oh, and stop by Wardrobe and have Aneena fit you with a proper Tangerine Cream wig. And since the Mayor has cheerfully splattered our plans with his poo-poo urgency, I'm cancelling scheduled rehearsals until your return. So until then, your time is your own."

Berlyn Twick departed the Purple Grotto, leaving Glix alone with a bad feeling churning in the pit of her stomach. Fortunately, Hans cheered her up with his incessant jokes and tales from Grapeskin's history, many of them at Twick's expense.

• • • • •

Mr Vane smiled at the figure slumped in the big leather chair. "So you find yourself in limbo, eh Miss Larue? I fully understand. One moment you feel grounded and totally prepared to go in some direction...and the next moment you are dangling from a skyhook, swaying in the wind, your shoes unable to get a perch."

Glix just shrugged and made a goofy face.

Grapeskin's Keeper of Stories certainly had colorful ways of describing things. In her current mood though, Glix found this description unsettling, particularly since it was a stiff, gusty wind that had driven her out of the Purple Garden while she was having a quiet stroll with Cinder. Now she was in the Library, stuck in some place called limbo and trying to ignore whatever her sigil was trying to tell her.

"Perhaps you should involve yourself in a research project, Miss Larue. Since you are going on an adventure to mysterious Miranza Vale with our esteemed Mayor you might find my special collection on help-fairies both interesting and useful. Just a suggestion, but forgive me if I might brag a little; you will not find many of the works I have compiled on these strange creatures anywhere else on Wyn."

The Rising Star made a different kind of goofy face and pushed herself out of the chair. "Okay, Mr Vane, show me the way. You're right: I do need a project."

By mid-afternoon the next day, Glix had picked up and put down at least a hundred documents from Mr Vane's special collection. Most were too specialized for her, although she had found one technical paper titled *Speculations on Help-Fairy Aerial Ambulation* had quaint ink drawings that showed how the author thought the machinery powering help-fairy wings worked. But the paper was dated 274 years ago, making Glix wonder if the author's ideas and his theory about Hallah's gravity were still valid.

My Helpful Life with Wings by Margeet-9 however, was a fascinating personal life story by a retired help-fairy who grew up in Sipshilly. Glix was still reading it when Willik, Mr Vane's assistant, shooed her out of the Library that night.

The nice, Quincian part of her insisted on staying a few extra minutes so she could write Mr Vane a note thanking him for the helpful project idea and promising to be back to finish reading Margeet-9's story in a couple days.

Things wouldn't work out that way. At all.

54

Overlarge, Overstuffed

FOUR BLASTS from the mighty Cobnose Bay foghorn shook the stone guard shack between Grapeskin Studio's two purple gates. The night guard shook the sleeper awake and went back to his post.

Glix shivered and rubbed her gloved palm, which for some reason felt abnormally cold. Even in her fur-lined leather pants and high-collared black blouse with the goose-down quilting, and even wrapped in her expensive eelskin cloak, Glix shivered. Wrapped around her neck, Cinder shivered, too.

Was it really that cold? Or was this bone-chilled feeling an after-effect of the dream that had been shaken apart by the guard? Probably a bit of both. Glix had dozed off and on for the last half hour in the guard shack and did the same once again, a fading echo of her dream refusing to give up and go off to the graveyard of used dreams.

• • • • •

She is conversing with a round-faced old woman with plump, rosy cheeks that dimple when she smiles. She has a just-right nose, kindly eyes, an assortment of friendly creases and a dense mass of steel-gray hair pulled back in a tight bun. Although she looks exactly the same as Lady Crocus, Dream-Glix doesn't recognize her. Just as she decides that this is the perfect grandmotherly face, it begins to morph.

Over a span of seconds it morphs into a gaunt gray face with hollow gray cheeks. Seeming neither male nor female, it has high, sharp cheekbones, a high gray forehead, a smooth gray skull and thin gray lips. It seems to be made out of something hard, with a dull sheen that reminds her of the polished round rocks in the bottom of a stream.

This is the face she saw when she held the cinder-egg, or one very much like that face. But in this dream it is a huge face that is both ghostly and ghastly. It is terrible to behold because it appears to be in terrible agony ... or could it be terrible anger? Or terrible madness? Whichever it is, the gaping wound of a mouth seems to be forming words that are always just beyond her understanding.

276

Almost always. Dream-Glix is certain that one of the words it mouths is her own name. But when she realizes that, a cloud of monstrous winged figures fly into the scene to hover in front of the mouth. The figures seem to be made of a black substance that feels like concentrated dread. Then the gray eyes roll back and the gray lids slide closed. Is it dead? wonders the dreamer.

No. A vast, hollow boom shakes her dream and a new piece of sky comes loose, falls slowly for a time before the relentless grip of gravity turns it into a missile. Then the ghostly face is back, superimposed over the latest gaping blotch. When the mouth begins to move, the winged black things fly over the mouth and the face dies again.

• • • • •

Shosh-shosh-shosh-shosh. This sound scattered the echoes of her dream scene. Glix opened her eyes again in time to see a dark face lit with six yellow eyes bursting through the fog. Her heart lurched when she first looked at the thing, then she took a deep breath, relaxed a little and gawked.

Dull black, with a tall and boxy superstructure but a rounded bottom like a boat hull, it stood on six rubber-tired wheels, each as tall as Glix on her tiptoes. The carriage itself was much taller and was fitted with numerous windows, some of which were dark, some of which glowed with amber light. To Glix, it first seemed a large boat on wheels — a boat with twin silver smokestacks rising from the roof in the rear.

From the middle of the carriage, a door opened and a small ladder was lowered. One of the Mayor's assistants appeared in the doorway and beckoned to Glix. "Quickly now," he hissed. "A bank of heavy squalls is headed this way ... even in Bigfoot, squall travel can be dangerous."

"You call this thing 'Bigfoot'?"

"Yes we do, Miss Larue. A large name for a large conveyance."

A nervous Glix climbed the ladder and was ushered to a booth built into one side of the entry lounge. "Breakfast will arrive soon. When you have eaten, someone will escort you to the salon, where the Mayor will be expecting you," said the man in terse, clipped tones. Moments later the contraption was underway.

As the carriage wound along the foothills of the Jawbottom Peaks that separate the Fogwit Basin from Fairdilly Commons to the north, the usual fog was blown to tatters by the incoming storm. Glix was treated to a rare view of the city and the bay. Her stomach lurched at all the black splotches that still smoldered — or worse — from skyfall bombs. She forced herself to eat an excellent mobile breakfast that she barely noticed. Several cups of roasted blickernut tea finally dissolved the last of her mental cobwebs.

A wind-driven drizzle was peppering the windows with a fine spray by the time the narrow foothill road intersected the main road at Kirpansy Pass. The Mayor's carriage turned and headed north. Presently another of the Mayor's assistants escorted her to the salon, where Glix was directed to an overlarge, overstuffed chair across from the Mayor.

278

55

All This Time

THE MAYOR of Fogwit City slouched in his own overstuffed chair, his tophat pulled low over his forehead. He cocked his head, made a tiny crisp nod in Glix's direction, then pointed to a now-familiar stack of paper on the small table that separated them: "This morning's *Lobster*, if you're interested, Miss Larue."

Glix shook her head and looked around the room instead. Yesterday's *Lobster* had featured a freelance newswing's pic of her in that outrageous blue-helmeted, boobaceous disguise as she was about halfway to the bar. She chuckled to herself: funny picture, for sure. But she wasn't up to seeing any more of herself in the newspaper at the moment. Her life needed more boredom right now.

Bigfoot's salon was handsomely decorated and felt more like a small room in the Mayor's mansion than a compartment in a giant steam carriage. Three of the Mayor's assistants occupied seats along the right and left sides of the salon.

By the time the carriage reached the undulating downs of Fairdilly Commons, the drizzle had become a downpour and the black of night had become the gray gloom of a stormy morning. A steady stream of headlights caused Glix to wonder why so many freight carriages were on the road at this hour. She said as much to the Mayor ... and soon wished she hadn't.

"The end of redfish season in Sipshilly," he explained. "There is great urgency to get fresh ones shipped into Fogwit before the height of lulu. Because this is not a safe time for seafaring along the coastal routes, the fools brave this road. 'The freshest redfish bring the freshest prices,' so goes the saying. I don't suppose you heard that much in a land-bound, tuck-away place like Quince, eh?"

Glix shook her head, too hypnotized by the steady parade of looming headlights and rain-spatters to speak. And things she had heard from Captain Barlett during their strange talk — about Hallah and its Keepers and what the Prime Keeper really was and about the Myn disaster on the other side of the world — were now starting to rattle around in her head. Somehow, hearing the Mayor talk about redfish prices as though nothing more important was happening was like something out of one of her dumber dreams.

The Mayor didn't appear to notice her distant mood and continued. "Too dangerous even for travel by road when the really big squalls hit, and their time is almost upon us. Any day now. After that, the Sipshilly fishers will have to process the catch into redfish balls and redfish cakes and redfish jerky and even redfish flour.

"Have you ever been to Sipshilly in high lulu when the fish factories are working at top capacity? No, of course you haven't." The Mayor wrinkled his nose in distaste. "The stench is appalling. Much the same in Wickelwharf, but it's bluefish they process there. We Fogwits much prefer redfish."

The Mayor scratched under his tophat, then continued. "Of course they pickle the eyes and the tails and make redfish sausage with the gut-parts and gills. And I hear they grind the bones to make a high-grade squarm-fodder." The mayor cast a twinkly eye at the girl, but evidently she had missed his little joke. Finally noting Glix's unresponsiveness, the Mayor fell silent and returned to his own thoughts.

Glix had not missed his squarmy joke; she just completely ignored it. The stupid squarm joke was just the latest thing making her wish she hadn't agreed to come on this stupid trip with this man who evidently had no idea of what she had been through in the last couple months. That was it, she realized in a flash of sour insight. The Mayor was still treating her like the clueless Quincian nicebody she'd been when they had first met.

Back in Fogwit, she might do something useful today ... maybe even wrap up her coin-dispenser and send it back to Zirk Macaller with a thanks-but-no-thanks note. But here she was stuck doing nothing ... or if not nothing, at least not what she wanted to be doing.

Presently, Glix roused herself enough to pick up the *Fogwit Morning Lobster* from the table after all. The bold headline on the front page was impossible to miss: "**Latest Skyfall Destroys Port Goodluck**."

According to early reports, the disaster had occurred just before midnight. Several thousand men, women, children and pets had been killed by the impact or by the huge wall of water that flattened what was left of the town and washed it into the Great Wet. According to reports of rescue crews from nearby islands, the disaster was so complete that it was almost as though the little sea-mining town had never existed.

Glix felt sickened and closed her eyes. Bad idea. Images from the Fogwit City skyfall surged up from her memory, but she pushed them back. Her sigil was not so easily dispensed: it suddenly pulsed with a chill that felt like icy needles. She dropped the *Lobster* on the floor and stuck her gloved hand under her bum. Then a brutal clap of thunder jarred her eyes open and she forgot about the pain. "Nice weather for windsharks," mumbled one of the Mayor's assistants from his seat at the wall.

Glix shook away the afterimages and was left with a sick feeling in her belly and immense confusion. Had the rebel Keepers lost? Should she have tried to connect with them? And could it have prevented the destruction of Port Goodluck somehow? It seemed unlikely that she could have made a difference; she didn't even know if Lady Crocus was still trying to destroy wynside. She set these thoughts aside as best she could, returned the fallen *Lobster* to the table and took a mint-coated blickernut from the tray on the table. Not daring to close her eyes again, she watched the storm.

The rain now made a muffled staccato drumbeat against the bodywork and everything outside became a shapeless mess of pelting water. More than once, sharp gusts blew Bigfoot several feet across the road and the driver up front had had to swerve sharply to miss oncoming vehicles. As if the sick feeling wasn't enough, Glix now felt a slow-rolling panic brewing inside her gut.

Across from her, the Mayor had become a picture of intense focus, apparently unaffected by the raging weather outside. He studied a small, familiar object that he held between two fingers: a cinder-egg.

Cinder-egg? A surge of wild outrage shouldered aside the sick panic she had felt only seconds before. "You! You pink-hatted scratchfinger. You stinking, leaking buttfester! You stole my cinder-egg! And you've had it all this time!"

56

From the Prow

THE MAYOR'S finger-snap stopped Glix's rant in its tracks. His facial expression and quiet intensity instantly claimed her full attention. "Enough! I am not in a mood for your vocal quirks, Miss Larue ... or Miss Cream, or whoever you are at the moment. Listen to me and listen well."

Glix shrank back in her seat. Empty of words for the moment, she could only nod, wide-eyed and fully attentive.

"I have given you my protection and the best of my table. Do you really think you would have survived in Fogwit City without it? Have you heard of the service-waifs locked in secret rooms on Viggas? Or the 'catchers' who steal them? No? Well it's better not to know. Those are not just stories, Miss Larue from silly, naïve Quince. There were catchers in the crowd where we rescued you. Did you know that, Miss Larue?

"I have offered you advantages and opportunities that no Fogwit child will ever have, no matter how deserving. Do you think I have created Tangerine Cream on an idle whim? Do you think I have recruited the very expensive services of Berlyn Twick out of the goodness of my heart?

"If it will sooth your concerns, the cinder-egg I hold in my hands is not 'your' cinder-egg. It is not actually a cinder-egg at all, merely a clever imitation, fashioned by the best Fogwit City artisans from images captured by eyebuttons and, ah, other information. I hope to use it to gain useful knowledge about the real cinder-egg you netted, and possibly obtain the missing item itself. *Your* cinder-egg if you insist."

The Mayor paused to catch his breath. "Disasters like what just happened to Fogwit City and Port Goodluck are just the beginning. And they could just as easily happen to Quince or anyplace else. If we cannot figure out how to stop what is going wrong, we are doomed. All of us. And I don't mean a hundred or a thousand years from now. As you yourself heard on Mullver's Rock, unless something changes soon, Hallah has no more than ten years to live. That means all life dies with it: you, me, your dear parents, your little sister Wixit and a few million other souls. Everybody. And your sodbunny, too."

For the first time in his speech, the Mayor softened his tone and allowed a faint smile to curl the edges of his ample mouth.

"Here is one more secret for you to add to the batch of secrets already stored in that not-so-innocent little head of yours. Your missing cinder-egg is quite possibly the key to whether Hallah and everybody in it avoids destruction. It is a direct connection to the hidden power and intelligence that keeps Hallah functioning ... and which is now failing us. Think on that.

"If my hunches are correct, those meddling blackhoods who call themselves help-fairies helped themselves to your cinder-egg and now have it in their possession. What are they planning to do with it? We don't know. What we do know is that the Grand Mother would not invite a Quincian Rising Star to her grottoes without a very good reason. And she never does anything just to be helpful or nice."

Glix was visibly shaken ... and perplexed. Did the Mayor really not know that we were at war with the Prime Keeper? Or was he just keeping that part secret, because she was just a naïve Quincian nicebody? He didn't seem to know about her interactions with Lady Crocus, which made her wonder if he knew all the stuff Captain Barlett had told her about. Certainly he knew about Septriq, though. What had shaken her was the stuff about help-fairies and their Grand Mother. None of the Fanglers had even mentioned help-fairies. Very confusing, all of that.

The Mayor noted Glix's reaction and paused a moment before he continued. "We have mysteries to solve, Miss Larue. And like it or not, you, a Quincian innocent, are a part of them. The Council of Notables — of which I am a member, by the way — has entrusted me with the task of retrieving your cinder-egg in hopes that it can be used to solve these mysteries and stop our planet from falling apart."

Glix remembered her interrogation by the Council of Notables during the Fairdilly Fair. She couldn't help blurting; "I don't remember seeing you when they were asking me all those stupid questions."

"Observant girl. In fact, I was unable to attend the fair. No doubt you remember the hawk nosed fellow with the pointy yellow beard? Captain Flanchett of the Mayoral Guard was kind enough to be my eyes and ears."

Glix nodded. She remembered the man, if not the name. He was the only one of the five Notables who ever cracked a smile.

"So. Now you know why I accepted the Grand Mother's invitation on your behalf, Miss Larue."

Almost offhandedly, he asked Glix another question. "While we're on the subject, is it really true that you actually held the real cinder-egg in your hands? Even for a moment?"

Her sigil began to tingle as she thought back to those sizzling moments at the Fairdilly Fair, the images that assaulted her brain and the black mark that had stained her hand — and her life — forever. "Yes, I held it," she admitted. "It was a very strange feeling, but the proctor snatched it away from me. And his hands were wrapped in a kerchief ...." Glix paused, realizing for the first time that the proctor must have been protecting his own hands. What might that mean?

The Mayor nodded and interrupted her wonderings. "Thank you for your honesty. Were I a guessing type of person, I might guess that the copper glove you wear on the hand that held it is something more than a fashion statement. Possibly ...." The Mayor let the word dangle unfinished, hoping perhaps that Glix would blurt out the truth.

Glix said nothing, but her mind flew back to Mullver's Rock. If Mrs Flagstaff was a help-fairy spy as Arrol Moon had thought, the help-fairies must know about her sigil. Was it possible that the Mayor didn't know about it?

"No comment, eh?" The Mayor visited Glix with a piercing stare, which she did her best to return.

The Mayor sighed, shrugged and turned to look out a window at the pelting storm. "Glix, Glix, Glix. What am I going to do with you? Well, no matter. What is, is."

Again, Glix said nothing. An uncomfortable silence dangled in the air for several thunderclaps before the Mayor continued.

"As your father and others correctly guessed, it is likely that a help-fairy — possibly in disguise — somehow stole the cinder-egg you held. The proctor has not been able to explain how it disappeared from his care, nor has he any inkling of who might have assaulted him behind the tents. Possibly he is lying. The fact that he somehow knew the dangers of handling cinder-eggs is a suspicious thing in itself, although he claims to have learned about cinder-eggs from a former help-fairy.

"If those curiosities were not enough to trigger suspicions, the help-fairies' early departure has never been explained to my satisfaction. Their 'sudden emergency in the grottoes' does not ring true to the Council. I represent the majority of the Council, those who are convinced the proctor is not the thief. We believe the meddling winged women are up to something. If all goes well, today we may get a better idea of what is true and what isn't. Here."

The Mayor held out the shriveled cinder-egg replica.

Glix shrank back into her seat and jammed both hands in her lap. "No thank you, Mr Mayor. You can keep it."

"Don't be silly, Miss Larue. It is merely a look-alike, not the real thing. If it were the real thing, do you think I would be handling it? So please ...." The Mayor gave her a look that Glix interpreted as meaning "I'm-asking-you-nicely-this-time-but-the-next-time-I-won't."

Glumly, she reached out and took it with timid copper-gloved fingers, more than half expecting the hot-cold burning sensation she had felt before. But this time, nothing ... other than a vague feeling

286

of wrongness. She shook her head and handed it back to the Mayor. "It's definitely not my cinder-egg. It's far too light."

"Too light, is it? That's certainly a useful piece of new information. So if the true cinder-egg should find its way into your hands, you will recognize it. I am now certain of that, at least. If I understand how these things work, 'your' cinder-egg 'knows' you, if that is the right word. And most likely you are attuned to it, which means you can ...."

The carriage named Bigfoot shuddered hard in a sudden gust and the Mayor stopped in mid-sentence. He turned away and spoke to one of his assistants. "Crawl up top and see if you can tell where we are. This accursed rocking motion is making me queasy. Perhaps Glix would like to see the view from the prow as well."

287

288

57

Final Wish

GLIX FOLLOWED the man up a ladder to a cramped chamber over-hanging the driver's compartment.

A band of narrow windows provided a 180° view of the rain-blurred landscape. The man selected the center seat and motioned Glix into the seat to the right. Aside from a cluster of mysterious le-vers, knobs and a grip-bar in front of each seat, there was little to see except blowing rain punctuated by occasional jags of lightning. Still, it was way better for Glix than the salon and the Mayor's relentless intensity.

"I am called Cloden, by the way." The man held out a huge hand.

"I am pleased to finally know your name," said Glix, clasping the man's hand with the strongest grip she could manage.

The man spoke into a mesh. "Cloden here, Mr Mayor. I judge that we are only a few miles from Fairdilly Forks. If the weather gets no better or worse, we should be at the cutoff to Miranza Vale in less than one hour. After that, our progress will depend entirely on the condition of the road up to the Vale. Cloden out."

Pointing ahead, Cloden now spoke to Glix. "But for the rain, we would be able to see the colonnade and the dome by now. If you keep a sharp eye out, you should soon be able to see the first bridge over the Bones. At the junction, we will take the first fork to the right. Then ...."

Glix interrupted. "You're talking about Fairdilly-Hiphollow Road, right? My friend Mr Hipskander lives in Hiphollow."

Cloden frowned. "Strange place, Hiphollow. No proper town, they say. Most live in the woods, in houses they grow from vines that they cover with plaster. Ildrits, they call them, or so I'm told. Never been there, myself."

A pair of blue-gray blurs streaked past the windows.

"Were those windsharks?" inquired Glix.

"Yes, those were windsharks ... wild and vicious ones, too; not the ones what've been bred and trained for towing skycraft or carrying riders. They'll be back. Some of the smaller fishers haul their catches to market in trailers hooked to a buggy. Windsharks can smell that bounty a dozen miles away. Weather like this, the people who should be guarding them will be inside the vehicles. Every season the windsharks make a raid or two during the early squalls. Sometimes they get some of the fishers as well as the fish. Smart, those windsharks. Too smart. Up to me, I'd clean out every windshark aerie in every mountain on Wyn."

Another pair of blue-gray shapes flashed by in the murk.

"There. We're over the bridge and onto the causeway section now. Off to the left you can see the Waystation. Some help-witches caught a group of young kjoas trying to loot their coin-catchers last year. Sent them back into the mountains naked as mole-snakes ... and with red stripes on their hides. You ask me, best to clean out the kjoas while we're cleaning out the windsharks. Then clean out the witches. Wyn would be all the better."

Kjoas? Glix was intrigued and decided to get some practice playing the naïve Quincian role. And maybe she would learn something new while she was at it. "What are kjoas? Some kind of animal?"

"No kjoas in Quince, eh? Well, you're lucky, you Quincians. Kjoas live like animals, but they're as human as you. Packs of no-goods that infest the roads in places, usually near the Waystations. Do some stealing and such, but not much harm otherwise. Evil exceptions, of course." Cloden paused, and changed the subject. "Look now. Quickly. We've finally made the Forks."

Now under the shelter of the copper dome over Fairdilly Forks, Bigfoot slowed, swung into the roundabout and then onto the first road to the right. Once past the dome the rain again pelted the windows, but at least there was no fish-hauling traffic here.

Fairdilly-Hiphollow Road was narrow and full of ruts and muddy potholes. The going was painfully slow and marred by frequent bone-jarring bumps and lurches.

After a time, Cloden spoke again. "About ten miles from the colonnade to our turn-off. Meantime, we're in for a rough, nasty ride. You ask me, I say the Hiphollow folk like it that way. Keeps people from wanting to travel there. To be fair, I've never traveled it further than the Waystation; maybe it's better beyond, but I doubt it. We won't be going that far this morning, anyways."

Glix was just barely listening. Most of her attention was focused on maintaining her white-knuckled hold on the grip-bar. But she nodded and Cloden continued.

"Just past the bridge over Juggerwood Stream is the road up the canyon to Miranza Vale and the help-fairy grottoes. We can be useful now since we have a better angle than Narek, our driver down below. Keep sharp eyes for rockslides and washouts. And also for a big jagged outcrop of jutting rocks on the downhill side. That's where the river cuts through the teeth of Jug's End and goes over the edge. Be roaring loud in this weather … can't miss it. We need to make our left turn at that place and onto the road that winds along the Juggerwood. Probably twice as bad as this road.

"You see any hazards, hit that red button." The man looked meaningfully at Glix, then back out the window. "People who feel the need to hide their faces behind cowls and tuck themselves away from everybody else in remote places must have something to hide, don't you think?"

Glix just shrugged, grabbed the grip-bar a little tighter and tried to set aside her growing fears about meeting the Grand Mother.

Looking for washouts, rocks, the bridge and the boulders gave her mind something more constructive to do.

The steep grade and watery headwinds blowing up from the southeast combined to slow the Mayor's carriage to a fast crawl. It was like driving through a continuous waterfall; the beams of its colossal headlights barely penetrated twenty feet ahead. When the wind slackened, thick tendrils of fog oozed up over the edge of the road, writhing like a colony of monstrous, misty cobras.

A quartet of twelve-foot long blue-gray bullets bored tunnels in the mists and disappeared. Glix blinked and watched as the tunnels unswirled, blending back into the grayness. There was something strange about those windsharks. They looked, what, lumpy?

Glix brought her eyes back to the road and screamed. The fog had thinned to reveal a line of cowled, black-robed figures spread out across the entire width of the road. All were swooping their arms in great circles as the carriage bore down on them. Cloden jabbed at the red button. A brass horn on the ceiling shredded the air with a high-pitched blast and Glix clapped her hands hard against her ears.

In the compartment below, Narek over-reacted, jamming on the brakes and spinning the huge steering wheel sharply to the right. The top-heavy vehicle tilted, skidded on half its wheels, and teetered at the very edge of the cliff. Up top, Cloden hung onto his grip-rail and kept his balance, but Glix didn't. She hit the wall hard, bounced once on the floor and then lay still. The carriage slid toward certain oblivion.

To the surprise of both the watchers and the occupants, the carriage slowed and landed with a jolt back on all six wheels. It bounced once and then skidded forward, still propelled by relentless momentum.

Cloden now saw the cavernous gap in the road where a bridge used to be. In his moment of doom, he saw it as a vast wet mouth intent on swallowing the Mayor's carriage and all inside. The black-robed figures now stood at the uphill edge of the road, helpless to do anything but watch Bigfoot's slide toward the gap.

Still slowing, its front wheels slid into empty air, hanging out over the gap as if suspended by an invisible crane. For a frozen moment the next pair of wheels teetered on the edge. To Cloden, it seemed as if only the force of the headwinds and driving rain kept them from falling into the flood. But perhaps if he crept back down the ladder he could shift the balance long enough for Bigfoot's passengers to escape.

He probably shouldn't have started forward to pick up the unconscious Glix. The precarious balance shifted; Bigfoot tilted forward, beginning a graceful, slow motion dive into the churning, boulder-laden waters of the Juggerwood.

293

Sliding forward, Cloden felt and heard the splash like an explosion going off directly under his feet. His head slammed onto the roof, but he flung out a meaty arm and caught the grab-bar in an iron grip. To his vast surprise, Bigfoot righted itself and was captured by the current. Down the flood-swollen waters of Juggerwood Stream it went, riding the thundering rapids like a whale-sized black canoe.

As Cloden watched, helpless, Bigfoot shot toward the giant teeth of Jug's End. A strange sense of exhilaration came over him and he wondered whether the carriage might make it past the teeth and go sailing through the air for a time before crashing down the slope ... or maybe even surf the waterfall to end up nose-diving into the narrow lake at the bottom. It would be a spectacular, glorious way to go out, he decided.

Closer at hand was a nasty churn of froth and spray hiding treacherous rocks. In the compartment below, Narek hauled on the steering wheel with his one good arm. Maybe the front wheels would act like a rudder and turn the carriage just enough to be spun by the river so that it made the last part of its journey broadside. Then, with luck, the carriage would get stuck, pinned between the two huge rock teeth of Jug's End. With even more luck they might ride out the storm and escape to safety when the floodwaters receded.

It was a worthy idea.

With Narek's final pull on the wheel, the nose of the carriage turned just enough to graze the nearest submerged rock. The craft shuddered at the impact, then spun and slid nearly broadside on the current. Seconds later it collided with the crags at full speed.

From his viewpoint on the upper cockpit, Cloden guessed what the desperate Narek was trying to do, but also guessed that the carriage would lose the battle with water and rock. He was right ... the crags of Jug's End tore Bigfoot apart as if its metal skin was no stronger than eggshells. For a few seconds, sounds of impact, crunching metal, shattering glass, exploding boilers and screaming humans shredded the air.

As the upper compartment was ripped apart, a leather-clad body was flung sideways into the soup of fog and pelting raindrops. It turned a few awkward somersaults, hit the muddy slope with a thud, slid over a small boulder and fell head first into a cragbush thicket.

Back at Jug's End, the remaining pieces of the Mayor's mangled black canoe were torn from the rocks to ride the raging current over the edge, surfing the waterfall to wherever it ended. Cloden got his final wish.

58

Between a Pair

A LITHE GREEN FORM squirmed out of the tattered remains of Glix's eelskin cloak and crawled to the top of the cragbush. His mistress remained unconscious. The sodbunny's sharp eyes and sensitive nose trolled the air for dangers, but fog and rain muted his senses. Moments later a deadly cigar shape with four pairs of wings bored a swirling tube of turbulence through the fog. Cinder dove back into the bush and crawled into what was left of his favorite pocket. The shape slowed, then shot off again into the murk.

Glix gradually came awake. Her new world was dominated by pain and gray: swirls of lead-gray fog shot through with sheets of pale blue-gray rain; tough gray-green foliage on gray-brown branches; gray-brown mud and mottled reddish-gray rocks of the mountainside.

Still groggy, she squinted and tried to wipe the mud from her eyes. Not too easy, since only her right arm seemed to function and it was caught in an awkward position between two branches. With small, sporadic movements she worked it loose.

Her left arm felt as though it had been ripped open from elbow to shoulder by a piece of jagged metal, which just happened to be true. Her black blouse was slashed and soaked with blood. Through gaping tears in her leather pants she could feel the bitter sting of wind and rain. Thinking about how that might have happened made her stomach churn, so she tried to think of something else.

The first something else that came to mind was that she was up-side down. Her battered brain decided it was highly un-nice for a Queen of Niceness to be in such an undignified position. Being an upside-down Tangerine Cream seemed no more dignified, so she made an effort to juggle herself into an upright position. Big mistake. Her yelp of agony pierced the rain like a gigantic spike and had the same effect: none. Glix closed her eyes and let the jags of pain in her broken right leg subside to a pulsing throb.

Further attempts at movement were postponed while she tried to take stock of the situation from her head-down posture. Besides possibly bleeding to death and having a broken leg, one other fact was unavoidable; she was woozy and a deep chill was settling into every corner of her being. Shock, the deadly twin sister of trauma, had come calling.

Trying to remember what had happened made her head throb; everything since she entered the Mayor's carriage this morning had become a tumbled stew of disconnected memories. Only one thing was certain: she wouldn't survive long here.

Somehow, she had to climb the slick, muddy slope back up to the road ... right after she somehow managed to get out of this spiny bush and get herself right side up again. And somehow she had to do all this with a useless leg and a useless arm ... and before the shriek-ing wind tore away all the heat left in her body.

Put that way, the task of saving herself seemed utterly impossi-ble. Maybe if she took a little nap the pain would go away and her strength would return. Seduced by this idea, she closed her eyes and let herself sink down toward a black pit of emptiness.

Somewhere up the slope, the wind and rain tore a canta-loupe-sized rock loose from the mountainside. It slid, rolled and bounced its way toward the water far below. A certain cragbush was directly in its path. The rock bounded into the bush, shaking it to the roots, grazed Glix's head and then continued on its downward trajec-tory. A jolt of adrenaline shot through the girl, shredding her deadly lethargy. The new pain in her head was a life-saving gift; something she realized only after the curses had stopped.

Head throbbing, teeth chattering and with half-frozen blood dripping into her nose and eyes from the gash on her left arm, Glix grabbed what she hoped was a strong-enough branch and began to pull herself through the sharp, brittle foliage down toward the roots. Progress was slow and each movement of her injured leg jabbed her with daggers. But at least she was moving again.

Other creatures were also moving again. Glix could not see four snouts emerge from the mist and come to a hovering stop directly over the cragbush. But what she couldn't see, she could feel and hear; the hard wash of frigid air and the menacing buzz of wings that could only belong to windsharks.

297

The mental image of those deadly jaws sent fear as sharp as the pain in her leg surging through her body. And where was Cinder? Before she could answer that question, something dropped down over the bush. Moments later boots and leather leggings appeared in her peripheral vision.

"Ho, there. You must be one of the folk from Fogwit City. Fools to be on the road in such weather, I think. But at least you are the lucky fool. If any others survived their long tumble, they are likely drowned by now. Be brave, lucky one; the Hiphollow Rangers will have you and your sodbunny in front of a crackling fire in two hours, no more."

Feeling more than a little foolish being upside down in front of an unknown male rescuer, Glix made another effort to right herself, but her injured leg became tangled in something and protested vigorously. "Aiiiee! Now look what you made me do, you squarm-sucking puddle of booger-slime. Can't you see my leg is broken? And my arm is bleeding all over my expensive cloak. What'd they give you for brains? Diddle-figs? Just tuck that monkey back where it belongs and go home! Who - needs - you!"

Glix clamped her teeth down on her wicked and foolish tongue until it hurt more than her damaged limbs.

The laughter of several unseen voices cut through the buzz of hovering windsharks. "Sounds like this one is a Fogwit for sure," bellowed one of the voices when the laughter subsided.

"Best leave it here ... or send it to Fairdilly by the downhill shortcut," rasped another voice still laced with mirth.

The voice attached to the legs in front of Glix ignored the others. "We cannot do much for your leg here, Orange-Hair. You must try not to move it."

While he was talking, the nearest Ranger was tying the edges of the net he had dropped around the main stem of the bush. At some signal there was a sudden angry buzzing of wings. Then a lurch and a ripping sound as the cragbush was torn from the slope. A shriek of mixed pain and surprise escaped Glix's mouth, only to be stifled by a gloved hand.

A pair of gentle — and now familiar — eyes caught her own in a grip every bit as firm as the hand that held her mouth shut. The Ranger's other hand reached through the net and brushed clumps of wet soil from Glix's wig.

In a voice just loud enough to be heard above the storm, he said: "Do you not recognize me, Queen? I am Javett. Your sodbunny has been keeping watch over you ... Cinder I believe you named him. A good one, he is ... one of our finest."

Javett sighed and stroked Glix's orange wig again. "My head is full of questions, Queen, but now is not the time. Only one thing: no more outbursts, please. I apologize for surprising you, but it seemed the best way to right your position in the shortest time. One of our number has already gone ahead to make preparations. When you have some hot tea in you and are tended by our healer you will feel much better about things. Two hours or maybe a little longer. But not three hours. You have the word of a Hiphollow Ranger."

Could this young Ranger really be Arrol Moon's cousin, the reckless daredevil windshark jockey from Mullver's Rock? And the Fogwit Air Tours pilot? And Mr Hipskander's shy son? Choked by a dozen conflicting thoughts and emotions, Glix could find nothing to say to him. The empty moment dragged on and on, until a whispered, "Thank you ... Javett," slipped past her lips.

Javett removed his gray slicker, draped it over the net that held Glix and the cragbush in a tight grip, and fastened it to the mesh. "This is the best I can do to shelter you. And this may help still the pain in your limbs."

The ranger's hand held a grayish-brown woody stick. He pressed it to Glix's lips. "It will help, Queen. Chew it. If you please." Against what was left of her better judgment, Glix began to chew on the stick. It was not tasty, but a wave of spicy warmth washed the cold and the pain away as if they had been mere grains of sand on a beach. Her eyes slid shut and her consciousness did the same.

Mission accomplished, the Ranger pulled himself up the rope and remounted his windshark. A few minutes later Glix, Cinder and their cragbush were hauled away from the mountainside, slung between a pair of windsharks.

300

59

Red Splatters

FLYING CLOSE to Hiphollow Road was the only way Javett and his two fellow Hiphollow Rangers could tell where they were going; the drenching downpour turned the features of the landscape into blurry ripples. It was the slow, winding route to Hiphollow, but the safest for their valuable cargo.

They were only a few minutes into their journey when the trio and their netted cragbush traced a tight bend in the road below to see a dozen giant black windsharks blocking their route. Their help-fairy riders wore heavy black cloaks with dark blue hoods and thick black belts studded with unknown implements.

Hiphollow Ranger patrols had reported similar squadrons of help-fairies in this vicinity, but always from a distance: never up close. These dark riders were arrayed in three tiers of four, one tier above the other. Despite his other feelings, Javett couldn't help but admire their sharkmanship; formations like that were not easy to manage. Not easy at all, and especially difficult in a storm like this. Before he could decide what to do, one of the riders in the top tier broke formation and approached the trio of young Rangers.

The strong voice that emerged from under the cowl was not unkindly, but bore an unmistakable note of confident authority. "Greetings Rangers," shouted the blue-cowled help-fairy. "Not a pleasant day to be carrying such tender freight, I would say." The speaker pointed at the netted Glix suspended between two of the Rangers' mounts.

"Our group has been dispatched from Miranza Vale to seek out your cargo. This girl and her entourage were on their way to an important meeting there when their vehicle encountered the washed out bridge over Juggerwood Stream. We are grateful that your help arrived before ours did, but we will now transfer Miss Larue to our carriage where she can be properly tended during the flight back to Miranza Vale."

"Carriage? I see no carriage Sister," responded Javett with what he hoped was a confident, manly bellow. He was irritated by the circumstances ... even though it was probably the help-fairies' right to take over care of the Quincian Queen. Still ....

"I suggest that you look behind you, young Ranger," responded the help-fairy. Her words were hardly inflammatory, but the note of condescension was unmistakable.

The young Ranger scowled and turned in his saddle. To his vast surprise, an ornate black coach-like affair now hung suspended in the air, rocking in the battering rain. A complex harness secured it to four of the hulking black windmules. Javett sighed. There was no doubt but that the help-fairies' coach would be a warmer, safer, more comfortable place for the injured Queen. But that didn't mean he had to like giving up his chance to become a hero for rescuing a Queen of Niceness.

It wasn't just the lost opportunity for heroism that bothered Javett. Help-fairies had a reputation in Hiphollow for being very strange folk, and not always, well, helpful. Actually, Javett had first-hand knowledge about help-fairy cruelty and had no good reason to like them. Still, what choice did he have? He and his fellow Rangers were vastly outnumbered, and besides, these help-fairies each had a menacing looking rod slung over her shoulder.

Not so helpful looking, thought Javett. Judging from the strange black rings that covered the last foot or so of the rods, he guessed this was some kind of weapon, although it was unlike any weapon he knew. His Rangers had no weapons at all, unless you counted their belt knives, short-bows and sleep-darts.

He turned back to the spokesfairy and shouted what he hoped was a measured, mature reply. "As you wish, Sister. We will entrust the Quincian Queen into your helpful hands."

Twenty minutes later the wounded Quincian Queen was strapped to an improvised stretcher and hauled deep into the grottoes below Miranza Vale. A trail of red splatters marked her entry into the Grand Mother's murky lair.

303

END OF BOOK ONE

Book Two: The Well of Life

304

Author's Note

I WROTE MY FIRST novel at the age of 12. Although I was quite proud, it took me many decades to write one that was longer than a single page. For practice with longer tales, I started telling fanciful stories to my kids as soon as they were old enough to properly applaud and cheer. My first full length published novel, *The Luck of Madonna 13,* came much later and won some awards, which are sort of like applause, but quieter and won't disturb a sleeping dog. Since then I've learned that writing novels is more fun than a barrel of acrobatic snails and I've written quite a few more ... including this one.

The story you have been reading was once called *Night Funnels* and had its beginnings in a greeting card to my youngest daughter. All that aside, thanks for reading ... and be sure to get hold of *The Well of Life*, the next installment in Glix Larue's story. My website will take where you need to go.

E. T. Ellison
www.etellison.com

306